GONNA
LOVE YOU

IF I'M GONNA GONNA LOVE YOU

RENÃ A. FINNEY

URBAN BOOKS
http://www.urbanbooks.net

This is a work of fiction. Any references or similarities to actual events, real people, living or dead, or to real locales are intended to give the novel a sense of reality. Any similarity in other names, characters, places, and incidents is entirely coincidental.

URBAN SOUL is published by

Urban Books
1199 Straight Path
West Babylon, NY 11704

ISBN-13: 978-1-59983-058-2
ISBN-10: 1-59983-058-2

First Printing: November 2008

10 9 8 7 6 5 4 3 2 1

Printed in the United States of America

Acknowledgments

With the culmination of a novel, this, for me, is sometimes the most challenging task . . . remembering to express appreciation for all those that were so instrumental in both the journey of this novel's preparation and in my daily existence. So, as always, I thank God, the most honored being in my life, for charting my course and blessing me daily. To my anchors and the persons who stand beside me, believing, loving, and sharing constantly, George, Chanel, and Gee, loving you guys is a treat full of splendor, amazement, and joy. To my parents, Alfred and Helen Anderson, and my siblings, Alfred Jr., Shirley, and Leslie. We have each other, we weathered the storm, and within this family are the strength and love to persevere. I must thank my spiritual parents, Dr. Michael and Minister Tamara Scott, who provide my spiritual shelter and support my endeavors with pride. To my extended family and friends, thank you for reading and telling everyone that you know, "Get Renã's books." I thank God for all of you in my personal fan club. There is always that special friend that comes along in the eleventh hour, just when you need a shoulder and reader the most. Mystery is intriguing, and I thrive on the unknown, so I'm not telling the world who you are. You know that I know, and that's what matters. You are my forever friend, and your friendship and love mean the world to me. Special thanks to Nicole Peters for your patience and understanding during my delays in finishing this work. You are a jewel. To my Urban family, I am honored to be a part.

This period has, without a doubt, been the most difficult time of my life. Living each day knowing that

I have lost a portion of my being and it will never be whole again until. . . It is because of my profound loss that these acknowledgments include a dedication:

I dedicate this novel to my brother Kenneth Antonio Anderson. Kenny, for all that you were, everything we shared, and especially because you loved me, *If I'm Gonna Love You* was created in the space where my pain resides and where your memory and the realization that you would want it to exist rest. That is the only reason that this work breathed life. Forever my love, RIP.

Now, back to all of you that are taking this literary journey with me. What can I say? . . . Enjoy!
Be 4-ever Blessed,
Renã

Prologue

There are people who, for whatever reason, prefer to conduct the affairs of their lives during the daylight hours. Heaven forbid if an activity should carry them well past dusk or beyond what is considered by some as the bewitching hour, aka after midnight. If you were to add a natural weather disturbance, complete with streaks of lightning, loud blasting thunder, and gale-force winds, most people would cease all movement and resolve upon the first deafening clap of thunder to stay indoors. I was quite certain that no sane, intelligent being would venture out in this kind of weather unless it was a matter of life or death. Yet here I was, Patrice Michelle Henderson, with a bright yellow, high-powered flashlight in hand, wandering around my bedroom on my knees, trying to find the other Nike sneaker, which I had kicked off hours ago after my workout at the gym. I had always considered myself a smart chick. Couple that with a good portion of what some old folk would consider "good common sense" and you would come up with a person who should have known better than to go out in this weather.

I had definitely gotten soft. A couple of months ago,

heck, strike that, a couple of days ago, I would have given anyone major attitude if they so much as asked me to get up off my comfy sofa and open my front door after a long, exhausting day. They could definitely forget me doing so if there was any kind of precipitation falling from the sky. My going out in the elements tonight was sheer madness, and I'd have to admit, if only to myself, it wasn't making any sense. Tomorrow I'd have a good long talk with myself.

I waited for almost an hour to see if the electricity would be restored, but it appeared that there would be no such luck. Don't get it twisted. I was not afraid of the dark by a long shot and considered myself one of the rare breeds who savored the dark tranquility of the night and considered it ideal for my sporadic escapades of creeping; however, I could have done without the heavy rain, thunder, and lightning. But I knew better than to question the good Lord's work.

"Dang!" I yelled out as I hit my forehead on the corner of the upholstered antique stool situated near the closet door and immediately dropped the flashlight on the floor. The sudden throb of pain caused me to rock back and forth for a minute, until the pain subsided. "That's going to leave a lump," I mumbled to no one. Any other time, I would have seen this mishap as a sign and forgotten all about going through with my plan. But, I was driven by a force I could only identify as a desperate need to get to my destination. I rubbed a little more across the spot I had hit before reaching to pick up the flashlight. I shined the light farther inside the closet, and there in view was the Nike, nestled between two pairs of pumps.

I didn't see my adamant search as time wasted, because I couldn't see myself wearing a decent pair of shoes out in this inclement weather. While my wardrobe was extensive and I adored shopping for clothes, it came in a slow second to my love for shoes. Shoe shopping was always good for whatever was ailing me, and there was simply nothing like searching for the right shoe to complement a particular wardrobe item. I wasn't really proud of my total absorption, but to be honest, there was nothing like the high of purchasing a pair of diva shoes. I didn't need to be judged for what I liked: there were worse things, and since a few had come and gone, I believed I chose the lesser of the addictive evils.

The room was lit up brightly for a fraction of a second as a streak of lightning zigzagged across the black sky. At almost the same exact moment, two claps of thunder resounded throughout the house with a deafening echo. Even with the storm in full force, there was an urgency that pressed me to get my other sneaker on, gather my things, leave the comfort of my home, and go across town.

I was willing to go the extra mile for someone in need. It was obviously the Good Samaritan in me. After all, a friend in need was a friend indeed. I was giving back because, God knows, my friend had gone the extra mile for me on several occasions.

In less than forty-five minutes, I pulled into the gated community, swiped the visitor's pass I kept secure in my glove compartment, and drove around the pond, toward the house. I made a sharp right into the driveway and pulled my car up behind the Yukon Denali. The rain was still heavy as I glanced around, noticing that many of the houses in this area were without electricity as well. A few of the elite had chosen to separate themselves even more from the average Joe by having their high-powered generators pick up where the local power-supply company had left off.

Rushing to the door, I fumbled to unlock it with my emergency key. Once inside the house, I took a deep breath and leaned my back against the closed door. The house was chilly and caused me to shiver as the wet hood and jacket clung to my body. Despite the short distance from the car to the house, I had gotten totally drenched. The idea of ending up in bed with another bug hit me. How could I have forgotten being laid up the previous two weeks with the flu, too weak to even get out of bed? "The things I do," I said to myself in a low mumble. The first thing tomorrow morning, I would drop by Wal-Mart, Walgreens, or someplace and get some of that ginkgo biloba. If it was going to help me stay mentally sharp and remember incidents that had happened only weeks before, then I couldn't see how it could hurt. Besides, I might mess around and call the wrong name in the heat of passion or end up at the right place at the wrong time or the wrong place at the right time.

Without wasting any more time, I slid into the first-floor bathroom, removed my wet clothes, and slipped into a cami and matching drawstring pants. As an after-thought, I brushed my hair up and placed an elastic band around it since it had gotten damp. The moisture from the rain on my body brought the scented body mist alive, and the fragrance of lilac and jasmine hung in the air.

I mentally pushed the impeding sign of exhaustion away, knowing I would probably be staying over. Lifting the flashlight off the counter, I started up the steps, being careful not to move too swiftly. Shining the light in the direction of the master bedroom suite, I called out, "I'm finally here. I know it took me a long time, but the weather is awful out there."

No answer came. Before I could call out again,

someone touched my shoulder from behind. I dropped the flashlight and turned around in a panic, all ready to let out a loud scream. With lightning quickness and before my eyes could fully adjust, I was pulled into a hard body and held so tight I couldn't budge.

I strained my eyes in the darkness of the hallway and blinked until they focused. "Is this any way to handle the person that just endured a major storm to come over here and take care of you?" My body trembled from the scare, and I inhaled deeply to restore my breathing to a normal rhythm. I had expected him to be in the bed, not lurking in the hallway, scaring the heck out of me.

"I actually feel much better, but I knew if I shared that tidbit of information, you wouldn't be standing here in my hallway." The response came without hesitation. His voice was deep and mellow. What hoarseness he'd had earlier, when we talked, was now gone. Left in its place was his usual baritone and seductive tone.

"So, there is no congestion, cough, runny nose, or fever?" I quizzed as if I was a well-trained health-care professional jotting down pertinent medical information. As I strained to look at him, I rubbed up and down his back, enjoying the feel of his warm body. "Does your body still ache?"

"I'd have to say no to most of your medical questions, but my temperature did rise the minute I pulled you into my arms." He was looking down at me. It didn't take the reassurance of electricity to see the longing that I heard in his voice.

I cleared my throat, hoping it would help steady my voice. "And you couldn't wait until tomorrow to pull me into your arms? Or at least, let's see, until after the storm had blown over?" I tried to act irritated, when in fact being in his arms was worth the price of weathering *the storm. Even if I was risking getting sick again with the bug that I had passed on to him a week before.*

"I just had to have you over here, in my arms, and since you were the one out in the weather, I knew you would be all wet and I'd get a chance to dry you off."

There it was again, the sound of desire in his voice. Even in the dark I closed my eyes and allowed his voice to carry me away to the place where I was at his mercy. "Hmmmm. That sounds so good. But I've already changed my clothes." I couldn't help but shiver at the mere thought of him hovering over my moist body, gently drying and caressing all my delicate places.

"Then you'll just have to get wet again." The lights flickered just as his lips were moving slowly toward mine. I inhaled deeply and waited for our lips to meet in the middle of our yearning, and then it happened.

"Patrice." There was a light tap on the hood of the hair dryer. "Have a seat in my chair. You should be all dry."

Chapter 1

With a little struggle, I opened my eyes, blinked a few times, and took in my surroundings. I had fallen asleep under the hair dryer and had been having a dream. But then it hadn't really seemed like a dream; it had been more of a flashback in time. I remembered the incident vividly and immediately realized that it had happened in my not-so-distant past. This pleasant memory from back in the day had remained tucked safely away with all the other remnants of my lustful adventures.

That was during a period of time when I had an extensive list of suitors and no problem at all entertaining whomever, whenever, with little concern if there would even be a repeat performance. I'd been selective, of course, and hadn't allowed just anyone to step to me. Those that did had played by my rules and understood that I had no intentions of being anything more than a good thing that they could enjoy every now and then. The arrangements I had going had worked for the most part, but I'd had to remind a few that getting caught up, enthralled, or totally obsessed with what I had to offer would cause them to end up on the fast track out, never to gain entrance to the land of Patrice again.

That hadn't always been the way I'd rolled; I hadn't always been this way, let me get that straight from the gate. Some things happen to spin one's life out of control, and I guess that was basically what happened to me. College had been a solo project, with no financial assistance from my mother or any other concerned family member. My father had left my mother when I was very young, and the minute he departed, she went from being a housewife to working a couple of jobs to take care of the basic things: food, shelter, and clothing. My access to those things was very limited. It seemed I was always the one that did without so that my two younger siblings could have the best that she could offer. She gave them everything, and I, well, I got what was left and often only a small portion of that. In my childlike mind, understanding why was so hard. I remembered when I was in middle school, my favorite aunt, Virgie Nichols, asked my mom if she could take me in since she had no kids. My mother's reply was a flat-out no. She went so far as to tell me that she'd said no because she didn't want me being raised to think I was better than my brother, Keith, and my sister, Selby. It had nothing to do with loving me. Aunt Virgie explained once that I was more like my dad in looks and actions, and my mother couldn't stand to see him in me.

There were many times when I would stay home from school because my mother would say she had enough money only to wash my siblings' clothes. I was too embarrassed to wear the same outfit I had on the day before or maybe the day before that. That was when I started washing the few clothes I had in the bathtub, with soap, and hanging them around the small room I shared with Selby. I was only twelve then, but I learned even at that early age to do what I had to do to survive. Years of doing things for myself had fueled my drive, and I resolved to finish college and not return home un-educated, defeated, and deemed a failure, which would have made my mother and my dysfunctional relatives happy. They had a thing for believing that apples didn't fall far from trees, but in my opinion, this apple had never belonged on that tree in the first place.

The minute I walked out the front door of the Hender-son house, I vowed never to return until I had achieved a measure of success. I did return for a few visits, so that pretty much said that in the time since I'd left my small town, I had done the darn thing. I'd graduated at the top of my class in both undergrad and grad school, was gainfully employed in the investment banking industry, and could boast of a financial portfolio that was more than adequate to handle not only all my needs but all of my wants.

There'd been obstacles, and like many people, I'd had a little help to make it through the rough times. My help had come in the form of my college professor and ad-viser Ben Giles. What started off as a four-year educa-tional, clothing, and recreational helping hand in exchange for many of my evenings and an exclusive physical relationship turned into a proposal of marriage just as I was ending my senior year. I was really fond of him and cared deeply, but I didn't love him, at least not the way he loved me. The truth of that was not received well by Ben, and he committed suicide because I had no desire to be his lifetime mate. The guilt I experienced from not loving someone who clearly deserved my love and had given so freely to make my life bearable was a scar I never recovered from. So, I cut myself off emo-tionally and only got involved with guys that posed no real threat to my heart. For many years it had worked, and I was actually happy that way.

So, you see life truly didn't owe me a thing. I had lived it upside down and inside out. In addition to having my physical needs met on my terms, I liked living well, plain and simple. Ever since I'd been old enough to call my own shots and had enough in the bank to make things happen, I hadn't allowed anything or anyone to deny me the privilege, which I felt had been more than earned. Being a continuing student in the school of hard knocks was for those who either couldn't do any better or didn't have the inner strength to make a change. It had only taken living without the simple things from the cradle to my teen years for me to know that it wasn't the lifestyle for me. Once I had been introduced to another way, I'd declared that I was never going back. That was a promise I'd made to myself over a decade ago, when my bank account had enough zeros to keep me from shopping at Goodwill and peanut butter and jelly was no longer my substitute filet mignon. Thankfully, I hadn't had to renege on my promise.

I was comfortable with the way I was and saw no real reason to change or adjust my lifestyle, that is, until Gina came along. In hindsight, in the midst of all that I had done and who I was, she was the best thing that had happened to me. The reality of adopting and raising a daughter had caused me to realign my priorities and to do things differently. It wasn't that I couldn't have my own child; I just had never married, and honestly, I thought I never would. But after spending so much time with Gina over the years as a mentor and coach at the youth center, I couldn't help but take her under my wing. When I met her, she was fourteen years old, cute, witty, and smart, a definite mini me. She became my shadow, and I adored her. From day one, I couldn't stand the thought of her living in a dysfunctional environment, with a mother who was an addict and who cared little about how her daughter was living or what she was doing to survive. After Gina was hospitalized with a sexually transmitted disease that could have ended up fatal, I became her foster parent. Shortly after that, her mother, without putting up an argument, allowed me to adopt her. Gina Webster became Gina Henderson, not to mention the center of my world. Because I was now a parent and concerned about the image I portrayed, no longer did I partake of spontaneous activities.

As far as my "male companionship for entertainment purposes only" philosophy was concerned, despite the best laid plans, life could sure enough give you something you weren't expecting. My unexpected delivery stood six feet four, was nicely built, with caramel brown skin that had not one blemish and was as smooth as it was chiseled. Not to mention piercing brown eyes and a smile that made me simply weak. Bryan Chambers and I worked in the same building, and while I made it a practice never to get involved with anyone that I worked with or around, when I saw him at a restaurant I frequented one evening, I asked him to take me home. For me, it was an evening like any other with a man that I was attracted to, but Bryan had another plan. For days, months, and even a year, he pursued me in an old-fashioned manner. As much as we enjoyed getting busy, he limited our physical contact and embraced me mentally and emotionally. I wasn't for the hand holding, walks in the park, long drives with no destination, flowers, jewelry, and calls just to say hello, but before I knew it, all those things meant so much to me. Bryan Chambers had captured me in a web of total bliss without warning. I was smitten, and I was not going to complain. In fact, I was happy and life was complete.

Now this. I had to wonder why I was having a flashback. And more importantly, why was I having it right now? Whatever it was, I'd have to think about it later. Right now I would complete my late afternoon of beauty and relish the last few hours of being thirty-seven. At 12:01 a.m. I would forever be older. The worst part was before I would have a chance to adjust to being an older woman, I would be thrown from one extreme to another with Gina going away to college. On top of the emotional roller coaster of aging, I would be experiencing empty-nest syndrome. If I still cursed, I'd say that life was a b——, but instead, I'd just pray real hard for better days.

Kim's presence and utterance brought me out of my deep thought. "Okay, Ma. There you go, all glamorous and cute. The highlights are definitely working for you."

Spinning around to face the mirror, I carefully examined my reflection and turned slowly from side to side. The loose curls hanging around my neck and falling on my shoulders made me appear almost exotic, not to mention the auburn streaks, which went well with my natural hair color. "Oh, my God, Kim. I didn't think I would, but I like it. It's not as drastic as I thought it would be, but it is different."

"So, tell me. What are you going to do for your birthday tomorrow?" Kim turned toward her counter and put the cap back on the can of hair spray she had just used to finish off my hairstyle.

"I don't really know. I believe that Gina and Bryan have made reservations for dinner. Where, I'm not sure. The big celebration is not going down until this weekend, when Kyra gets back in town. But you should know that, since you received an embossed invitation complete with an RSVP request, which you returned two weeks ago. I know this because it was included in the stash I lifted from Gwen's."

While my best friendship with Gwen went back to grade school, we had added Kyra Simmons to the mix our freshman year of college. Our circle had grown with Andre, Marcus, and Vince, who were the best guy friends a girl could have. We all hung out together and were inseparable. Kim had come along a little later, quite by accident. I happened to be shopping one day, and she was looking me up and down. It didn't take much to irritate me, and I immediately asked her if there was a problem. She apologized and mentioned that she was a hairstylist and couldn't help but notice how beautiful my hair was. Kim said that in this era of hair weaves, she was mentally giving me props for having my own. We chatted a bit, and she slipped me a business card and offered a complimentary visit. I was so impressed by her skills, Kyra and Gwen soon followed. Along with having the best hairstylist in the city, we had developed a friendship, and Kim was now a part of the posse. The best part was there was no shop gossip. She didn't get involved in petty gossip and didn't allow any to be exchanged, regardless of how much money was being spent in her establishment. There was always some catty stuff going on between women, and many times the beauty salon was a haven for much of it.

"You are too much. Does Gwen know you've been playing private eye?" Kim continued cleaning up her station, which was double the size of the other stations. She had four-by-six photos around the mirror of some of her young clients sporting their special occasion dos. Wouldn't you know that Gina would be right up there with the other girls, all dolled up?

"Actually, she doesn't. And I'm expecting you to

keep my enlightening, well-planned search and seizure between us. At least until after I get my bounty. After that you are free to spill your guts." I stood up with my back to the mirror, holding a smaller mirror to get a view of the back of my head.

"I'll do my best. But, now, if your birthday gift from Bryan tomorrow is something in the neighborhood of three carats and you are sporting it on your left hand, drop by here tomorrow and let a sister see it, because it will probably be as close as I'm going to get for a while. Derrick's trifling hide is moving like molasses." Kim sucked her teeth and brushed off the chair I had been sitting in with the cape she'd removed from around my neck.

"We'll see. I'm not ruling the possibility out, but to be honest, I don't know if I'd be clicking my heels in excitement." I pulled at a curl that was curved over my right eye.

Kim tapped my hand and adjusted the piece of hair again. "Girl, you must have inhaled too much hair spray. There isn't a woman I know in her right mind that's going to turn down no carats. And need I remind you that Bryan is as fine as they come, has got money to burn, adores you and Gina, not to mention he embraces all the clan that surrounds your butt, even me? Patrice, you have hit the lotto, and you don't have to scratch around no more. Sweetie, I love you and you are forever my girl, but you are a piece of work and are as high maintenance as they come. I'd say you should be giving him a ring, and a big one at that." Kim chuckled.

"Well, Ms. Thang, I didn't ask you. And I'm a trained receiver and not a giver," I replied pompously.

At least that was the way it used to be, but Bryan had brought about a whole new way of life, and I had found myself giving as much as I took, at least sometimes. I had to snap back to reality periodically and check my rules of engagement. When I got too close or cared too much, I had to readjust my emotional gadgets. Midway into our relationship, I only had to adjust every three to four months; of late, it had increased to once or twice a month. I was going back and forth like a yo-yo. We were in an active relationship, had been for a while, and still sometimes I couldn't completely let go. Gina had made me turn a complete one-eighty, but I wasn't ready to allow Bryan to turn me quite that much.

I looked around the shop, which was empty since I was Kim's last customer of the day. All the other stylists had finished their last client and had cleared out more than an hour ago. Kim's shop was totally upscale, and the hues of soft lavender, brown, and beige blended together well. Overhead, the chandelier lit the reception area and spattered diamond-like rays on the high-gloss floor. The wall behind the counter held various types of hair products and accessories. Upscale Salon had a fully equipped day spa with signature spa products made exclusively by Kim Monroe. Her years of studying chemistry had not been wasted, despite her parents' belief that going to cosmetology school after receiving a master's degree was a waste of good money and time. She could never get them to see that spending her days in a lab, with a white coat, would not be rewarding or fulfilling. It was, after all, their dream and not hers.

That decision paled, though, when she hit them with the biggest change of all. The day that she decided to go to cosmetology school, she also visited a medical facility that would end her years as Kenny Monroe and physically create Kimberly Monroe. The day the total transformation took place was the last day that she saw or spoke with her parents. They came to the hospital, pleading for the last time for Kenny to remain. Accepting that he was gay had suddenly become easy for them: it was the lesser of the two evils. But having a son who would be changed physically and turned into a woman was more than they felt the good Lord could forgive, and thus much more than they could condone.

Kim had stood her ground and refused to change her mind, realizing that it was true liberation that she needed and acceptance for who she really was. It was not about her parents, not really about anyone else; there was no known significant other. It was just her desire to live out the rest of her life honoring the woman on the inside, who felt it time to shine through. If anyone had asked her why she wanted a sex change, she would have told them that she'd simply been born with the wrong equipment and she had to take the necessary steps to right the wrong.

I went on. "That's just it, Kim. If I had to answer any serious, life-altering questions right now, especially one as weighty as spending the rest of my life as a married woman, my response would begin with *if*."

"Patrice, you know I know all about contemplating one's life. But, what is it with the *if?*" Kim looked at me with a raised eyebrow.

The response came slowly, but methodically. "If. Two letters that are loaded with no guarantees, some uncertainty, and, if I'm lucky, a few possibilities."

"Girl, you are too deep for me." Kim leaned over the counter to make sure I was penciled in for my regularly scheduled day and time. I handed her a check. "No, this one is on me. Enjoy your birthday, and I'll see you Saturday night at your party."

As I left the salon, I turned the word *if* over and over in my head, not sure where the response I'd given Kim had come from. It hadn't been there before that moment, or had it? Maybe I just didn't want to think about the possibility of Bryan asking me to marry him. Sure, we had browsed around jewelry stores, and he would call me into the room whenever he surfed the Net, checking out information about diamonds. We had talked about settings, carats, and shapes, but wasn't that just FHITBRL, for his information to be retrieved later . . . much, much, much later? I thought about Bryan handing me a velvet box, which would hold more than just a circle symbolizing eternity: it would hold a commitment to a life of adoration, understanding, forgiveness, and undying love—all wrapped up in a red bow. If he chose this occasion to pop the question, I just wasn't sure if I would be ready to say yes. It had nothing to do with love, and everything to do with timing.

Chapter 2

"We've been thinking of making you an offer for the past six months. It was more about coming up with a salary that would make you think twice, maybe even three times. We knew you wouldn't take on the added responsibility for peanuts." John Briggs, the senior partner of America Investments, laughed along with his new young partner, Chris Harvey.

I had been summoned to the executive conference room the minute I'd arrived. There had barely been enough time to put my briefcase down, open the blinds, and listen to my voice mail. It was a good thing I'd driven through the Starbucks drive-thru and picked up a Caramel Frappuccino. With this unexpected meeting, I would have been deprived of my early morning run around the corner to get my caffeine fix. It was Friday, and we never did Friday meetings. Everyone was finishing up paperwork or looking over figures so they could exit early and start the weekend on a high note. It wasn't normally my custom to exit early just because it was Friday, but today I had planned to be among those rushing out shortly after noon.

After my birthday dinner last evening, I'd ended up

going to bed long after midnight. I was exhausted, to say the least. Bryan and Gina had planned a special evening just for me. We'd started off with dinner at Bistro Twenty Seven, one of my favorite restaurants. Then they'd whisked me away to the Funny Bone Comedy Club. We were entertained by a gospel comedian who was appearing for that night only. The three of us laughed until we cried from the time she hit the stage to the time she said good night. By the time I climbed into the car and relaxed into the seat, the thought of the evening ending had set in and my heart had started beating double time. All the way home I wondered if Bryan was going to pop the question. In the weeks prior to my birthday, we had talked about little else except our future together. The signs were there, and I would have had to be blind to miss them. Bryan was ready for the next level. I wanted to be with him and didn't want to see anyone else, hadn't for years, but the thought of forever with anyone was frightening. Not a late-night fright kind of fear, but a fear that stemmed from not knowing if I was making the right decision. I'd always been a risk taker, but this was different. I just didn't think I had the key ingredients that would yield a happily ever after.

After we arrived at my house and the moment of truth hit, I stood at the open door of my home office, taking in the sight of my new wall plasma television. Bryan didn't say a word, but I knew that he had to notice the look of sheer relief on my face. The ending of our evening hadn't exactly gone as I thought it would. There'd been no cuddling on the sofa or talking over coffee, only an announcement that he had a headache. Please!

I turned my attention back to Chris. He'd already been a part of the company when I started ten years ago. We'd become fast friends, and as much as I liked him, I liked him even more when I learned that he was married to someone of African American descent. It somehow sent me a message that he wasn't prejudiced and that with him the table would always turn on the side of fairness. There was an undercurrent in the city that race was still sometimes a factor in many of the hiring practices and promotions in the investment banking arena. I was just glad that I had never had to encounter that undercurrent with John, and I knew I never would with Chris.

"I'm listening," I said and leaned forward in my chair.

John continued. "We'd like you to accept the position of senior vice president for Acquisitions. As you know, I already announced that Chris will be taking Ben's position as partner, and thus leaving his very lucrative position open. We are willing to offer you two hundred thousand dollars as your base salary, plus all the administrative-level perks. Of course, we had to have a great meeting of minds to come up with an adequate incentive." John nodded at Chris, who nodded back. "We finally decided on an attractive stock-option package in the new company we are opening in Europe."

I tried to act unaffected by what John had just said, but my eyes opened wide as I turned to Chris and he smiled, confirming that the offer was indeed real. "I would be pleased and honored if you would consider our offer, Patrice. You've worked hard as a senior analyst and senior consultant, and even harder as a managing director, and you deserve this opportunity. Now, the stock options are up for debate. If you'd prefer something else, say the word. We just couldn't come up with what to give a person that has everything." John paused, as if he was mentally going over the assets he knew I had. "You just bought that Benz last month, so that is hardly broken in. Now, if you'd like a new one in a different color or a Jaguar, we can discuss it."

"You guys are too much. I can't say I haven't dreamed of becoming a part of the top administrative team and moving upstairs, but this is so sudden," I said. I didn't want to bop to it, but the theme from *The Jeffersons* was playing in my head. "We just cut the retirement cake for Ben three weeks ago, and I had just gotten used to Chris leaving me and going upstairs with you, and now this."

I sat back in the burgundy leather swivel chair that was situated at the end of the cherry and oak conference table. My eyes captured the three large wooden frames hanging on the wall. The first two frames bore the likenesses of the founding partners, who have been at the helm of the company since its inception thirty years before. Chris's likeness was below the two, along with the other four vice presidents. He had been the latest addition, contributing seventeen plus years to the success of America Investments, and yet he had been offered the partnership. Phil, Chuck, Windsor, and Sadie had been beside themselves last week when John announced Chris's new position. Now, Ben's photo would move over to the emeritus wall, and Chris would take his place.

I couldn't believe that if I were to say the word, answer in the affirmative, my likeness would be framed and would grace this wall of distinction. Me, Patrice Michelle Henderson, in all her African American beauty on the wall of the executive conference room, announcing to those that walked through the doors that I was someone of great importance. *Wouldn't that be something?* I thought.

"We know that Ben made some significant contributions to our company," said Chris. "But you know as well as we do that things have to continue to make this company a vital contributor to the investment sector. The wheels of progress must not stop. You are our logical choice. In fact, Ben agrees that you would be an asset. Patrice, we all know you've made a name for yourself, and this change would make several of our biggest clients happy." Chris beamed at me.

"Yes, and my being a minority and part of the top administrative team in the company would definitely enable the company to gain more minority business and would make us look even better," I interjected, not wanting to leave out the obvious.

"Don't think of it as us using you. Think of it as you using us," Chris replied. "Seriously, we don't mind at all. And you know I'm not caught up in color whatsoever. In fact, the blacker the berry . . ." He started to laugh.

"I know that for you, the juice is sweeter, Chris," I said.

"You know that's right," Chris responded, with a loud chuckle. The partners had never expressed a concern regarding his preference; in fact, they appreciated it, especially given his handle on the firm's African American clients.

"I'm honored to have your and Ben's vote of confidence," I said. I decided to discard my modesty, state the obvious, and blow my horn. "I am the only logical choice." I knew Wanda Young would be furious. How she thought she could waltz in a couple of years after me and be the know-it-all in investing was beyond me. Not to mention prancing around like the company was lucky to have her. Up until Wanda came through the revolving doors to join the team, I'd been the only African American female face in management. That alone was enough to cause Wanda to view me as her arch enemy. It didn't matter to me. I didn't need anyone else in my fan club; nor was I searching for another friend. What I did instead was use my business savvy to rise above her pettiness, and it had worked for all these years. We were civil, and that was about all we needed to be and all we would ever be. As I thought of Wanda, I knew I would gladly accept the new position just to see her reaction and would relish all the perks, rights, and privileges that came with being a senior vice president. However, to appear in control, I wouldn't send up the yes flares just yet.

"That's the Patrice we know. Cocky and self-assured," said John. He took a sip from the burgundy company mug.

"I would like a little time to think it over, if you don't mind," I said matter-of-factly and watched each of them for any sign that they had changed their mind because of my request for more time.

"Of course. We realize that it is a big decision, so by all means, take your time," said Chris. He stood up and moved around the table.

"I'm leaving on vacation for two weeks, so I'll have a little time to think while I'm relaxing in Kingston, Jamaica," I replied.

"That's right," Chris exclaimed, snapping his fingers. "You are taking Gina on a precollege vacation. I swear you take that young lady on more vacations."

I couldn't help but smile, because I actually did. From the trip to Paris we took after the adoption was complete to birthday and Christmas getaways. I wanted to give her all the things that I had never had and to introduce her to places she had never been but had only dreamed of. When she finally met Mr. Right, I wanted her to know her worth and not give in to someone showering her with material things in exchange for her physical affection.

"Well, my baby is worth all that and then some," I

said. But, this actually wasn't my idea. It was Bryan's."
I slowed my speech as his name rolled out of my
mouth. I hadn't thought about how this offer would
affect our relationship. He was not one to go on a male-
dominating power trip, but he had been talking more
and more about starting his own investment consulting
firm. Because we were both in the same business, he
had talked about me joining him as partner in a company created by and for the two of us. In addition we
were still waiting for Gina to leave for college in the
fall and choose a major that would hopefully complement what both of us did. Not wanting to pressure her,
we stood by silently, praying and checking every piece
of paper with the UVA emblem, hoping it would give
us a clue or hint.

"Well, if you should decide before you return and
want us to set everything in motion while you are away,
just call," said John. He stood up and leaned his belly
on the back of the chair he had been sitting in. I tilted
my head a little as I looked at him. I was trying really
hard to stay focused, but John Briggs reminded me of
all the mall Santas I had ever seen. His big belly was as
round as could be, and his cheeks were always rosy red.

"I will do that," I responded.

The phone on the conference table rang, and Chris,
who was closest, leaned over to get it. "Patrice, Tina
just rang to let you know that Gwen is waiting for you
downstairs."

"Oh, okay. I'm sorry, guys. I've got to run," I said.

"Patrice, tell that fine girlfriend of yours that I still
got love for her," Chris joked and laughed.

I couldn't help but laugh along with him, because it
had become a habit of his to flirt with Gwen whenever
she came around and to chuckle whenever she came up
in a conversation we were having. Besides that, listening

to this Ivy League white boy who sounded just like a brother always amused the heck out of me. His dialect was spiced with a little Ebonics, and obviously from the way April hung on, he had some other physical attributes that were common among men of color. That last piece of information I really hadn't had to get from April. Sarah, the benefits coordinator in human resources, had dated Chris before he got married, and she was hopelessly sprung. She'd run Chris's butt all through the Donovan Building, and when he'd got married, she'd sat in the back of the church, crying like somebody had stolen her 401(k). To get over Chris, she finally got another lily-white stud. I was not sure if this one was well endowed or if she had just decided that licking was as good as sticking. Either way, Sarah was still smiling, so I assumed whatever it was, it worked for her.

I had never been interested in sampling another flavor. In all the time that I had worked alongside Chris, and despite his early advances, I had always kept things between us in perspective. I'd have to admit, though, I used to be curious, and on a couple of business trips I wondered, but one evening of play was not worth an awkward business relationship. In short, back then I knew what I was working with and had heard about his sexual skills; putting the two together would have caused a major disturbance in the order of the sexual universe. On the other hand, pride had told me the first time this thought occurred to me all those years ago that I didn't want to turn him out, and fear had said not to venture out into the unknown. So, I didn't.

"Hey, girl. Why you bust out of the elevator, grinning from ear to ear?" Gwen asked. She walked over to me, leaned her cheek against mine, and gave me a hug. She looked absolutely radiant. Very few women looked good pregnant, but pregnancy looked good on her. Her hair had grown out and hung around her neck in loose curls. She had taken a leave of absence from Wescott and Windsor when, at her last doctor's appointment, her blood pressure was slightly elevated. Scott had instantly demanded that she stay at home and put up her feet for the next six months. Gwen knew the decision was really personal for him, since he had been a premature baby and had almost lost his life. Not to mention that as a pediatrician, he knew all too well that some preemies didn't make it or suffered long-term damage to their frail organs. Because of those two factors, she didn't bother to put up a fight. She didn't ask me what I thought, and it was no use. My godmother vote had been cast on Scott's side of the tally. Her health was my main concern.

I still considered them newlyweds, since they'd been married only a year. Everyone in the crew joked to Scott that he hadn't wasted any time. The truth was at thirty-six, Gwen was concerned about her age affecting the odds of having a normal pregnancy. For that reason, Scott, of course, had consulted the best obstetrician in the area, and both were taking every measure necessary to ensure that all went well. I had immediately made a call to the physician of all physicians and had it on his authority that everything would be all right. Call it what you like, but I called it trusting in someone bigger than us. I hadn't always gotten it right, but I'd always known who to call.

"We need to celebrate. Chris and John just offered me Chris's old position," I said. I kept moving, even though I knew Gwen was cemented in place, ready to ask me to repeat myself.

When I turned around, just as I'd predicted, she was standing there, with a questioning look on her face. "Patrice, what did you just say?"

I walked back to her and spoke with a straight face. "They offered me the position of senior vice president for Acquisitions. But it's no big deal. I mean, a little extra money and some stock options in the new overseas firm. I'd move upstairs into a bigger office, and my portrait would be on the wall in the conference room. Stuff like that." I moved the piece of hair from over my eye and continued to look at her as if none of what I had just said fazed me the least bit. "Come on. We really need to feed the baby." I rubbed her stomach.

Without saying a word, Gwen let out a scream, and everyone within close proximity glared at us. "Oh, my God, Trice. I'm so happy for you. If I could, I'd jump up and down. Oh, my God!" She grabbed her cell phone from her purse and began to scroll through some numbers.

"Gwen, what are you doing?" I looked at her, trying to figure out who she was getting ready to call, but I couldn't help feeling the same ripple of excitement that she was experiencing. This was my best friend, and her excitement was not a put-on. I knew that she really was happy for me, and proud to boot.

"I'm calling Kyra, Scott, Dre, Tori, Marcus, Vince, Mama Bea, Ma Elliott, my parents, TJ, your mama, the twins, heck somebody, anybody." She was still scrolling and grinning from ear to ear.

"Slow your roll. None of them need to hear you now, Ms. Verizon. If you blab it to them, they will start calling around to everybody, and it will beat me home. FYI . . . I'd like to talk to Gina and Bryan about it. In fact, I haven't even accepted the position yet." I felt a little uneasy because while the decision was mine to make, it would impact the two people I cared about the most. Gina was easy and would be just as excited as me. Anything I did was a reason for her to brag about

the accomplishments of her mother. I just wasn't sure
how Bryan would take it. So, for now I wouldn't allow
myself to go over the top with excitement.

"Oh, I'm sorry." Gwen put the phone away. "I was so
excited, I didn't even think about Gina and Bryan not
knowing yet. I'll just put my excitement on ice until
you tell them."

"Thanks for understanding. I probably should have
told them first, but you know I would not be able to
have lunch with you and not spill my guts. I've always
shared everything with you first."

"Same here. Scott has gotten used to you being my
left lung, but it still caused a little friction between us
when I slipped and told him that you were the first to
know that I was pregnant. If it will make things better,
I will act as if I didn't know. I promise." Gwen crossed
her fingers to show that she would be true to her word.

"No need. Bryan and Gina know how close we are.
They wouldn't be shocked that you found out first. But
to make them feel super important, keep it between
us until I tell them. For right now, though, we need to
feed my godbaby." I reached into my purse for the keys.
"The excitement has caused me to work up quite an
appetite myself. You know what else?" I didn't wait for
her to reply. "I see no reason to return to work today."
I strained to look at the front doors of the building. The
weather report had forecast a beautiful day, and from
where I was standing, on the inside looking out, it appeared that the report was right on the money. "Let's
say we have a long, leisurely lunch, and we can go over
the last-minute details for the party tomorrow night. I
don't want you to wear yourself out, since you are in
such a delicate state." I busted out laughing. I had
waited for just the right time to let Gwen know that the
surprise party was not a surprise, after all.

"You knew? How? We worked so hard to keep it a surprise." Gwen looked like someone had told her that she was a half inch too short to ride the roller coaster at the amusement park.

"I know. But if it helps, I'll act really surprised as I open up all my gifts. See." I threw both hands up and opened my mouth really wide to show her my birthday surprise look. "Especially when I open the purple and white wrapped box and pull out the black Dooney & Bourke tote you got me. There is one thing I can't understand and maybe you can enlighten me. Why did you tuck it away in Scott's walk-in closet?" I was curious to learn the answer.

"What I want to know is why in the world were you all up in my husband's closet?" Gwen asked, with arms folded and an inquisitive look on her face.

"That's easy actually. Remember when you two went to his conference about a month ago, and you called and asked me to get a folder off the shelf in your office and drop it by Wescott and Windsor?"

She nodded that she recalled.

"Well, I couldn't let an opportunity like that go by and not use it to snoop. You always shop early, so I knew you had my gift. After I checked the closets downstairs, the spare room, and your closet, I decided to check Scott's closet. It was the one place you would never expect me to look. And there it was, my birthday gift. That was sheer genius, though. I almost didn't check there. I mean, I was all the way downstairs and almost out the door when the possibility hit me."

"I knew you would snoop around, and it was Scott's idea to put it there. He assumed it would be the one place you wouldn't look. He figured you would respect his privacy. Scott just didn't know we were dealing with supersnoop. You are such a bloodhound when it comes to a gift with your name on it."

"You know it. And as for my news, we can share it at the party. I wouldn't let an opportunity like that go by without letting all my friends know that a sistah done made it to the top. By then I would have told Bryan and Gina."

"You've got everything planned to a tee. Are there any other arrangements you want me to make? Is there anything else that you've planned exclusively for your special event?"

"Not a thing. But should I come up with any other additions, I'll be sure to let you know." I rummaged through my oversized bag, looking for my sunglasses.

"I don't mean to change the subject, but Bryan called me this morning. The new forty-two-inch plasma for your home office and dinner were only part of your gift. It seems your real gift wasn't ready. He is planning to give it to you tomorrow night," Gwen stated coolly, confirming what I had suspected.

"I assumed as much. I'm just not sure how I feel about a proposal at this point in my life. I mean, it's the next logical step, but I'd be giving up who I am. Isn't that what he'd expect?" I stared at my best friend, wishing she could help me make sense of what I was feeling.

"Bryan would be asking you to share your life with him. That's not a death sentence."

Gwen looked at me. I could tell she was attempting to sense the deeper reason for my question. She knew me well, because while that was part of what I felt, at the core of my being there was so much more. My mom hadn't shown me love, and my father had never returned, which in and of itself had sent me the message that there'd been no love lost when he walked out.

How could I function in a marriage when genetically I wasn't sure I possessed a forever gene?

"Listen, we need to talk," Gwen added. "But let's wait until we get to the restaurant. We are absolutely famished." She rubbed her stomach.

Thoughts of Bryan popping the question came and went. I had been thinking about it so much lately and had spent so many restless moments wondering how I would respond when the question was out there and the ring ready to be placed on my finger. "No problem, Boos. Let's be on our way."

I was hungry as well, but I knew I would have to do something about the anxiety and the nervous energy in the pit of my stomach. The ring was only one of my concerns now. The job offer was something else entirely, and I wasn't sure how Bryan would react to the news. All of it, the known and the unknown, had my mind going around in circles.

Chapter 3

Instead of the alarm clock waking me up, I awoke to music blasting, with lyrics that were hardly recognizable, and the entire second floor thumping. I gingerly got out of bed, realizing it was a little later than my normal Saturday rising time. My bare feet trembled from the surround-sound bass as soon as they hit the floor. Usually, I would have been slightly irritated at the volume, but Gina would be leaving in a couple of months, and I would yearn for some noise, any noise, to flow from behind the closed door of her room, letting me know that she was on the other side.

Sure, Bryan would be spending time with me in the evening, but we did all we could to practice control. We'd had a heart-to-heart several months ago and decided that we loved each other enough to wait. At the time it had sounded like a plan. At that time I had thought that I would be able to marry Bryan without blinking twice. Who knew that I would have a revelation and I would be plagued with the Henderson loveless curse. In addition to trying to do the spiritual thing and wait, he'd wanted to display the workings of a real relationship and give Gina an example of the true measure of a man.

For a while I'd avoided Bryan and would only see him if we had something planned with our friends. There had been no candlelight dinners, no late-night movies, no listening to love ballads while the rain beat against the windowpane, no out-of-town escapades to quiet bed-and-breakfast inns or secluded places, where we'd indulge in each other and leave our cell phones behind. When we had ventured along our newly altered path, I'd detested him for even suggesting this be our new lifestyle. Bryan had always been very spiritual, but when he was involved in a terrible car accident and remained hospitalized in a coma for weeks, the Bryan that emerged from that close call, with no permanent damage, was totally committed to God. So, when he'd said it would strengthen our relationship, I knew he believed that we would one day be standing at the altar. My spiritual commitment was not as deep as Bryan's, at least not initially, but I'd agreed with him that we show Gina something completely different from what she had known. I needed her to recognize her worth as a young woman and realize that giving it up did not seal a relationship with a stamp that said forever. Her first sexual encounter had been when she was only twelve, and it had been with the neighborhood drug dealer, Q. It had been so toxic and anything but healthy for her emotionally or physically, especially since she narrowly escaped permanent damage from some disease the low-life thug had given her.

I had been preaching for years that someone could be totally into another person and not be sexually involved. If I was going to talk the talk, I had to walk the walk. So, that was exactly what I had been doing. If nothing else, it had kicked my prayer life up to another level. There were many times that I ended the day wondering if I had made the right decision in waiting, but when I weighed everything and realized that my relationship with Bryan hadn't suffered, I decided that we had been thrown a lifeline.

I went down the hall to her room, knocked lightly, and waited. You'd think I'd have known better than to expect her to hear me over the noise. I went back to my bedroom, grabbed my cell phone, and hit the number set to speed dial her. After only a few rings, she picked up.

"Holla," Gina screamed into the phone.

"Holla. Girl, you better start checking the ID and know who you talking to." I always got on her for abbreviating her greetings or talking like everybody that dialed her number was her peeps, as she called them.

"Oh, my bad, Mom. I just hit my Bluetooth. I didn't even look to see who it was. I'm sorry." She was out of breath. "I was cleaning my room. Is the music too loud? I'll turn it down right now." Just like that the music went mute, and I could suddenly hear myself think.

"It is. But I wasn't going to say anything. Soon enough it will be so quiet in here, I will be going crazy."

"Let's not talk about that. You know I've never been away from you that much since we've been together. My only overnight stays at friends' houses are because you are out of town on business."

I closed my eyes and flipped through some of the times we'd had together. I couldn't believe that my baby would be leaving home. I didn't know how mothers who gave birth did it. I hadn't given birth and had had only five years with Gina, if you counted the years that I'd mentored her, and I was having some serious doubts about allowing her to fly away from the nest. "I know. I guess I should have let you go a little more."

"No, you shouldn't have. I wouldn't change anything about the way you've raised me. You've done a great job, and I'm glad that you are my mom. Most people have no choice about who they have as parents. I know I was one of them. But I was blessed because I got a second chance and was old enough to tell the judge that I wanted you to be my mom for the rest of my life."

"Gina, enough. You are going to make me cry, and I'm too much of a diva to be crying. And besides, you talked me into getting these eyelashes, and crying may cause these darn things to stick my eyes together or something."

"They look hot. Wait till Auntie Gwen and Aunt Kyra see them. They are going to want me to take them to get the same hookup."

"Well, be sure to share your beauty advice with your aunties and see if they are interested in getting the hookup. But right now, I need to run out. Bryan has to go to the office and pick up a package. I've got to talk with him before tonight, so I was going to meet him." I stood in my closet, which was strategically arranged according to clothing types, and pulled a pair of sweat-pants off the shelf while holding the cell phone in place against my shoulder. Last night over pizza, I'd told Gina all about the job offer, and as I'd expected, she was excited and supported me 100 percent.

"Hang up the phone, Mom. I'm right here." Gina stood behind me, with phone in hand, snickering.

I clicked the phone closed. "If the music hadn't been so loud, I wouldn't have had to communicate with you via an electronic device." I playfully hit her butt with my sweats as she turned around and moved toward my bed.

"I came in last night and placed the sheet and duvet cover back on the bed. You were really tossing and turning. Are you worried about the proposal or the job offer?" Gina pulled one of the decorative pillows from the top of my bed, placed it under her head, and reclined.

"How did you know about the proposal?" I asked quickly.

"Oh, Auntie Gwen told me. But I also assumed that since I helped him make arrangements to get the plasma television in your office, there had to be a ring lurking around somewhere. It just seemed like it was time for something permanent. Besides, I've gone to Jared with him a couple of times and pointed out what I thought you'd like."

"What? And you didn't tell me?" I put my hand on my hip and narrowed my eyes at her.

"I was sworn to secrecy." Gina laughed. "Enough. I can't disclose everything. The man will never trust me again. So, chick, what had you tossing and turning? Bryan popping the question or the job offer?"

"It's both really." I ran my fingers through my hair. "I'm worried that Bryan won't understand why I want to jump at the opportunity with the firm, and I'm concerned that I won't be able to answer in the affirmative if he should pull a ring from his pocket and kneel down in front of me."

"The ring part is easy. You love him. He loves you. You both love me, and I know I love you. That equates to us being a happy family, so that case is pretty much closed. But why wouldn't he want you to take the job?"

"Well, he's been talking about starting an investment consulting firm, and he would like for me to be his partner." I spoke to my daughter, hoping she could provide a reassuring solution to my problem. Something I hadn't thought of or some way I hadn't yet examined things. I was a wiz with money and number crunching, but matters of the heart sometimes had a way of confusing me.

"That would be so neat. Why didn't you tell me?"

"It's just a future plan. It's not like he is going to open

it tomorrow. Although, I'm not sure working together is a good idea. Imagine working together all day, coming home together, and getting up the next day to do the same thing all over again. I'd be in serious Bryan Chambers overload."

"And that would be a bad thing?" Gina turned over on her stomach and propped the pillow under her elbows.

"I don't know. But I do know that if I take this job, it would be like sending him a message that I don't believe in his dream and that I'm not interested in being a part of it."

Gina held out her hands and examined her brightly polished fingernails. It appeared that she wasn't listening to me.

"Gina, did you hear me?"

"Oh yeah, Mom. I'm listening to every word. You are all worked up over this, when the solution is simple. Talk to him and tell him that you believe in his dream and want to be a part of it, but for right now you'd like to gain as much experience as possible so it will make the firm you two will have together even better."

I stared at Gina for a couple of minutes without speaking. The child had made the solution seem so simple. I was making everything all complicated and trying to analyze it, when it really was as simple as Gina made it. "You know what? You are growing up too fast. The wisdom you just dropped on me seemed to have come from someone a whole lot older than eighteen."

"Well, I have excellent teachers. I happen to hang around some very profound and wise women. Don't sweat it, Mom. You will make the right decision. Your heart won't ever lie."

* * *

I rolled the window down instead of turning the air on. I knew the humidity wouldn't be good for my hair, but I needed a little fresh air. Not that Richmond air could be considered fresh, but I was hoping for at least a few breaths of something that resembled fresh air. I gave up the attempt after a few minutes and opted for manufactured air. I rode in silence, not even wanting the radio to keep me company. I replayed my conversation with Gina and the midnight conversation I'd had with Kyra and Gwen on a three-way. While they hadn't said it exactly the way Gina had, the summation of what they'd said was the same. They thought I was not giving Bryan enough credit and that I was underestimating his ability to understand my reason for wanting to be promoted within the ranks of the company I had given so many years to. Kyra had added that the promotion was rewarding because the investment banking industry was very racial, and many of the upper-level managers were very prejudiced and rarely promoted women of color to their highest ranks. That was indeed a legitimate rationale. Before I hung up, Gwen had urged me to tell Bryan as soon as possible and trust him to understand and be willing to share in my excitement. As far as the marriage was concerned, they'd seen no reason for me to delay what was to them inevitable. There was a shortage of good black men. And the ones that were available either wanted to live off of what you brought to the table or felt that you should make less than they did. No amount of sexual healing could make up for a black male with issues.

The downtown area was extremely busy this time of day. Buses were pulling in and out of traffic, stopping every other block letting people on and off. I could have used the expressway to get there but had thought the extra riding time would afford me the opportunity to get my thoughts together. Now, I sat behind yet another bus and wanted to scream, knowing that at this rate, although I could see the top of the Donovan Building, I wouldn't be pulling into the parking garage for another fifteen minutes.

I reached for my phone to speed dial Kyra, but after hitting the button, I quickly clicked off the phone. I wanted to rehearse what I would say and have Kyra play Bryan and tell me what wanted to hear. It sounded like a plan until Gina's words came rushing back to me. I was really making way too much out of the whole situation. It wasn't a big deal, and I needed to just chill the heck out. I was acting like I didn't know Bryan Chambers, when in fact we had been in an ongoing relationship for almost five years. He had never, ever gone off on me for anything, not even when I'd pressed all the wrong buttons. Our disagreements were always minor, and because I could be so bullheaded, he was usually the one to mend the fence and make the extra effort to be the stable bridge over our troubled water. In short, I knew he loved me. He had proven that on numerous occasions, and I had to trust that the job offer wouldn't be that big of a deal.

The first floor of the parking garage was nearly empty. Only a few cars were parked inside. There was no need to reach into the backseat for my briefcase, since I wasn't here to get any work done. Work was the furthest thing from my mind, and since I'd left the office on Thursday, I hadn't given two thoughts to anybody's portfolio. Don't get me wrong. My clients were important. It was just that I was good at what I did and conducted my job between the hours of 8:00 a.m. and 5:00 p.m. If something ran over, 8:00 p.m. was the cut off time, and that included traveling and meeting over dinner, but that wasn't a normal practice. Since it worked for all parties concerned, I wasn't about to change an arrangement that was working for me.

I walked along, humming one of the tunes that I'd heard blasting from Gina's room, and smiled to myself. That girl and her world were such a huge part of me. If she'd known which song I'd chosen to hum, she would have gotten a kick out of it. A peaceful, calm feeling was coming over me when, out of the corner of my eye, I spied Wanda's Mercedes sports car. The "It" loomed somewhere on our floor, and I glanced up as if I expected to find a cloud of blackness cloaking the building. Hopefully, I would be in and out of the lobby and elevator and wouldn't run into her. I glanced at my watch and mentally noted that I had about a couple of hours to kill before the girls were meeting at my house. That would give me enough time to talk to Bryan, get a big kiss, maybe a tight hug, and be on my way back across town.

"What's up, Jordan?" I smiled at the weekend security guard, who worked at our building and attended Virginia Union full time. I had recommended him for the job about six months ago, and I had not regretted it. He was not only handsome but very bright, and he had things together. A rare combination for a twenty-year-old black male. Virginia statistics would have him anywhere else and doing just about everything else, but he was serious about his education and used the job to help pay his tuition, not wanting to be a financial burden on his single mother. "I see you got your head in the books." I leaned across the counter and pushed the book up a little to take a glance at the title. I nodded at the American literature textbook. "I like to see that. You inspire me to be more."

"Oh, thanks, Ms. Patrice. But I aspire to have it together

like you and Mr. Bryan. I've got a long way to go, but I'm determined to get there. How is Gina doing?"

"She's good. You know she finally decided to attend UVA in the fall." I knew he liked Gina by the way he looked at her whenever she came to the office with me on weekends. But he never approached her. I didn't know if it was because he didn't know what she would say or if he was more concerned about what Bryan would say. Bryan played the protective father role to the hilt. Jordan had even asked me if Bryan was Gina's real father, since he knew we were dating but not married. "I'll be sure to tell Gina you asked about her." I watched him smile, displaying all of his pearly whites. If there was a question of whether or not he thought my daughter was a catch, his face just confirmed it. "Well, I'll check with you on my way out. I'm going up to talk to Bryan." With that, I continued toward the elevators.

I leaned against the wall of the elevator and glanced up at the mirrored ceiling, listening as the elevator audibly told me which floor I was passing. Once it got to the eighth floor, the eight lit up and the doors opened wide. I swiftly got out of the elevator, glancing at my watch again. I knew not much time had passed since the last time I'd checked, but I checked it just the same.

I heard voices coming from down the corridor. Obviously, someone other than Bryan had to use their off-hours to pick up something important or to work on a project. Their workload was as hectic as ours, and while I considered our company tops, theirs was right up there with us. A familiar giggle came from the hallway just as I turned the corner, and there was Wanda, leaning against the wall, with Bryan standing in front of her, with his arms folded.

I took a couple of deep breaths and tried to see past how the scene appeared to my naked eyes. I inhaled slowly and exhaled as I walked toward them. Bryan looked up first and smiled his usual smile. "Hey, sweetie. I didn't know you were coming by."

He really didn't look like someone with their hand caught in the cookie jar, but he was standing in the hallway talking to "It," and she was smiling up at him like he was a juicy steak. That trick had seen us together on numerous occasions and at every function our company had. And yet she dared to stand there talking to him when there wasn't a soul around to judge whether it was a purely aboveboard conversation.

While Bryan might not have been aware of her intentions, I was, and I was pissed with him for being so darn naïve about the fact. "I didn't expect you to be standing here talking to Wanda," I grumbled. I dragged out her name and let the last syllable escape my lips like it was torture just to let it out.

"Good to see you, too, Patrice," Wanda retorted and smiled a sly smile.

Before I could say something, Bryan interjected, "I was on my way to my office when Wanda came up to deliver something to Joe. We started talking and realized that her father is a frat brother of my uncle. They both pledged at Virginia Union."

"Oh, what a coincidence. Imagine that," I said. My reply was laced with a twist of sarcasm, and I knew neither of them missed it. "Well, we better be getting a move on. You don't want to miss the party."

"Oh, you two are going to a party? That must be nice. I will be spending my evening with a pay-per-view movie and a big bowl of popcorn," said Wanda. She looked down at the floor and glanced back up at Bryan with sad, puppy-dog eyes. "Is it a birthday party or a party for some other occasion?"

"It's a birthday party for Patrice. Me and a couple of her best friends are hosting it," Bryan replied.

He was providing "It" with too much information, and I couldn't wait until we were alone so I could tell him just that. She didn't deserve to know anything about me. I cut my eyes at her and looked at Bryan. "It's just a small gathering with my closest friends," I interjected. I moved closer to Bryan and tucked my arm under his. To drive home the point that this prize was mine, I leaned my head on his shoulder and stared at Wanda with a threatening look in my eyes. I knew better and should have displayed a Christlike attitude, but her presence here alone had dug under my skin. I didn't have time to ponder what Jesus would do, and I hoped He would forgive me for the shortcoming.

"Oh, well, since it's a party, I guess you will be celebrating Patrice's promotion as well," said Wanda. She showed her two oversized front buck teeth and grinned much too hard. "Bryan, I was green with envy, but I'm glad they offered it to someone of color. That she's not the most qualified person really didn't matter to me. I was just glad they gave a minority an opportunity to serve in such a highly esteemed position."

My heart dropped. There it was, my news, and it was being told by my arch enemy. "Well, I believe they realized that they would be getting both, a minority and the most qualified person in the company," I retorted.

"Bryan, you must be very proud of your little Patrice," Wanda said.

He pulled me in closer and held me tighter than he really had to. "I am very proud of her. She is something else and never ceases to amaze me. Not to mention being full of surprises." The last words he uttered dripped with harshness, which was uncommon for him to use, especially toward me.

"What I don't understand is why you haven't accepted the offer yet, Patrice," Wanda snapped. "I would think that you would have taken the offer and run with it for fear that they would offer it to someone else." She flipped her hair weave from side to side. "I know I would have."

"We are two different people, and my decision is not one that I will be making alone. When you have a significant other, the decision should be made together." I wanted to shout, "In your face, Wanda." That was a great recovery. She had dropped the news like a bad football pass, and clever me had picked it up and run for a touchdown. I just hoped it would end the game.

"Is that right?" Wanda muttered. She looked down at her fake Gucci watch. "Oh, my goodness, where has the time gone? I still need to complete a report for a new client."

"Well, it was nice talking to you, Wanda," said Bryan. He turned around and grabbed the file on the nearby counter. "And I'll see that these get on Joe's desk."

"Please do. And the pleasure of talking was really all mine. I've admired your work for a while, so it was great telling you so in person," replied Wanda.

This trick was acting like I wasn't standing there. "Take care, Wanda, and I'll see you at the Monday morning meeting," I said. "I hope you'll be on time for a change. There may be an announcement, and I know you don't want to miss it." I would be back in the office on Monday since we had changed our vacation plans. Bryan's uncle would be having emergency surgery, and since he had reared Bryan from the age of ten, after his parents were killed, they were extremely close. His uncle Abe didn't want us to postpone our vacation to celebrate Gina going off to college, but we had assured him that staying in town to take care of him was more important than a vacation we could take some other time.

We both watched as Wanda retreated in her run-over Reeboks. Someone should have told her that she should always dress to impress, even if she was dressed down. A look like that would definitely not warrant a second glance. She turned the corner, and we waited for the elevator to open and close, signaling that she had left the floor. She had stayed longer than she should have and had dropped my news like it was her own.

"Is there something you need to say?" Bryan walked toward his office. By his swift steps, I could tell he expected me to be right behind him.

"Actually, Bryan, I came to tell you about the offer." I entered the spacious office and took a seat in the large cushioned chair against the wall. It wasn't across from his desk, but it allowed me to take in more than just his upper body. It gave me a view of his feet. I needed to see his feet because when he was a little upset, he nervously patted them. While I waited for him to say something, I leaned over slightly and looked under his desk. Sure enough, he was patting his right foot.

"How long have you known? When did they offer you the promotion?" He picked up a folder, and before he could open it, he threw it back down on his desk and looked directly at me.

"Just yesterday. And as I mentioned a few minutes ago, I haven't made a decision, because it was one I needed to talk to you and Gina about. You two are important, and how you feel about it matters to me. It matters to me a lot." I was telling the truth. I just hoped he believed me.

"And what did Gina say?" He was still looking at me.

He was making me nervous. I didn't even feel comfortable blinking; he might assume that it was a sign that I was leaving something out. "She was pleased. Gina sees it as a chance for me to serve as a top officer in a company that I've worked really hard for. She also mentioned that I would gain even more experience for the company we will eventually start." I was using Gina's take on things and hoping it would help to bail me out of the fix I had gotten myself into.

"Oh, you remember that, do you? I'm surprised." He picked the folder back up again and started flipping through the sheets within it.

"Every conversation we have ever had stays tucked away in my mind. I have never played you that cheap. I never thought they would consider me for Chris's job, not in a million years. Heck, I didn't think America Investments was ready for a black face at the top. So, there was never a reason to talk to you about it. What was the use of playing 'let's plan for the black girl to take over the investment world'?" I laughed and waited for him to join in, but he didn't. I placed my hand over my mouth and coughed.

"But they did make you an offer. That was the time to talk to me about it, when it happened. Not twenty-four hours later, after the entire city of Richmond knew. And here I am being informed by a bigmouthed coworker that you are not even overly fond of. Did you stop to think how that made me feel?"

"It wasn't supposed to happen this way. I came over here to tell you," I said. He was not making this easy for me.

"Didn't you think I was serious about our firm, or did you think it was just a pipe dream? News flash, Patrice. That's not how I do things. I wasn't dreaming in black and white. It was actually in color, complete with a list of possible investors, a plan ready to set in motion, and a date for my resignation from Rutgers Investments."

"Bryan, how could I have known that you were ready to set things in motion?" I rose to my feet and walked over to the edge of his desk.

He handed me the folder he had been flipping through. "Here. This is the reason I had to come back to the office. I was planning to give this to you later."

I reached for the folder, half expecting it to burn my hand the way his glare was burning a hole through me. I silently read the entire first page and then flipped to the second and then the third and fourth. "Bryan, why didn't you tell me? You've leased office space on the west end, and you've filed all the papers, complete with start-up capital from you and several sound investors."

"Patrice, I've been working on this for the past year. And tonight it was part of my gift to you. I was not only planning to ask you to share your life with me, but I was giving you half of Chambers Investments as well."

I reached for his hand, and he pulled it away. "But didn't you think that if it was going to be our business, I would want to invest as well? I can't let you float everything, with no financial input from me. That's not how a partnership works. Or did you want me to be only a silent partner?"

"Don't go there, Patrice. You are anything but silent. I just thought you would appreciate someone giving you something as significant as a partnership, with the only requirement being that you move into your office suite and do what you do. It was important that I be able to offer you what I worked hard to create, not just for me, but for us. Is a man being able to take care of his woman fully foreign to you? I mean, don't get me wrong, but I was taught the old-school way. That a man should not ask for a woman's hand in marriage unless he can take care of a wife and a family." He turned away and looked out the window and then back at me.

"Not that you need anyone to take care of you, and for the record, I knew you could afford to front your half and then some. For once, I didn't want you to have to work for it. I wanted to give it to you."

"Bryan, this is great." I held up the folder. "And I'm glad that you want me to be a part of this. I've been used to doing things on my own for so long, it's hard to just accept someone giving me anything. Please don't take this the wrong way, but for right now, I'd like to take John and Chris up on their offer. I'll ask for a one-year contract."

"They will never go for that. They are businessmen and they have negotiations to make and anything that your name is on ties you in." Bryan put his head down and held it in his hands. "This offer changes everything."

My heart sank. The touchdown I had made back there hadn't been a very good one, because I was losing the game. "It doesn't have to. Bryan, look, it's time for me to meet Gwen and Kyra at the house. Can we just talk about this later? I know it's important, and I also believe we can work it all out."

He looked up at me and gave me a weak smile that was barely there. "You go ahead. I'm going to check my e-mail and then go on home. The housekeeper is there to let the caterers in, and everything should be all decorated by the time I get there, just for you."

I knew he was being a little sarcastic. Unusual for him, but he was probably thinking that me not sharing after we had come so far was a little unusual as well. "You want to give me so much, and I appreciate it, but you have to know that I'm just not used to letting someone else set my life up." I walked to the large window and looked at the surrounding buildings. I thought of the last time that had happened and the end result. A man had killed himself trying to love me. "You are asking me to become an extension of you, and I'm just not sure . . ." I opened my mouth and waited for the next words to come out.

I heard him push away from his desk, and I closed my eyes, waiting for him to embrace me. He didn't. Instead, he walked across the room and sat in the chair I had vacated. "For us to go the rest of the way, you will have to trust me. More than anything else, what you are saying and what you are not saying boils down to a matter of trust."

I felt the weight of the world on my shoulders, realizing that he was right. It was time for me to trust him. If he was going to go through with asking me to marry him and if I was going to consider being his business partner, I was going to have to trust Bryan with all of me. If I were doing a psychiatric self-evaluation, I'd ask myself, "How does that make you feel?" And my response would be, "It makes me feel like I'm not in control." I was no professional in the area of psychiatry, but I did believe that response would land me right back at the two-letter word *if*. No guarantees, some uncertainty, and if I was lucky, a few possibilities. I had just stumbled upon uncertainty.

Chapter 4

My head was pounding by the time I pulled in the driveway. The traffic had been just as hectic on my way back home as it had been on my way downtown. Expressways were supposed to be for those in a hurry, yet every driver I'd zoomed past was a senior citizen who seemed to just be out for a Saturday afternoon drive. I hadn't been quite sure what kind of mood I'd be in after telling Bryan about the job, but I hadn't expected someone else to tell him while I stood there looking like I was stuck on stupid. Had I known the building crier was going to be there, armed and ready to release my news, I would have stayed at home, taken a beauty nap, and waited for Bryan to come to my domain.

I turned the corner and found my neighbor's boys playing in the middle of the road. I stopped, gave them a threatening look, and blew the horn. The bigger boy picked up something and was ready to throw it until he saw that it was my car. He dropped it quickly, and they both ran around the corner. Those two boys were demon possessed. Their mother had told me that her husband had left because the boys were so bad that they had set fire to his pickup truck. It seemed one hot afternoon he came in from work and they wanted to go get ice cream. Needing time to take a shower, he told them to wait. By the time he finished his shower and came outside to take them, his truck was ablaze. He insisted that they had some major problems and needed to be sent away. Being a protective mother, she wanted to believe they weren't that bad. Her stand to protect the evil ones had caused her to become a single parent, raising not one but two problem kids.

If I were to consider moving, it would be because of the two fire starters that lived next door. They had done everything in the neighborhood, from kidnapping cats and dogs, and writing ransom notes for their return, to spray painting sidewalks and fences. They had even set on fire the trees that lined the entrance to the subdivision. They had terrorized everyone except us. It had taken only one threat when we first moved in for Gina to meet them at the curb on her way to school one morning and tell them about the projects she'd been raised in. Of course, they had talked stuff and called her out of her name. The next day I spied them sitting on their front step with their Pomeranian, who doubled as their guard dog. As I was pulling in the driveway, I almost ran into the garage when I noticed that their ball of fur had been shaved, with only a little hair left on the top of his head. Gina never told me a thing except that we wouldn't be having any trouble from them. She had been absolutely right: while they held everybody else hostage with their pranks, they wouldn't even blink an eye in our direction.

Kyra's car was already there, and since Gina's Honda Civic was in the center of the driveway, I was unable to pull into the garage. The fact that I couldn't get in my own garage was getting ready to irritate me until I caught the negative emotion and dispelled it immediately. It had nothing whatsoever to do with my crowded driveway or not being able to get in the garage; it stemmed from what had just happened between Bryan and me. While Wanda had been the mouthpiece that relayed the tidbit of information, I couldn't even blame her, as much as I wanted to. I had played with time, and when I decided to tell Bryan, it had simply run out.

As I jumped out of the car, my cell phone rang. I reached across the driver's seat, pulled my bag from the passenger seat, and grabbed the phone.

"Hello." I didn't bother to look to see who was calling. I knew I sounded irritated. If it was someone important, I'd apologize later.

"I know you're getting old." Gwen's voice came through the phone.

I walked to the rear and opened the trunk and pulled out a couple of bags I had left in the car the night before. A little last-minute shopping. "Can I ask why you are bringing that fact to my attention today of all days?" I closed the trunk and walked toward the front door. Maybe Gina had heard the car pull up and was near the door. Otherwise, I'd have to put the bags down, get the keys from my pocket, unlock the door, and pick the bags up again. Too much work.

"You were going to pick me up," Gwen said.

I stopped in my tracks. "Oh, my God, Gwen, I truly forgot all about picking you up." I looked up at Gina as she opened the door. She didn't say anything but held the door open wide so that I could walk in. "Give me a minute to put my bags down, and I'll be right over to get you." I was going to just drop my bags off in the living room, use the bathroom, and head over to Gwen's, but then I looked up and saw both Kyra and Gwen sitting on the sofa, sipping lemonade. I closed the phone. "You hoochie. I can't believe you were messing with me like this. I wouldn't put it past Kyra, but you?"

Gwen stood up and walked toward me. "I'm sorry, sweetie. You are blaming Kyra when your darling daughter was in on it, too. They convinced me that you would see the humor." She touched both sides of my arms to steady me so she could look carefully into my eyes. "I don't think you see it." She busted out laughing. Kyra and Gina joined in, cracking up.

"Ha-ha. Very funny," I muttered. I dropped my bags by the recliner. "I'm going to use the bathroom. I've had to go ever since I hit the expressway." I started walking toward the bathroom but turned around and went back into the living room. "Wait until I tell you guys what happened."

"Hurry up then. You could have saved that last part until you came back," Kyra yelled. "Now, we got to wait until you come back to find out what happened."

I listened to Kyra complain and laughed to myself. She was going off, apparently, just to hear herself. I'd be back in the living room in record time. Obviously, I wasn't the only one on edge. I knew my reason, but to keep misery company, I'd ask about hers.

When I plopped down in the recliner, Gina came into the room and handed me a glass of lemonade, kissed my forehead, and sat on the arm of the recliner. "Tell us what happened, Mom. Wait a minute." Gina leaned closer and pulled the top corner of my tank top open. "What the heck is that on your breast?"

Before she could conduct a closer examination, Kyra and Gwen were right in front of me, yanking my tank open even farther. "Is that a tattoo?" Kyra asked as she peered over her glasses.

"You are correct, Professor Simmons. And here I was thinking I had wasted money on your education," I said.

"You got a tattoo, but you told me last week I couldn't get a belly-button ring. What happened to 'your body is a temple,' young lady?" Gina said and folded her arms.

"Your body is a temple. I still stand by my speech," I insisted. "I don't know what happened. I left Bryan, and I was just so out of it. I've been feeling some type of way because of my birthday. Gina, you will be leaving me in a few weeks. I just realized that I'm getting old, and there is nothing I can do about it."

"Your age has never bothered you before. And besides, you don't look your age, Trice. You know that," Gwen added before returning to her seat.

"Lately, I've been feeling old," I said. "I don't know. Maybe I'm just going through some emotional stuff. I needed something drastic, something major to make me feel, I don't know, younger."

"And a tattoo of whatever that is will make you feel younger?" asked Kyra, always the voice of reason.

"It's actually two hearts connected," I explained. "Anyway, enough about the tattoo. It's done, and I can't really undo it. So, I'll have to live with it. What I need to tell you is about my visit to Bryan's office."

Gwen started to get up.

"Where are you going, Auntie Gwen?" said Gina. "Uncle Scott asked me not to let you move around a lot, and you are supposed to have your legs up."

"I just need a snack," replied Gwen. She leaned back again and shifted around and put her feet in Kyra's lap.

Instead of complaining, Kyra began to rub Gwen's slightly swollen feet.

I went on. "Well, my plan of telling Bryan backfired. I got to the office and that big mouth Wanda was in his face, flirting. Before I knew it, she had told him all about the job offer. Talk about egg on my face." I threw my hands up helplessly.

"What?" Gina was the first to speak. "What was she doing all up in your business? She don't know you like that." She was holding a plate of fresh fruit and a yogurt.

"I know that's right," I muttered. "I could have given her a beat-down, but I remembered that I don't roll that way anymore." Bringing it up again and visualizing the pleased look on Wanda's face had me just as upset as I'd been when it happened.

"Forget her. What did Bryan say?" asked Kyra. She looked up from the *Essence* magazine.

"He was not pleased. He saw the whole thing as a trust issue," I told them. "I apologized and explained that my purpose in coming to the office was to tell him, but I don't think it mattered. After she shared what I should have, the damage was done." I looked at them and hoped that they could say something that would make me feel better.

I went on. "On top of all that, Bryan tells me that he leased a building and is already making plans to open his own investment consulting firm. I knew he was thinking about it, but I had no idea that he had already taken steps to make it a reality."

"Isn't that a good thing?" Gwen asked and picked a piece of watermelon from the plate she was holding and placed it in her mouth. Kyra reached for the plate and speared a pineapple with the fork and took a bite.

"It is. But his vision included me working alongside him, day in, day out," I explained. "If I accept the offer at America, I won't be able to join him right away. Hence part of my dilemma." I rested my back against the cushion of the microfiber recliner, totally exasperated.

"So what happens now?" Kyra asked.

"We didn't finish the conversation," I replied. "But the look on his face was enough to let me know that if I don't say something that he wants to hear, what I didn't say then or now will be making a statement for me."

"Mom, as I told you earlier, your heart won't lie. You're just not in tune to what it is saying. Tell him how you feel, and I think he will understand," said Gina. She pulled her micro braids up and turned her head from one side to the other as she looked at herself in the oval mirror above the sofa.

Everybody in the room looked in her direction, with mouths open, including me. This was not the first time she had exposed me to her newfound wisdom, but Kyra and Gwen had not been privy to her wealth of relationship knowledge.

"Yeah, she credits us for all that she has learned," I quipped. We all chuckled.

Gwen rubbed her stomach. "I'm still hungry, guys." She looked at the empty plate.

"Come on in the kitchen," I said. "I will put together a chef salad for all of us. Hopefully, that will keep you and baby full until the party." They all followed me into the kitchen.

"I still can't believe you know," Kyra complained. She then told me how nosy I was and how she wasn't going to help plan anything else for me.

"Kyra, I know what my problem is," I replied. "But tell me. What has your bloomers in a bunch?"

"I'm cool. Let's just eat, shower, and dress," said Kyra. She went to the refrigerator and started pulling out ingredients.

"Okay," I said. I glanced at Gwen and Gina, who both looked away. "I've got enough problems. If you should need to join me on the bench of what the heck, just let me know." I loved Kyra, truly I did. But maybe her keeping her problems to herself was a good thing. Today was not a good day for me to share. I didn't mean to be selfish or consumed by my self-imposed issues, but I had more than enough on my plate to give me a few sleepless nights.

Usually when we didn't see eye to eye, Bryan would call just to say we could work it out or to reassure me that our love was enough. His sensitive side was always in play, and I had come to depend on what he brought to the relationship. Here I was, a few hours before my party, and I didn't have Bryan to reassure me that all was well. I had worked so hard to keep some semblance of peace, control, and balance in my life, and now things were spiraling downward, and I could hardly keep my head up.

Chapter 5

Everybody was on the floor, dancing to Frankie Beverly's "Before I Let Go." It reminded me of a college frat party with bodies dancing all over the place. Bryan's game room had been converted for the purpose of partying, and even though the guest list was limited, it seemed that everyone I had ever known was here to celebrate with me. Scott was even letting Gwen dance for the first time since the party had started. I didn't know if you could call what she was doing dancing, since the only body parts she was moving were her arms and head. It didn't make a pretty sight: she looked like she was getting ready to go into a fit. Gwen wanted to be a part of the fun so badly, and for that reason, we all just mimicked her dance steps and cracked up while we did it. She was supersensitive, and had she known we were mimicking her moves, she would have busted out in tears.

We had already experienced a crying spree earlier, while we were getting dressed. She had brought two outfits and had assumed she could fit into both. The second option was only to be worn if option one didn't yield the look she was going for. The pants of her outfit were not maternity, but just a few sizes larger than what she normally wore. She got them up as far as her thighs, and they wouldn't budge beyond that. None of us said a word but continued to busy ourselves with dressing, not wanting to react until she reacted. Instead of pulling the pants off and moving on to the other outfit, she sat on the edge of the bed and started crying. Gwen cried so hard that her mascara started to run. After we had comforted her and assured her that she looked great in her second option, she was okay with her pregnant state. Either way, Kyra and I had agreed that it was going to be a very long six months. Like the morning sickness, which hadn't lasted the duration of the first trimester, we were hoping that the crying spells wouldn't last through the remainder of her pregnancy.

The party was the best I had ever had. The food was great, and my gift table was covered with gifts of all shapes and sizes, just the way I liked it. Gina had been designated the human money tree and was prancing around with twenties, fifties, and a few Ben Franklins pinned all over her. The rest of the evening was a formality, since I had made my rounds, kissed cheeks, given hugs, taken photos, danced with all those that asked, and indulged in every delicacy that was created for the occasion. The crab canapés were so delicious, I grabbed an entire tray from a server, ordered a glass of ginger ale with extra ice from the bar, and took the back steps to the second level. I pushed Bryan's bedroom door open, turned on the lights, and sank into the wing chair in the corner of the room.

I took a bite from a canapé and put my feet up on the ottoman. Bryan was acting bubbly and was the perfect host, but he had said very little to me. It probably wasn't obvious to anyone else, because he was floating around and making sure everyone had what they needed, but I had noticed a difference. He had touched my arm lightly at the right times, smiled for the cameras, and talked endlessly about whatever topic he was asked to chime in on. Still, there was a part of him that just wasn't Bryan. I probably would have felt better if I didn't know why. If I didn't know, I probably wouldn't have hidden up here, wondering what was going to happen next. But I knew it was our earlier conversation that had him out of sorts, and at the conclusion of this evening, we needed to have a heart-to-heart. If we were going to make it, I guessed I had to trust him completely. How did I end up here, having to make the most difficult decision of my life? Nothing I had been through compared to this. I had worked hard all my life to be independent, to stand on my own, not needing anyone to hold my hand or validate me. Love had always come at a price, and I had always chosen the "care on the run" package, that is, until Bryan came along. Then I'd adopted Gina, gotten closer to Bryan, and caring and loving came without saying.

"Why are you hiding up here?" Kyra stood in the doorway.

"I don't know. I just needed to be alone for a few minutes." I placed the tray on the nearby nightstand and took a sip of ginger ale. "How did you know where to find me?"

"Bryan saw you sneak away and asked me to come up and check on you." Kyra stood in front of the oval full-length mirror in the corner and turned to look at her backside. "Girl, I'm getting so wide. Pretty soon I'm going to need blinkers and signals to let people know I'm in motion."

"Stop joking about yourself. You are not that big. And as I've told you before, if you feel that your weight is getting out of hand, start working out and change your eating habits. I'm not a fan of working out, but I indulge occasionally when the scale goes slightly beyond one hundred thirty-five. I can always join you, though. Just say the word." I was attempting to engage in this conversation about Kyra's weight, and yet I wondered why Bryan hadn't come to get me himself.

"It's easier said than done. My schedule is just so crazy. I don't have time to plan my meals, and you know I hate working out. Always have and I don't see that changing."

"It would help a lot, Kyra. I can't understand how you can have so much book sense and not enough common sense to know that not doing anything isn't going to make the weight go away." I didn't intend to be so mean, but here she was, talking crazy and acting like the weight was just going to fall off because she had suddenly recognized that she was wide. I loved her to life, but she needed to leave my presence if she was going to be negative.

Kyra came over near the chair I was sitting in and stood against the wall. "I'm going to get a membership at the Gold Fitness Center, and as an incentive to help me, I'll pay for your membership as well. You know how I feel about my hard-earned money. If I pay for both of us, it should show you that I'm serious and I'm tired of being overweight."

"Good for you. You do know that you are a beautiful woman, and I don't want you to lose weight for someone else. It's all about you, sweetie. It's about being healthy." I meant what I was saying. I wanted her to be healthy and happy with the woman in the mirror. I wasn't up for a workout two to three times a week, but if it was going to jump-start Kyra's workout plan, I was going to be right there sweating with her. "You know Janet is still there. I'm sure she would be willing to be our personal trainer."

"That's right. I forgot all about Janet working over there. That would be great. It should be easier with someone I know to guide me along. Sounds like a plan. For right now, I'm going to help you with this tray of crab canapés, and then we need to get back downstairs. They are ready for you to cut the cake and open your gifts."

I didn't need any help with the canapés, but I saw it as a chance for her to indulge all she wanted before the workouts started. "I'm not going to open all of them. We'd be here forever, and I'm sure everybody is tired of eating, dancing, and talking."

"Well, cut the cake, listen to them sing 'Happy Birthday,' and then announce that you will open up all the gifts at home and send thank-you notes. It sounds like a plan to me." She reached for my glass, drank, and then handed it back to me. "I know that you are having some major anxiety about this part of the evening. And even though you are not opening the gifts, Bryan is still going to want to give you his gift."

"I know, and believe it or not, I'm ready." I smiled. These few moments alone had helped me, or at least I wanted to assume that they had.

When we got back downstairs, Bryan met me, and we walked over to cut the cake. After the "Happy Birthday" song, everyone ate cake and mingled for a while longer. I waited for Bryan to say something or to make a special announcement, but instead we began saying good night to our guests. We stood at the door, along with Gwen, Scott, Kyra, and Gina, and thanked everyone for coming. I felt a little empty. I had expected Bryan to go along with the engagement announcement, and yet because he didn't think I was ready, he hadn't.

"Well, girly girl, we are out." Gwen looked at me and then Bryan. "Thanks for hosting the party, Bryan."

"It wasn't a problem. I think everyone had a good

time." That was all Bryan said. He looked away before meeting our gaze. His plan had been aborted, and even though he didn't say so, I could tell that it had left him uneasy.

"We will drop Gina off and make sure that she is all locked in before we leave her. I'll have her set the alarm," said Gwen.

"Okay, Trice," said Scott. He hugged me tightly. I believed even he could sense my disappointment.

Kyra rolled her eyes at Bryan and reached to hug me. "I'll see you at church."

"Okay. Make sure you get there in time to help me out with Sunday school. The kids like it when you join in," I said. I felt like crying. But didn't I bring this on myself? I would have loved to point a finger in another direction, but there was no one to shift the blame to. I played back the recent hours of my life. While I had told the girls and Gina, I had never told Bryan that I wasn't sure I was ready to get engaged. Somehow, though, he must have picked up on it. I knew he wouldn't delay our engagement because of the job offer. He must have sensed more.

Bryan closed the heavy oak door and looked at me as I began to tidy things up. "You don't have to do that. The cleanup crew will be here later this morning, and by noon my game room will be returned to its normal function. I'll be ready to beat you at a game of pool right after brunch."

That was our usual Sunday afternoon pastime. I hadn't known a cue ball from an eight ball when I'd first started hanging out with Bryan, and it had been one of the first things he'd wanted to teach me. I'd enjoyed the feel of him cuddled behind me as he showed me how to hold the pool stick. His patience had always been evident as I proved to be anything but a good pupil. I remembered lingering close, attempting to focus on the game as the smell of him intoxicated me beyond safe measure. He would remind me that there was no rush to master the game since we had all the time in the world. We would laugh together at all my failed attempts and he would cheer with me when I actually hit the right ball in the right pocket. It had been with him, in that game room, that I'd released my inhibitions and allowed myself to thirst after what Bryan offered and be quenched by how he fulfilled all of me. Because of Bryan, I had become pretty good, not only at pool, but at life. I just hadn't realized it.

"In your dreams, Chambers. I may be another year older, but I still got game. The pool table is my territory, and the last time I checked, I was still reigning pool queen." I gave him a weak smile, which made me feel sadder. Tonight, the ending of our evening, should be like so many other nights, an anticipation of something good. Instead, I didn't know exactly what to expect.

"Patrice, come with me." Bryan took my hand and led me into the living room. I thought we would sit on the sofa, but instead, he had me sit in the matching oversized chair across from it, and with little effort and without releasing my hand, he sat on the floor in front of me.

I felt like Cinderella getting ready to try on the glass slipper that would forever change my life. I crossed my legs and the wide pant legs of my chocolate slacks displayed my gold, ankle-wrap Vera Wang sandals. The sleeveless, gold, sequined drape-neck tunic hung loosely over the waist of my slacks, displaying a gold chain belt. My jewelry was modest, with only diamond in my ears and a diamond necklace that Gina had me during my birthday dinner. My hair had suf- the humidity, and Kim had been too hot with me when she had to come to the house and put it in an updo. I looked birthday good, if I said so myself.

We shared an intense stare, which neither of us broke for what seemed like forever. It seemed we looked behind this evening, desiring to go back to another time and place. I continued to stare at him, while he said nothing for a minute but just stared back at me. I wondered what he saw and craved to know what he felt. My personal feelings were somewhere between a desperate need to gain control and an emotional desire to experience a total freeness within, one that would let me love this man the way he deserved to be loved.

Bryan's BlackBerry signaled an incoming text, and he leaned over and grabbed it from his belt. "Gina is just letting us know that she is at home, the door is locked, and the alarm is on. She loves us and told me to tell you not to come home without her engagement ring."

"That girl is something else." I tried to laugh, but it came out as a nervous giggle. This was a first. I'd thought I was in control, and this encounter or the delay of what I had expected had proven that I was not. Tomorrow I would look back on this as an enlightening experience, but tonight I wasn't sure how to describe me or the experience. "She should know the engagement ring is out of my control."

"It's not about control. We just need to be sure that we are both on the same page. I know we are reading the same book, but dag, baby, I'm not sure we are even on the same chapter."

I looked into Bryan's eyes and felt my heart do a double beat and then skip. He had an effect on me that hadn't changed much from our very first night together. Being this close to him reminded me of why we limited our alone time. His lips were curved to perfection, ar⁣ every time his eyelashes blinked, they revealed p⁣

brown eyes that always pulled me in further than I imagined possible. His cocoa brown complexion was smooth and without one blemish—the telltale signs of someone whose daily regimen included well-balanced meals, exercise, and a little self-indulgence. There was, of course, the smell of him, and although there was a slight distance between us, my nostrils pulled him closer, and I inhaled to bring him even closer.

"Do you know how long it took me just to tell you that I love you?" I asked. I was not usually the romantic one, but before I had thought twice, I had asked the question and reached for his hands, pulling them tightly between mine.

"I should, since it only happened recently. I mean, I knew you did, but it took you a while to verbalize it." Bryan smiled. "You have been one complicated lady."

"I've never meant to be. Look, it's taken a while just to get to this point of our relationship and to dissect what I feel for you and what I feel about us. The short of all this is, it's going to take me some time to take down this wall completely."

The look on his face didn't encourage me to continue, but I needed to go on. "It has nothing to do with loving you or you loving me. History has a way of erecting stone, and once it's there, it can be almost impossible to take down."

"I know you have a wall up, and I've spent years trying to understand why. But I also believed that one day you would be willing to take it down. I guess that day hasn't arrived yet."

I ___ my head down, not knowing what else to say. ___ t on. "It's the same way with the job. You've ___ building your reputation and erecting it in ___ ven if it means venturing out on your own ___ going to take a while to walk away from what you've built." This time he looked away, and after a couple of minutes of silence, he looked at me again. "If you need to take this promotion to prove something to yourself and them, I'll have to understand. And while you are doing that, I will build my empire."

There it was. He had given me an out. I knew I should take it and run, but in all that he'd said, he hadn't mentioned where we stood. If I took the job, where would it leave us? "I want you to understand my reason for staying at America. I do need to prove something to myself and, heck, to them, too. But I really need you to be okay with my decision. I'm not saying that I won't ever come to work with you. Just not right now. Please don't let it cause a problem in our relationship."

"There is no problem between us. Know that." He opened the leather ottoman next to the chair and pulled out a box. "This is for you. And I believed tonight was the right time to give it to you."

I held my breath and blinked back the emotion that threatened to show itself.

He went on. "But after what you just said, I know now the time isn't right. I wish it was, but what stands between us is too major." He put the box back where he had been safely keeping it. "We aren't ready for this step."

I looked at him and still couldn't say a word. He was right. As badly as I wanted him to be wrong, Bryan was right. I just didn't want my not being ready to be the end of us. And somehow I sensed an impending decision that wouldn't necessarily be in my favor.

"Until you are completely ready to trust me and feel comfortable with giving me a part of you that you will no longer control, we can't really move forward. Patrice, it will mean believing in me enough to know that I will never hurt you and that I will take care of your heart." He touched my tunic right where my heart was.

"But what if—," I began, but Bryan kissed his finger and touched my lips with it.

"Now get out of here before Gina texts me back and tells me that you have missed curfew."

I wrapped my arms around his neck gingerly and just held on tight. The fragrance of him serenaded me, and I mentally allowed him to take me to the place that I wasn't ready to go to emotionally. What could I say? Bryan had already said so much.

Chapter 6

I was seated between Chris and John in the executive conference room as the staff filed in. Many of them were complaining about the need for an early Monday morning staff meeting, and many just needed to have at least one more cup of java before dealing with missed deadlines, status reports, and the teamwork effort of ensuring that America Investments was giving each client top-notch service. The three Rs that had become our motto were being resourceful, extending respect for the customers' needs, and fostering relationships to make our clients feel like family. That was the platform that made America tick. What had started as a family business led by John's father and brother had changed when the elder John died and the brother was killed in a car accident. There had been no family left, so John had offered Ben partnership in the firm. He had shared the helm of the business with Ben, who had become like family. It had worked and made all those in upper management work harder, knowing that the business was as much a part of them and no longer solely a family business with blood ties. Now, here I sat, two weeks after they had offered me the job, ready

to be added to the upper administrative cabinet. I
hadn't wanted to appear too eager, so I'd waited the
customary time allotted to such business decisions
before I'd given them a positive response. I'd also taken
extra time to go over the pros and cons. The pros had
won, but the one con was huge and would affect me ad-
versely for a while. That con was my relationship with
Bryan and the business he wanted me to be a part of.

I badly needed the vacation we had postponed, but
even after Uncle Abe's surgery, Bryan hadn't felt it was
a good time for us to go away. Instead, he'd promised
Gina Christmas in Jamaica. He'd sweetened the change
of plans by suggesting that she bring one friend. Even
though she hadn't thought the postponement was a
good idea, it had worked in our favor. The day we would
have left, Gina had a severe asthma attack. When we got
her to our doctor, he told us that it was good she wasn't
out of the country and that he was able to treat her so
quickly. Being aware of how severe her attacks could be
and knowing the exact dose of medication necessary
to end the terrible symptoms had been crucial. I was
beyond relieved; the last thing I needed was for her to
be away from home and have an attack with no one
there to administer medical attention.

Ever since our conversation, well, actually his conversation, since I hadn't contributed anything meaningful,
Bryan had been distant. Our telephone conversations
were rushed, dinner plans were cancelled, and his visits
were brief. I believed he only came by to check on Gina
and to put on a show for her that everything between us
was okay. She knew better and could tell by my actions
that things were not okay. In a nutshell, Bryan was
asking me to change and to change quickly.

What use would it be to deny that I didn't know how
to fix us? I knew I would have to change if we were

going to make it work, but right now, at this particular moment, accepting the promotion and being in total control of my destiny, without having to consult with anyone, felt good. Like I was in the power seat and was calling all the shots for me, myself, and I. Who would understand that? I wasn't sure I understood it myself. It was like having six in one hand and half a dozen in the other. I wanted Bryan and I wanted control, end of story.

Earlier, I had crawled out of bed, fueled only by the announcement that would be made during the staff meeting. I missed Bryan and didn't know how to tell him. And Gina had demanded my attention all weekend as all the asthma symptoms hadn't gone away. Despite my telling her to get back in bed and wait for Gwen to come take care of her, Gina had come to my bedroom to help me pick out a power outfit. I could have done it on my own, but she swore I hadn't known a thing about dressing until she'd moved in. She had forgotten all the compliments she had given me about my style of dress when I was mentoring her.

"Mom, here. Wear the navy pin-striped Tahari suit with the sleeveless button-down Anne Klein shirt. Hit that with your navy slingbacks and some silver jewelry, let your hair flow and tuck it behind your ears to show your silver and diamond hoops, and you will make a definite statement." Just that search to find the right outfit for me had worn her out, and she'd pulled back my bedcovering and climbed in my bed.

I'd let her rest until it was time for me to leave. I'd helped her get down the steps to the lower-level guest bedroom so Gwen wouldn't have to go up and down the steps. That was where she was when I'd left the house, all curled up with her auntie Gwen. I'd wanted to stay at home, but Gwen had talked me out of it, knowing this morning would mark the formal announcement. She'd also mentioned something about needing the practice. I'd begged to differ. She had done well with Barren and Darren, her twin nephews, and God knows, she had been my mother on too many occasions. But I was glad that Gina was with her other mother and just as comfortable as if I was there.

I was pulled out of my morning reflection as the meeting started. "Good morning, everyone. I hope all of you had a great weekend. As always, it's Monday and time to get back to the grind. It's time to lend some money and make more money. That is, after all, what we do and why we are here." John's scratchy voice was at its usual octave. The Monday morning speech had started just like all the others over the years. You'd think he would use something different, since everyone's lips moved along with his. They had heard these words so many times, they were etched in their psyches and could be repeated on the dime. Still, I just laughed inside, because he was as sweet as punch, and no one could argue that he wasn't.

I looked over at Chris, who was obviously thinking what I was thinking. The chuckle under his breath gave that away. As I looked around, I noticed Wanda staring right at me. Other than being Monday, I was sure she knew what day it was, and my smirk in her direction and the slight lift of my head, a display of arrogance, should have confirmed it. She had heard about my promotion purely by coincidence and probably hadn't shared it with anyone in the office, hoping that the partners would change their minds at the eleventh hour and give her the job, which she didn't think I deserved. That was probably why no one eyed me suspiciously or even realized that the seating arrangement sent a message. I often ended up between John and Chris. They both chose not to position themselves at the head of the table;

this, too, they felt fostered teamwork and a "we are family" style of leadership.

John continued. "Before we move on to status reports, client rosters, and all that other jazz, Chris and I have an announcement. We were trying to give Ben a few minutes."

Just as he mentioned Ben's name, Ben came strolling into the conference room. "Forgive me, John. I'm a man of leisure now, and I completely lost track of time this morning. The minute I left here, my wife took my watch, vowing never to give it to me again. But she did give me a dose of Viagra last night, and I'm just a little exhausted."

Everyone in the room busted out laughing. I believed all of us were aware of how happy his wife was that he was retiring to spend more time with her; however, she looked a little too meek and mild to be peddling Viagra. But if that was what it took to get what she needed, I wasn't mad at her. Lily was so nice. She was a retired principal of one of the area high schools who now spent her time mentoring and volunteering. She was all too ready to jet set and spend time with the grandkids in California and Texas, and from Ben's latest tidbit of information, she had some other plans for him as well.

"It's cool, Ben. John was just about to make the announcement," said Chris. "Man, I'm loving the golf attire. When the meeting is over, you've got to tell me where you picked that outfit up at. I need to hit the course with some gear like that. Also, just in case I have some problems later, I'd like to get a couple of those tablets." Again, everybody busted out laughing.

I just looked at Chris and hit him with my elbow.

"My bad. I was just saying, if he got some extra, I could use them," said Chris.

John was redder than ever. "If we can move on, Chris,

I'd appreciate it. We don't want to spend all morning handling shop. There is money to be made and money to be saved. Now, as I was saying, Chris and I, along with Ben, would like to announce that Ms. Patrice Henderson has accepted our offer and will be stepping into Chris's vacated position of senior vice president for Acquisitions here at America."

Everyone clapped, cheered, and looked at me, smiling. Everyone except Wanda. She didn't clap; nor did she join the rest in extending a smile my way. In fact, the minute John made the announcement and everyone started to clap, she faked a couple of coughs and left the room. That was good. I didn't need her here to rain on my parade.

The Monday morning meeting was concluded with a private catering service, which brought in a celebratory breakfast. Instead of the usual pastries, muffins, bagels, bottled orange juice, apple juice, and coffee from the downstairs cafeteria, they were serving Belgian waffles, scrambled eggs, bacon, sausage, home fries, and toast, complete with freshly squeezed orange juice, apple juice, and coffee. What an early morning feast, and it was all just for me.

I mingled and ate, chatting with everyone. Just as I was refilling my juice, Wanda walked in and went straight to get a cup of coffee. After she stirred in a couple of sugars and a creamer, she pranced my way.

"Here it goes," I said to myself. "Wanda, sorry you missed the end of the meeting. Are you feeling well? You still look a little green."

"Don't you worry about how I'm feeling. I guess I should be saying congratulations, so congratulations." She sipped her coffee and moved the cup away quickly. "This stuff is too hot. What are they trying to do? Burn the roof of everyone's mouth?"

I looked around at the people mingling, still eating and sipping juice and coffee. "Actually, no. It doesn't look like anyone else has burned their mouth. Maybe you sipped, instead of blowing and sipping. That's what I normally tell my preschoolers in Sunday school to do when I bring in hot cocoa."

Her right eye twitched. I knew her temper was boiling almost out of control. Still, I couldn't resist sticking the dagger in further. "Oh, a quick update. I'm going to be assuming many of my duties immediately. That would include your division. So, Wanda, you will be answering to me. Please clear your schedule this afternoon. I'd like to go over your client list and check your status personally to see what tips I can give you to improve your division. There is some concern that your division is lagging behind."

"This is the first I've heard of it. Chris has never said a word. In fact, he's always telling me what a great job I've been doing. We even discussed me increasing the territory for my division. I'm also interested in handling some of the overseas accounts we are going to have when the new firm opens." Her eye was still twitching, and her head kept jerking. I had never noticed it before, but she appeared to have some kind of nervous disorder going on.

Okay, maybe it was time for me to ease up. She had better be glad that I was a saint. If not, I could keep this up and drive her all the way over the edge. "Well, the overseas thing is out of the question right now. Let's just focus on the stateside stuff. You are not ready to go global." I drained the last of my juice and turned to throw the cup in the trash.

"We will just see about that," Wanda snapped. "I'll just talk to Chris and see what he has to say." She twitched again, and both her eyes were blinking like the flashers on a car.

"Did I hear my name, sweethearts?" Chris walked between us and put his arms around both of us. "What can I do for you two beautiful women?"

"Chris, I'm glad you are here. Patrice just informed me that she will now be supervising my division. No one shared this with me prior to—"

"That's correct, Wanda," Chris replied. "I will be heading up several new divisions for the new firm. It's been real, girl, but a brother got to move on up." He laughed at his own humor.

"Well, that's great. I'll just move over to one of the new divisions," said Wanda. She turned to me and smirked.

"It doesn't work that way," said Chris. "There is no transferring at this point. You will continue with your division, since that is your baby. And you will answer to Patrice." I waved at her and smiled.

"So, I'm supposed to just work with Patrice without question?" asked Wanda. She looked away, dispirited.

"Wanda, start it off on a good foot. You know we promote a spirit of teamwork here, but for all administrative purposes, you will be working for Patrice." Chris said it without a thought. It sounded direct, and I believed that was for a reason. Wanda's perception of me had never escaped him. On many occasions, he would tell me to retaliate and not take her bull. He never formed an opinion of anyone, but like me, he was not one of the members of her fan club. "Now, if you two will excuse me, I need to return some calls. Later."

Just as Wanda was about to walk away, I made an attempt to make her feel better. "Wanda, this doesn't have to be difficult. I will show you the same respect that

Chris did. Despite what you think of me and what you assume I think of you, I'm very professional."

"I don't need you to cut me any slack or do me any favors. I can handle my own, thank you." With that, she walked out the door and didn't bother to hear what else I had to say.

"Oh well, I tried," I said aloud. The room had begun to clear out, and like Chris, I had some calls to return. But before I did that, I would call to check on my baby and call to say good morning to Bryan. He knew the announcement was being made this morning, so I would gauge by the way he sounded if he wanted to hear the details. I'd give him the short version of the meeting and tell Gina all about Wanda. Being a female, she would understand the catty business. Bryan would tell me to ignore her and keep it moving. He just didn't know, and I wasn't about to tell him, how that wasn't going to be possible. I'd been there, tried that, and I wasn't planning on going through it again.

Chapter 7

It had been a long week, and my body was in need of a long shower or maybe a soak in the Jacuzzi. I was in serious need of a stress-free getaway, without really getting away. I did something I never did: I kicked my shoes off the minute I hit the door. I didn't care where they landed, and I had no intention of picking them up anytime soon. I might not pick them up until the weekend was over. The days were speeding by, and before I knew it, Gina would be leaving. For that reason, my focus was on her. Bryan had called me and asked if he could hang out with us for the weekend, because his house was being painted inside, and his allergies would not allow him to stay in the same room with paint fumes. I was too eager to say yes. I had hoped that at the conclusion of the weekend, we would be on better terms. He hadn't changed his mind about going with me to take Gina up to Charlottesville. We had even planned to take off a few extra days to help her get settled. I was going to take full advantage of being in Charlottesville by taking in the scenery with him. It wasn't Jamaica, and there wouldn't be any white sandy beaches to relax on, but I would make the best of it.

There was another small disagreement between us. He was all for Gina moving away and embarking upon a new life. I wasn't for the new life. I felt she could have a life right here in Richmond and go to Virginia Commonwealth University. It was where I had gone and where her auntie Gwen and Kyra had gone. I had given her the lecture many times: if it was good enough for me, it should be good enough for you.

Bryan was on her side and wanted her to go where she felt she could be the person that she needed to be. He felt Richmond wouldn't allow her to grow up and blossom. He was a man, and I had never heard anyone say that men went through the empty-nest stuff. Whenever we got on the subject, I would end up mad at both of them. It was two against one, so they always won.

I walked toward the voices and watched in the entryway of the kitchen as Gina and Bryan laughed and joked while they prepared food to put on the grill. This was a glimpse of how my life was supposed to be daily. They got along so well, and it was so noticeable that they adored each other. There was no getting around that truth. This kitchen scene was perfect for a Mahogany card. I stood there, not wanting to interrupt them or the moment.

"Oh, hey, Mom. We were getting ready to put the steaks on the grill. The salad has been tossed, and the potatoes are in the oven, baking. I did them just the way you like." She walked over to where I was standing and hugged me.

I leaned toward her to see if I could hear any wheezing. "How are you feeling?" I rubbed the side of her face.

"Fine, honey bunny," Gina replied. "It's been a week since the attack. And the symptoms only really lasted three days. I've been cough free, congestion free, and all the other frees for a week. And because you were so concerned, Auntie Gwen has been watching over me and giving me my medicine as prescribed. She's also been giving me so much orange juice, if I see an orange, I'm going to scream. Who told her that orange juice was good for asthma?"

Bryan and I started laughing. "I don't know, sweetheart." I said. "She is good at the mothering thing and pushes medicine like an old grandma. Her and Kyra." I walked over to Bryan and stood at the counter, beside him. He didn't say anything, so I playfully hit him on the butt, and he just smiled.

"I know that's right," replied Gina. "The other old grandma came by every other day, and they both double-teamed me. It was even worse when Uncle Scott came by and checked me over at the request of Auntie Gwen."

"That's my team," I said. I reached in the salad bowl and pulled out a cherry tomato and put it in my mouth. It was very tasty and made me even hungrier.

"They were all in overdrive. Tripping like I was in the hospital," Gina complained. She sucked her teeth. "Auntie Gwen wouldn't even let me talk on the phone. Imagine that. It was an asthma attack. It didn't affect my throat or my ability to talk."

"You needed your rest, precious. I'm sure you have more than caught up on all the gossip and the goings-on," Bryan added. He finished seasoning the steaks and turned around, throwing the towel over his shoulder. "Why don't you go take a quick shower? It won't take me long to grill the steaks." He was casually dressed in jeans and a red IZOD polo shirt, and still he looked like he could strike a pose.

"Sounds like a plan," I replied. "Did Gwen and Scott take you up on the offer of dinner? I know Kyra is out of town again. By the way, I'm beginning to get suspicious. She is in and out more than she normally is."

"You are being nosy," said Bryan. "You and Gwen. I heard you two on the phone last night when I came over to check on Gina. Kyra is a big girl, and if she has met someone, you should be happy for her."

"If she has, I'm happy," I said. "But if she is keeping us in the dark, we should be concerned. He could be, I don't know, someone on *America's Most Wanted* or something."

"Your mind is too vivid. And it doesn't take but a minute for you to get carried away. Kyra is smart. She wouldn't get caught up in anything foul," said Bryan. He pushed the door open as he went out on the deck. "Leave it alone, Patrice, and let the girl be."

"Whatever." I turned my back and headed out of the room.

He popped his head back in the door. "Gwen called to say she isn't feeling well and for you to call her when you got in. I called Scott, and he said that he was going home early and would put her in bed."

"Why didn't she hit me on my cell phone?" I suddenly remembered that it was on mute.

"She said it went straight to voice mail. Call her and see how she is feeling, but, Patrice, don't you two play Momma or investigators. Kyra doesn't need you or Gwen tracking her down."

"We won't. I promise." I crossed my fingers behind my back.

Gina was sitting in the corner, flipping through a *Cosmopolitan* magazine. "Ohhh, I saw that. You are wrong."

"Girl, mind yours. I'm just going to call her and ask if she is okay. I don't want Gwen to worry. That is the last thing she needs," I said and smiled.

"It's the same as being nosy, and you've been warned," Gina replied. "My future daddy said to let Kyra be." She added some bass to her voice as she repeated what Bryan had said.

"I smell blackmail," I muttered. I stopped, leaned against the counter, and waited.

"Well, now that you have mentioned it. There is a pair of pastries that I would love to have."

"Pastries. What the heck?"

"The sneakers that Reverend Run's daughters created," Gina explained. "You've seen them in the magazine, haven't you?" She threw the *Cosmopolitan* magazine down and picked up the *Essence* and walked over to me. "Here, look at these. I have a couple of outfits that they would work well with. You know that shoes make an outfit."

"You are a mess. You can pick them up in the morning. I had already planned to take you to the mall to pick up a few things. Blackmail wasn't even necessary. You are scandalous, just like your momma."

"You know it. Can I have some cash to go to the movies?" She fixed me with a pleading look.

"Bryan gave you money for the movie already and a little something extra to get something to eat afterwards. He even gave you money to pay for Zaria. Don't try to play a player. I'm always a couple of steps ahead of you." I started laughing and left the room, ready to take a shower.

I'd wait until after dinner to check on Gwen. And I'd call Kyra first so I would have something to report. Bryan called it being nosy; I called it sister/girlfriend obligations. He needed to understand that Gwen, Kyra, and I had made a pact a long time ago to always look out for the well-being of the others. Especially if good sense was not being used. If Kyra was running around all over the country with some good-for-nothing, someone she didn't think we needed to know about, then it was time for me to take care of my obligation to find out the when, what, and who. On second thought, I needed to handle this before I showered.

Kyra's cell phone rang a couple of times before she picked up. "Hey, Trice. What's going on? Is everything okay?"

"Everything is fine. I was just calling to see if you were okay. You left town so abruptly. Gwen called your office yesterday morning, only to find out you were out of town. That's not how we roll. So, we were just wondering if everything is cool."

"It is. The new vice president wasn't able to attend a conference and sent me in his stead. He gave me all of one day to prepare and pack. My flight was around noon. I was planning to call you guys later to let you know." She sounded out of breath. "You just beat me to it."

I strained to listen for background noise. There was a faint sound of a television, but nothing else. "Well, we were just concerned. Scott called Bryan and told him that Gwen wasn't feeling well, and he put her in bed. I knew she would ask about you when I called her, so I thought I'd get a report." I still wasn't convinced that things were as cut and dry as she was saying they were. This was totally out of character for her. She was such a creature of habit and would not detour from her normal way of doing things. Our Kyra would have made a zillion reminder notes the minute she found out she was leaving town and would not have been content until she had addressed every single one of them. The first of those would be to let one of us know the details of her trip. She never wanted to be out of reach in case of an emergency.

"Please tell Gwen I'm just fine. A little tired, but other than that, I'm good. I won't bother her tonight, but let her know that I will check on her first thing in the morning. My session begins at nine a.m."

"I'll do that. When will you be back in town?" I had to ask, since she didn't volunteer the information. Again, this was an indication that Kyra was not her usual, informative self.

"Oh, I'm sorry." She inhaled and exhaled loudly. "I'll be back on Wednesday. By the way, I did some shopping for Gina last weekend. I just haven't had a chance to bring the packages by." She yawned loudly.

Yet another reason I knew something was wrong. She never put things off. "The child has more than enough. I can't think of a thing she needs."

"I'm sure she doesn't need a thing, but there were a few things she wanted. That's where godmother number two comes in. Look, I'm really exhausted. I'll give you a call tomorrow night. Love you. Bye."

"Oh, okay. Bye." I held the phone before she disconnected it and heard a male voice in the background, asking if she was ready.

If she was so tired, who would be asking if she was ready? Better yet, what was she ready for?

I stood in the center of my bedroom, still holding the phone, shocked that she had ended our call like that. And even more shocked that I'd heard a male voice in the background. Life was getting crazier by the minute. What was the world coming to when a straitlaced, always predictable person like Kyra suddenly became secretive and evasive?

I needed time to think about this turn of events. Thinking about it was one thing; hearing about it was quite another. I'd report to Gwen later. There was no need to alert her just yet. I closed my bedroom door, stripped down to my matching black satin and lace Victoria's Secret undergarments, and grabbed a towel from the linen closet situated beside my bathroom. I reached for a matching washcloth and closed the door. The latte color of my bedroom blended into my soft cream bathroom, which was accented in khaki. A hint of remaining daylight shined through my parted blinds, and the skylight made the room appear warm. I enjoyed this time of day almost as much as watching the sun rise. The remaining hours of daylight right before the sun would vanish always made me think of savoring what was left of that day and making the most of it.

Reaching inside the shower, I turned the brass handle and adjusted the temperature so that I wouldn't have to do so once I was in. Situated in front of the vanity, I removed a make-up wipe from the container and wiped off what was left of the make-up I had applied early that morning. After I brushed my teeth twice, I looked at my body in the mirror and turned to the side to see if anything was sagging. Ever since my birthday, I had been doing a daily inspection. I was thinking that the effects of aging would slip up on me without warning and alter what I had worked hard to preserve. If that happened, I was afraid I wouldn't be able to stop the aging process with creams, old-fashioned remedies, or whatever advice I could get from an "ask.com" Internet search. I refused to allow old age to catch me with my drawers down, so to speak. I needed everything to be tight when I finally slept with Bryan again. I didn't want him to be totally shocked if it didn't look like it had prior to our saving ourselves.

Just when I thought I was safe, I noticed something in the mirror. I took a couple of steps backward and looked down, way down. There, sticking out like a sore thumb, was the longest gray strand of hair I had ever seen. "Jesus Christ!" I yelled out loud. "Lord, no, not

there!" I screamed at the mirror. That was all I said
before I collapsed on the floor.

I came to with Gina and Bryan around my bed.
"What happened?" I looked up at them and blinked a
couple of times.

"We aren't sure. It was taking you so long, Gina
came up to check on you and found you on the floor of
the bathroom, with the shower running. I called Scott,
and he is coming right over."

"Mom, let me get you some water." Gina ran out of
the room and down the steps.

As I watched her exit the room, the memory of what
had happened flooded to the forefront of my mind. I
remembered everything and felt so silly. The trauma
of discovering the hair had caused me to pass out, or so
I thought. There was no way I could tell them that. I
had to figure out something before Scott got here. "I'm
okay now," I informed Bryan. "I was feeling a little
dizzy. I guess because I didn't eat anything all day. You
know how I can get if I go too long without eating."

Bryan nodded his head. "I know. But it's never caused
you to pass out before. Not since we've been together.
Has it ever happened that way before?" He reached
down and rubbed my forehead gently.

"Yes, years ago." I prayed silently for the Lord to forgive me for not telling the total truth. I had passed out
before, but it had had nothing to do with eating. We had
gone on a trip to an amusement park, and I had got
overheated and had passed out from heat exhaustion.
Even that had happened so long ago, I had almost forgotten it. I would tell him the complete truth later.
Right now, I just needed to head off Scott. "Listen, call
Scott and tell him I'm okay. If I start feeling worse, I'll
let you call him back, but for right now I'd feel better
knowing that he is over there taking care of Gwen."

"Are you sure?" He looked a little skeptical.

Gina walked in and handed me a glass of water. "Maybe she is right. Besides, Uncle Scott needs to take care of Auntie Gwen. Let's just keep a close eye on her."

"Okay. Let me call Scott back." Bryan left the room, and I listened as he relayed everything to Scott. "Thanks, man. I'll call you. Don't mention this to Gwen. She will only worry. Yes, I agree, she should probably see her doctor as soon as possible to be on the safe side. I appreciate it, man. Later."

I felt even more like a complete idiot. Then again, I didn't. The trauma I had just experienced was enough to cause any sane woman to lose it temporarily. If Gina and Bryan weren't in the room, I would either be cracking up at myself for being so melodramatic or crying through the hysteria. I wasn't sure which emotion would take center stage and couldn't understand why I had become an overnight drama queen. Maybe it was a combination of turning thirty-eight, the empty-nest syndrome, and the gray hair. Whatever it was, I was an emotional wreck. On top of that, I was lying here ringless when I could be rocking a three-carat diamond on my left hand and a promise from Bryan to have and hold me, in sickness and in health, until death did us part. Here I was, acting like I had youth on my side and assuming that Bryan would wait when my biological clock had accelerated and was ticking away like a hormonal time bomb. Kim was completely right. I should have been giving *him* a ring.

I lifted my head off the pillow and felt the pain of a sudden headache hit. Now, I had not only a gray hair but a huge headache from hitting my head on the floor. Go figure.

Chapter 8

The sun's rays came streaming through the blinds, an announcement by Mother Nature that morning had arrived in all its splendor. The only thing I missed about living in the country was the birds that used to chirp outside the room I shared with both my siblings. I'd rush to the window, throw back the tattered curtain, and watch them fly away at my sudden interruption of their morning ritual. I'd wonder how far away they would fly and what it felt like to be free. Even now, I would often feel the emotional strings that had tied me to the place that used to be home and all the pain I had suffered being there. Love was not supposed to hurt, but for me it did. At the hands of my mother, I had been stripped of love, but thankfully, Gwen and her family had given me all the love that I had missed. Still, it wasn't the same. I furrowed my brow and tried to relax against the brightness that penetrated through the blinds. I knew it was probably well past seven, my usual Saturday morning wake-up time, but I didn't care. The headache hadn't gone away, and while I knew I needed to open my eyes, I delayed the act for a couple more minutes. Responding to a few body aches,

I stretched and spread my legs, and both of them met some resistance. Now, I would have to open my eyes to see who had decided to take over my bed.

I struggled to open my eyes against the slight pain and raised my head up a little. Bryan was lying on top of the bed, next to me, in a white T-shirt and shorts, and Gina was at the foot of the bed, with Mickey Mouse shorts on and a white fitted T-shirt. Her braids covered part of her face, and she had her thumb in her mouth. She rarely did that anymore; however, if something stressful was going on, she would revert back to the habit of her childhood. The therapist we'd been assigned to see as part of the adoption process had mentioned that for Gina the thumb sucking was like a security blanket. Obviously, she was worried about me and had chosen not to leave the room but rather to cuddle up at the end of the bed in case I needed her.

I turned to Bryan. He was lying on his back and breathing evenly. Apparently, he'd been watching television before falling asleep, because he had his glasses on. He made it a practice of taking his contacts out in the evening before resting.

He'd had on glasses the night I met him at the restaurant. It hadn't been the first time I had seen him, but up until that night, he'd just been someone that I had noticed and knew only a little about, such as the fact that he was gainfully employed in the banking industry for Rutgers Investments. The grapevine could be an informative tool, should one partake of its usefulness. I had never been one to initiate gossip, but I had been on the receiving end a time or two. On that night at the Top of the Tower, he'd captured my attention, and over dinner I'd let him know that I liked what I saw. By the time I left the restaurant and got to his apartment, it was obvious that he liked what he saw, too. That night had opened the door to what would become a sexual obsession, a cool acquaintance, a friendship of sorts, and when I got tired of denying that he was more than all these things, a relationship. That realization hadn't come easy, and I'd fought it like crazy. Very similar to how I was fighting the next step for us now.

I lightly touched his cheek and traced an invisible line to the hint of the dimple in his chin. His eyes opened instantly, as if he had not even been asleep. "You okay?"

"I'm okay." I covered my mouth, knowing my breath had to be kicking. "You and Gina been camped out here all night, keeping an eye on me?"

"As a matter of fact, we have. You slept through a couple of hands of deuces, Monopoly, and a couple of reruns of *Martin*." Bryan attempted to smile, but I could still see the worry in his eyes.

"So, Gina didn't go to the movies?" I propped myself up on my elbow, trying not to show signs that my head was busting. I needed to go to the bathroom, but I didn't trust my legs. I'd wait a few minutes and see if the pain would subside.

"No, she didn't want to leave you. I told her that she could go ahead and I would keep an eye on you, but she wouldn't hear it. She even refused to leave your room, and we talked until she fell asleep." Bryan got up from the bed. "I was given the rare treat of watching both of the women I love sleeping like beauties. That is, except the snoring."

"I don't snore." I threw the pillow he had been lying on at him.

"Yes, you do," Gina mumbled in her sleep.

"You are one to talk," I said. I took my pillow and threw it at her. I was feeling some major pain. There was no way I was going to be able to make it through the day without telling them. I would probably have to call my physician or Scott. Hopefully, it wasn't anything major, but I knew I would need something stronger than over-the-counter Tylenol.

"Anyone who looks as good as I do could never snore by night," replied Gina. She leaned up and replaced the scarf that had fallen off.

"And vain too," I retorted and giggled. She was correct, though. She was a pretty girl. She kept her ego and diva like attitude at home, never allowing them to venture out with her. She was anything but stuck-up around her friends or at school. She had her share of rivals, but their hang-ups where Gina was concerned had to do with what they thought she should think of herself. They had a problem with the male attention she received and with the fact that despite not trying, she turned heads. Because she had attended a school on the other side of town, her new school had given her an opportunity to turn over a new leaf. Since I still mentored, she still hung out with some of her same friends and had started mentoring a group of six- to eight-year-old girls. I gave back because what had started as a mandate for my job had ended up being a passion. But Gina never wanted to forget where she came from. I had given her a silver spoon, but she looked at it as a blessing, and because of that, she appreciated the chance to change her life.

"Are you hungry?" Bryan had showered and changed into a pair of sweats and a Dallas T-shirt.

I was just coming out of the shower myself. Since I was a little light-headed, it had taken me longer than it should have. "Bryan, I think I should see my doctor. I didn't want to say anything, but the headache hasn't gone away. In fact, it is getting worse."

"Already ahead of you. I could tell when you didn't jump up out of bed that you were still feeling bad. Dr. Langston is going to meet us at her office at noon." He stood there, obviously pleased that he could read my body language so well.

"You know me that well?" I asked while brushing my hair. A ponytail was going to have to do for today. I had no desire to do anything more than put an elastic band around my hair. I had missed my regularly scheduled hair appointment because I had to work late, and I'd planned to drop by Kim's this morning and get something quick done. That plan was definitely out, and I would have to nag Kim as soon as this headache was dealt with.

"Sure do. Come on downstairs and eat. Gina is cooking, and you know once the food cools off, it's going to be harder to eat it." Bryan frowned at the idea of eating Gina's cooking. In spite of the many cooking lessons under Gwen's tutelage, Gina hadn't managed to perfect one entrée. If it wasn't instant or didn't require a simple boiling, it wasn't something that would end up appealing on the plate and pleasing to the palate.

"I'm with you. I've never been that much of a cook but the simple things I've helped her cook have been a little difficult for her to master." I watched as he lifted an eyebrow. "Okay, not just challenging, but many times what ends up being served is hard to recognize." I peeped around him, making sure our discussion of Gina's cooking skills was not being overheard by Gina. She knew she wasn't a good cook, but I didn't want to completely dampen her culinary spirit.

He guided me downstairs, and we were greeted by a whirl of smoke and Gina humming like she was in culinary heaven. The smoke must not have affected her vision or set off the smoke alarm, since she didn't move to open a window or a door.

"Just in time. I'm finishing up the home fries now," declared Gina. "I've got ham, cheese, and green pepper omelettes in the oven, warming. I even squeezed some fresh orange juice."

"I could smell it all the way upstairs," I said, trying to say something positive as I moved toward the kitchen table, eager to sit down. While we normally sat around the breakfast nook on stools for an informal breakfast, I needed the support of a chair against my back.

"Bryan, I made coffee. Would you like me to pour you a cup?" Gina asked. "I used the blend that Mom got from Chris. I believe he brought it back from England. Anyway, it's supposed to taste real good."

It was a good blend, not to mention expensive. I didn't mind her making it for us, but it cost way too much to mess up. I was sure she'd used too much or too little. The exact measurement was a little tricky, even for me.

"I'll get it. You just finish up those potatoes," Bryan said as he walked to the coffeemaker, which was positioned under the cabinet. The kitchen always reminded me of something out of *House Beautiful* colorized in black and white. It was large and spacious, and while it wasn't my favorite room in the town house, it had been dubbed Gwen's domain.

I poured a glass of juice from the carafe and sipped slowly. It was actually very good. I refilled the glass and watched Gina place the potatoes on a serving platter and Bryan add creamer to his cup of coffee.

As if shocked and surprised, Bryan spoke louder than necessary. "This is good." He picked up the coffeepot and held it up to the light and looked at the liquid curiously. "This is the best cup of coffee I've had in a while." He returned the coffeepot and drank from his mug again, as if he was making sure the second taste would yield the same response.

"I'm glad you are enjoying it. Mom, would you like some?" Gina placed the platter on the counter and reached for a mug from the center cabinet.

"Yes, I would," I said. If that stuff was making Bryan respond like that, I had to taste it. I watched as he picked up the container that held the coffee. He was reading the blended ingredients that were listed on the back. Since the second sip of coffee, he hadn't moved from in front of the cabinet.

Gina added my preferences to the mug and placed it in front of me. She waited, with towel in hand, for me to drink. I stirred the coffee a little and raised the mug to my lips. The liquid went down smooth, and I savored the taste of it for a few seconds. I immediately drank again and could only smile as Bryan nodded in my direction. "My God, Gina, this is great," I exclaimed. I had used the blend only a couple of times, but it surely hadn't tasted like this. She had to have added something else to it. "Did you add anything else to it?"

"Nope. I guess I'm just good at making coffee," she replied and turned to remove the omelettes from the oven, very pleased with herself.

The rest of the breakfast was a pleasant surprise. Everything was delicious. The omelettes had been made to perfection, not undercooked or burned. The spice was just right, and it was of restaurant quality. The home fries were seasoned well, and since I knew I didn't have any Bob Evans or some other brand in a bag ready to cook, I realized she had peeled, diced, seasoned, and fried the potatoes. I kept waiting for Gwen to come out from around the corner and give Gina away. Bryan ate everything on the first plate and then helped himself to a hefty second helping. The first plate he'd fixed had had a smaller portion. I was sure he'd been leaning on the side of caution.

"Sweetheart, you have done a wonderful job with breakfast," I declared. "I can't believe you can throw a breakfast together like this, and just when I'm all set to enjoy your skills, you are getting ready to leave."

"Mom, Bryan, I have a confession to make," said Gina, sounding very serious and looking even more so.

I dropped my fork and quickly reached for the napkin in my lap and wiped my mouth. My attention was not on chewing the remainder of the food in my mouth but on listening to what Gina had to say. In just a few seconds, my mind had raced from drugs, to pregnancy, to studying abroad, to having time to find herself and to changing her mind at the last minute about the university where she wanted to receive her academic preparation. I glanced at Bryan out of the corner of my eye. He, too, had stopped eating and was looking directly at her. Along with Bryan, I waited for my child to say something that hopefully made good sense.

"I don't know how to tell you this," Gina said. "I guess I should have told you a while ago, but the time was never right." She stopped as if going on was too painful.

"What in the world is it? You should know that whatever it is, you can trust us," I said reassuringly and hoped it was enough to push her to finish.

"Okay. I just don't know how you are going to take it," Gina replied. She reached for my hand, and I reached toward hers and held it tightly. "Mom, I could always cook. I just didn't, because you assumed I didn't know how and Auntie Gwen thought it was a special way of spending time with me." She started laughing. "But I'm glad that everything has met with your approval this morning. I must do this again soon."

I squeezed her hand until she let out a yell. "For five

years you've eaten whatever I've cooked, good, bad or in between, when you could have put an end to our suffering and whipped up something next to spectacular for us?"

"I wouldn't say I'm quite that great," Gina admitted. "But I can hold my own. A quick soufflé, double chocolate cake, the homemade kind, biscuits with country gravy, champagne chicken, crab cakes, a few other dishes. Simple stuff really." Again she laughed.

"Gina, where did you learn to cook those types of meals?" I asked. "No harm, but I know you weren't cooking those types of meals at your mom's."

"Actually Q's mom taught me. She is a chef at a restaurant on the west end," Gina explained. "Despite being a single parent and raising the boys alone, she cooked those kinds of meals for them. The owner of the restaurant thinks she's the best, so the pantry and the freezer at work were open to her at the end of her shift." Her last word sort of emptied into silence. The memory of Q settled on her face, and as quickly as I saw it, I knew I had to remove it.

"Don't matter. Wait till I tell Auntie Gwen you can cook her under the counter," I said. "Uncle Andre should have extended a partnership to you instead of Vince. You could go in that kitchen and give those well-trained chefs a run for their money."

At the mention of Andre, I suddenly missed him. He and Tori had decided to move to Atlanta just when the restaurant and club were doing so well. But Andre's Two Spot was doing just as well. In fact, they were due to come to town in a couple of weeks to check on Gwen, see Gina off, and spend a week or two with everybody. We were looking forward to seeing Andre Jr., who would be turning one. Thoughts of Andre, of course, brought Marcus to mind. After Gwen had married Scott, Marcus finally decided it was time to move on. Against our pleas, he'd gone back to the West Coast and was continuing things there with Mama Bea at his side. If he couldn't have Gwen, then he would take his number two lady with him. I knew he was dating, from Vince, but obviously, it wasn't serious enough for him to bring his current lady to Virginia to meet the gang.

The wonderful thing about friendship was, when it was real, it lasted. Marcus and Gwen still talked, and one or the other of them always made regular calls. Now that Gwen was pregnant, Marcus hardly gave her a chance to give him an update but was on the phone weekly to *get* updates. You'd think the unborn child was his, judging by the plans he was making and the way he was acting. Scott was a true trooper, because not many men would understand the unique relationship that Gwen and Marcus shared. He was secure and not threatened in the least bit. Not even Gwen's wish that Marcus be a godfather had thrown him over the edge. The only compromise necessary for Gwen was to have two godfathers, since Scott had chosen Kip to assume the elite position of godfather. It was going to work out since Gwen had chosen two godmothers, me and Kyra, of course. I'd had no trouble telling Kyra that she was backup to me. We'd laughed about it, but she knew that Gwen and I had much too much history for anyone to think that they could come before me.

I often had to trip myself. If we had to explain our dysfunctional, totally workable friendships/relationships with anyone on the outside of our circle, they would think we were a black soap opera. Though they suspected, no one knew for sure that Andre and I had kicked it for a quick minute. The problem? We loved each other too much to chance messing up what we shared.

"Well, I'm not interested in preparing meals or

telling others how to do it," Gina declared. "I'm strictly a behind-the-desk kind of girl. Listen, Mom, while Bryan takes you to the doctor, I'm going to meet my new roommate. She called me yesterday, and she is from right here in Richmond. I'm going to pick up Kennedy and meet her at the Commons."

"Oh, that sounds good," I replied. "What else did she tell you? What school did she go to, and where in Richmond does she live?" I was throwing out questions left and right.

"Slow down, honey," said Bryan. "She only talked with her a few minutes, and I don't think she had time to do a full investigation." He started clearing the table.

"I'm sure she will tell me all that when we meet. I just know that she went to St. Catherine's and her name is Courtney Andrews, but they call her Coco," Gina called over her shoulder as she left the room. "Coming from a private school, I'm sure she is all preppy and stuck-up. Just the kind I want as a roommate." She turned and came back to stand in the doorway, needing us to listen. "She probably doesn't know anything about the real world or how we live." Gina folded her arms across her chest and looked at me and then at Bryan, who had turned away from the dishwasher and was giving her his undivided attention. She walked away again. "I'm surprised she didn't invite me someplace for tea and cookies. That's what I get for wanting to attend a predominately white university." She was still mumbling when she went up the steps.

Bryan and I both laughed, imagining the kind of girl that Gina was talking about and also knowing that our Gina was nothing like that. The experience of mixing the two would be like mixing oil and water. It felt good to be laughing with Bryan, and for a moment, it seemed our problems had evaporated and we were able to just enjoy being together and being with Gina. This was the way it was supposed to be. Times like these shouldn't be overshadowed by job offers, control issues, merging identities, pending marital vows. Just relaxing and letting the affairs of life just be were important, too.

Chapter 9

"Patrice, you have a call on line three." Kandi's voice rang through my private conference room, which was part of my new office suite. The decorators had finally completed my suite, and it was all that I desired for it to be. While Chris's and John's suites were masculine and dark, my domain was soft, bright, and totally upscale. Gone were the large mahogany desk, the credenza, and the matching bookcases left behind by Chris. In their place were pewter and glass pieces, spread around so as not to dominate the room but to give it a very classy, elegant appeal. The color regal blue covered the love seat in the corner, the side chairs, and my executive chair. This color was offset by a soft mauve, which made the work environment both relaxing and stately. I'd been a little concerned that my executive sidekicks would think it was a little girly, especially when I'd shared my vision of what I wanted and received a questioning stare. However, when the decorators had completed the suite and rolled out the crème carpet and hung the last art print by Andre's cousin Chanel, who had become a nationally known art wonder, Chris and John had been pleased with the end result.

I was deeply engrossed in a spreadsheet for one of my

clients. My workload had doubled, since I had assumed the management of all mid-level divisions for all acquisitions, had taken on several merger projects, and had continued to work my client list. I had absolutely no problems with most of the divisions, and because the staff members knew I was deserving of my position and had always treated each of them with the utmost respect, everything was going well. Wanda's division was another story. She had made it clear that she had no intention of making my transition to the upper echelon of America Investments an easy one. Both Chris and John had already instructed me to do whatever I had to do. That was the green light I needed, because what I really wanted to do was fire her butt for insubordination.

Somehow, though, I didn't want to do that, because she was of color. And besides, she was good at what she did; she just didn't desire to work for me. I couldn't say the feeling wasn't mutual; that was probably the only thing that we would ever agree on. At every turn, she made a dramatic exit from a meeting or my office and left me struggling to display the epitome of the businesswoman I knew I was, cool, calm, and collected. On the inside, though, I was about ready to kick her butt, but it seemed that type of retaliation was no longer in fashion. It was much more up to date to go postal or to hire someone to do a drive-by.

"Good morning, Patrice Henderson." As I answered the phone, I took my reading glasses off and rubbed my eyes. I had been reading the reports for only an hour, but my eyes were tired and I was having trouble focusing. A couple of weeks had passed and I had taken the migraine pills religiously and yet a headache still managed to sneak up on me more often than it should have. Dr. Langston had diagnosed what I was having as severe migraines. I thought I had passed out from the shock I experienced the night of my life-altering discovery, but Dr. Langston had given us a medical explanation and had instructed me to take the prescription and to rest when I felt the onset of a headache. I couldn't afford to stop all production at the first sign of a headache, so I was really hoping that following one of the two orders would be enough. As I saw it, it was just one more issue I had no control over.

"Hey, girl. How you feeling?" Gwen said softly.

"I should be asking you that. You are the one with child and on bed rest." I pushed the executive chair away from the table and twirled around to face the large window. It was raining out, and the weather didn't help lift my spirits at all.

"Semi-bed rest. I can go places," she said in her defense. "In fact, I'm in the hallway of my doctor's office now. But I had to tell you what and who I just saw."

"Do tell." I leaned my ear closer to the phone, not wanting to miss whatever it was that she had to tell me.

"You know that Dr. Reese's new office is around the corner from the college," she said.

"Yes, I haven't taken you there yet, but I remember you telling me just in case I needed the information. Go on."

"I just saw Kyra with some guy, leaving Hunan's Restaurant at the corner of Grove."

"That's not really shocking. She was probably just having lunch with someone she works with, or it could have been someone regarding the fellowship," I pointed out, thinking that Gwen was just a little over the top with this one.

"That's exactly what I thought, until they started holding hands, and when she got to her car, he kissed her for what seemed like an eternity. Now, I've been kissed by a friend, and I've been kissed by someone who is more than a friend. Trice, this was no friend."

"What?" I stood up and walked to the window. If Kyra was locking lips like that, we should be in the know. There was nothing casual about Kyra, and she would not have gone that far unless she cared about the person. "Did she see you?"

"Nope. She was too busy grinning, kissing, and hanging on to this guy for dear life," Gwen responded.

"Were you close enough to see who he was?" I knew I was asking a lot of questions, but we had both known that Kyra was up to something and this had to be it.

"I wasn't that close." I heard them call Gwen's name. "Listen, I have to go. This shouldn't take long. They only need to take a few tubes of blood, and I'll be out of here. I promised Scott that I would go right home as soon as I finished. So, I'll call you when I get there."

"No problem. I will be in the office. Remind me to tell you about that trick Wanda," I added, knowing that I would need to vent later.

"Stop calling that woman a trick." She laughed and disconnected our call.

Just as I hung up from Gwen, I noticed that my private line was forwarded, which was the reason Gwen had to be transferred. I took my line off forward and started to organize by dates the spreadsheets I had been looking at. The phone rang, and I leaned across the table to answer it. I let out a breath and hit the speakerphone feature, and spoke. "Patrice Henderson."

"Ms. Henderson, it's been a while. We must not be friends anymore. You don't call a brother or show any love no time." A deep baritone voice came through the phone and caressed a memory from long ago.

This had to be a nightmare. I couldn't believe that Jason was calling me here at the office. Forget the office. I couldn't believe he was calling me at all. I hadn't talked to him since I'd started seeing Bryan. We had an "if I don't call you, don't call me" understanding. And since I hadn't called him in five years, he should have known not to call me. "Hello, Jason. How's it going?"

"It's going. I was in your area this morning on a service call and thought about you. So, I thought I'd call and check on you."

"Actually, I don't live in that area anymore. I haven't for a while. But I'm glad that you thought enough to check on me. I've been great. Look, I'm really busy, but you take care of yourself."

"Oh, you going to blow me off just like that? After all we've done to each other?" He was really pushing it. That was so long ago, I had forgotten it and him.

"Jason, we've never been more than friends. You know that. And what we had was an arrangement that worked. Now, I'm asking you to forget it, because I have."

"I know you haven't forgotten how I used to rock your world. The way I used to roll by your place and take care of you whenever you needed me. What I'm trying to say is, I need you like that now. I've been with a few, but, dag, can't nobody put it on me like you."

I could hear the longing in his voice: He was on the verge of sounding like someone trying to get off on a phone conversation. It sounded so vague to me. I must have really been living foul, because it hadn't bothered me back then. In the light of the sanity I had now, I wondered how I could have been that bad a judge of character. I had never hung out with him in my comfortable circle of friends, but I had occasionally met him for dinner. We had been part of the after 10:00 p.m. crowd, whose primary purpose had been just to get something to eat or to pick up carryout. It hadn't been about hanging out and gazing into each other's eyes or lingering over an intimate dinner. That hadn't been part of my act with Jason. We would order, eat swiftly, and go directly to my place. He'd be lucky if I said more than ten words to him during any get-together.

"That won't be happening. Now, I'm going to hang up, and I'm going to ask that you lose my number." I had leaned closer to the phone, trying to avoid raising my voice. He was getting ready to press my last black nerve.

"No, I'm not going to lose your number. I'd rather come by your job and lean your sweet asset across your desk and . . ." Before he could finish, I clicked the speaker phone feature off and stood up.

"My, my. Is that someone making an office appointment for love in the afternoon?" Wanda said and slithered up behind me like the snake she was.

I turned and narrowed my eyes at her. Not wanting to work for me was one thing, walking out in the middle of a meeting was another, but entering my office without knocking and eavesdropping on my conversation were not acceptable. "Why didn't you knock?"

"I didn't think I needed to. I thought you had an open-door policy." She walked over to the conference-room table and took a seat directly in front of me.

"That would be if my door was open. It was not. Never, I repeat never, come into my office or my conference-room without knocking." I was livid. As soon as she left, I was going to go directly to Sarah's office and write her up for insubordination and whatever else I could file. Unbeknownst to her, I had given her the benefit of the doubt up until now, but it stopped today.

"Oh, I'm sorry. You probably have an appointment or something that you need to prepare for." I couldn't believe her nerve. She got up from the conference-room table slowly, picked a piece of invisible lint from her black A-line skirt, and smirked. "Did you want me to ask Kandi to hold your afternoon calls and have your visitors come back at another time? I'd be more than glad to do that on my way out. Anything for my boss lady."

"Leave my office this instant!" I screamed louder than I knew I should have. There was no way she could miss the rage in my eyes as my temple throbbed. I knew it was throbbing because I'd felt it erupt from the inside, like an exploding volcano. If she was referring to Bryan, she knew nothing of our relationship. He trusted me, and because I wasn't sure if Jason would pose a threat, I'd tell Bryan about his call and every- thing he'd said, in case Jason wanted to go crazy later. Did she honestly think that I was in a relationship that wasn't secure?

Wanda looked a little shocked that I'd yelled. She turned and walked out of the conference room, opened my office door, and didn't even bother to close it.

I had to get out of my office. It felt as if the walls were closing in on me. Again, I turned to the phone, hit the speakerphone feature and dialed the number to reach Kandi. "Hey, reschedule my meeting with Chris, and tell him I had to run out. If you need me, or if Gwen or someone important needs to reach me, tell them to call my cell." I didn't give her a chance to reply but placed my cell phone in my blazer pocket and grabbed my keys. I would definitely be locking my door on the way out.

By the time I got to the elevators, I knew exactly where I needed to go. Bryan hadn't mentioned that he would be out of the office today when we'd talked early this morning, and right now I needed to talk with him in the worst way. Our relationship was not com- pletely back on track, but after my medical ordeal, some of the tension had eased. Maybe because we avoided all conversations regarding my new job and the progress with his business plans, and not once had he said anything about getting married. It was as if we had taken several major steps backward. We were past getting to know each other, and yet we were unable to enter into a serious relationship.

I got off the elevator on the floor that housed Rutgers Investments. There was a new face at the reception desk. I wondered where Ms. Edna was. She had been a permanent fixture forever, and from what Bryan had told me, she never got sick, took a vacation, or spent any length of time away from her job. Despite her primary assignment of answering the phones, she was the first to arrive and the last to leave every single day.

"Hello." I smiled at the lady who was positioned behind the reception desk. "Is it possible to see Bryan Chambers?" She looked to be about my age, with shoulder-length hair that appeared to have been inherited. Her eyes were a hazel color. Now those were questionable. I didn't compliment many women on their looks. It was not that I was so vain that I couldn't recognize other beautiful women; I just didn't make a practice of it. But this lady, I was sure, turned many heads.

"May I ask who you are?" She gave me the once-over, checking me out from head to toe. For someone assigned to work the front desk, she wasn't at all friendly. Maybe she was having a bad day or a severe case of gas.

"My name is Patrice Henderson." Again I smiled. I didn't bother to add that I was Bryan's girlfriend or his significant other. This was definitely one of the times when I would have loved to place my hand on the desk and display the ring that Bryan was going to give me. What's more, I would have loved to say, "His fiancée." Thanks to self, that ship had sailed, and I'd have to wait by the water and hope that it would sail again.

"He really is busy. Maybe you can leave a message for him, and I'll see that he gets it. Usually, Mr. Chambers only sees people if they have an appointment." She glanced down at an appointment book.

I was trying to stay calm, even though I was still on the edge from dealing with Wanda. "Why don't you call him and just tell him I'm here?" Sure I could have called from my cell, but I wanted this chick to do her job.

She raised her voice a couple of octaves. "As I said, he's very busy, but feel free to leave a message."

I stared at her and didn't say another word to her. Instead, I pulled my phone from my pocket and made sure she saw that I used speed dial. Bryan picked up on the second ring. "Hey, sweetheart," I said. "I came down to see you, but the receptionist says that you're busy and I don't have any appointment."

The receptionist's mouth opened and then closed quickly. She acted as if she didn't believe I was talking to him.

"Okay." I closed my phone and placed it back in my pocket. Leaning forward, I folded my hands, placed them on the counter, and grinned at her while I waited.

A few minutes later, Bryan came around the corner. "Hey, sweetheart," he called. He closed the distance between us and hugged me. "You look very nice today."

I hadn't thought much about the outfit I had on until he said something. I glanced down as if to size up what I was wearing. "Thanks, honey." I placed my hand on his chest.

"Oh, let me introduce you to Faith. She will be assisting Ms. Edna at the front desk. I forgot to tell you Ms. Edna had hip replacement surgery. Faith, this is Patrice Henderson."

"Hi," said Faith. She didn't add anything else. No apology for not granting me access or a simple "nice to meet you." Nothing. She eyed me like I had a serious odor.

"So very nice to meet you, Faith," I replied and faked

a smile. "When Bryan visits me upstairs, the receptionist knows that he has a standing invitation. I would hope that as Ms. Edna does, you would grant me the same privilege."

Faith didn't say a word but went back to whatever she was doing. I looked to see if Bryan had noticed, but he was standing at the other end of the reception desk, picking up messages. That was probably why she decided to ignore my last comment. I would have thought that she would be more professional in front of one of her bosses. But that was not my issue, or my problem. I had one of my own upstairs. I wanted to ask Bryan why he hadn't said I was his girlfriend and soon-to-be fiancée. But I'd bring it up later.

We walked the short distance to his office and turned and went in. Once the door was closed, I spoke. "How has your morning been?"

"Busy, but busy in a good way. Have you had a headache today? You look like you don't feel well." He pointed to a love seat situated against the wall. Bryan's office was polished and well organized. Many of the pieces were custom-made and gave the decor his personal imprint. I took a seat, and he sat beside me and held me in his arms for a minute. "Patrice, you are shaking. What's going on, baby?"

"Bryan, you know I am usually a very astute businesswoman, but something happened a few minutes ago that affected me big time." I rested my head in my hands and shook it a couple of times. I was just glad that he was in tune to me and knew that I'd made an impromptu visit because I needed his reassurance that I could weather this recent storm.

"What happened?" Bryan asked.

"Let me back up a little. Before you and I started talking, I was seeing this guy named Jason. You already know my definition of *seeing,* so I'm not going to go into all that." He smiled and nodded. "Out of the blue, he called my office today, asking how I was, saying it had been a long time. He asked if he could see me." I paused and then continued. "Of course, I told him absolutely not and to lose my number. Maybe he was always crazy and I just didn't know it, but he started to tell me how he wanted to come by my office and do things to me. I quickly hung up the phone."

"That's exactly what you should have done. There's no telling what he has been into since you two saw each other. But don't worry. He probably got the message." He hugged me again.

"To make matters worse, Wanda came into my office without knocking and heard part of the conversation. I had him on speakerphone. Anyway, she stood in the conference room, challenging me and threatening me with the phone call." I jumped up and turned to face him. "I couldn't believe it, but she was actually acting like she had the right to come into my office unannounced and eavesdrop on a conversation I was having." I paced the floor. "Bryan, I am simply livid."

"What did you say to her?" he quizzed.

"I ended up having to raise my voice and tell her to leave. Which she took her time doing. I'm going to go see Sarah in HR as soon as I go back up."

"You should. She took it too far, and you need to call her on it. I'm not sure how far you need to go, but you definitely need to start the paper trail going. She is a piece of work and, based on what you are telling me, psychotic to boot."

"No, you were busy smiling all up in her face a month or so ago," I reminded him.

"I didn't know she was part crazy." He started laughing. "Dag, Trice, you just don't know anymore. I'm used to dealing with your kind of crazy, but that's a whole other breed."

"Oh, so I'm crazy?" I closed the distance between us and stood in front of him. I had been in such a rage when I'd arrived that I hadn't noticed that he was looking really nice today, too.

"I hope you are crazy about me." He kissed me on the cheek.

"I am and you know that." I stepped away, sensing that we were too close together.

"I'm glad you trusted me enough to tell me all this."

I realized what he had just said. I had shared something with him that I really didn't need to. In relationship terms, I had trusted him. Dag, it must be the medicine. What the heck was I even doing here? I had handled Jason, and I knew I could handle Wanda, yet here I was, a part of me needing to have Bryan say that it was going to be okay.

"Are you free for lunch?" I asked as I started walking toward the door.

"If we can make it a late one, yes." He walked a couple of steps behind me.

"Good. I'll call you. Right now, I'm going to see if Sarah is in." I kissed him lightly and turned to leave. "Oh, sweetie, you look really nice today, too. I definitely noticed." I winked at him and left.

It was getting harder to be around him. It seemed that after we were at odds, a unstated truce had been reached, and I was hoping that what I felt right now was because God had seen what was in our hearts for one another, had looked beyond all my hang-ups, and was sealing our relationship on a different level. Even after I'd faced not being ready, more times than I'd cared to, I had thought about a life with Bryan. I wanted to attribute my feelings to the age factor, Gina, and now the medicine, but it just seemed harder to dispel the notion that a large part of me was ready to be his wife. The drawback was still the control equation. How was I going to balance it all out? He was willing to make it all work, but on mutual terms. All I had to do was say the word and release my strong hold on my heart. Why couldn't I just accept that? I was making something so easy, extremely hard.

My cell phone vibrated in my blazer pocket. Glancing at the caller ID, I noticed it was Kyra. "Hey, girly girl. What's going on?" I asked. Now that she was calling me, I couldn't wait to ask about the details of her day.

"Patrice, Mema just called. Poppa is dead." She began to sob.

"Oh my God, Kyra. Where are you?" I was about to get on the elevator but moved to a quiet corner instead.

"I'm still in my office." I could barely understand what she was saying. Kyra was very close to her grandparents. They had raised Kyra so that her mother, who was not even nineteen at the time, could go to college the way they had planned she would. They wanted more for her than they themselves had had, and if it meant raising her newborn to afford her the opportunity to see what life could offer, then they were willing to make that sacrifice.

"Stay put. I'm on my way." I clicked off my phone. I would go directly to Gwen's house and tell her face-to-face the minute I made sure Kyra was okay. In the midst of all that was going on and knowing that Kyra would need all the emotional support I could give, I was glad that Bryan and I had talked, especially given my emotionally drained state of mind. I needed an anchor, and he was there.

I quickly dialed Bryan and told him what was going on. He listened as I told him how Kyra's world had suddenly come to an abrupt halt and how the man that had provided for her when her mother couldn't had died suddenly. While Kyra's grandfather had been getting on in years, he had been as healthy as anyone his age could be. This made it even harder. Nothing had warned them to prepare for the impending end. So, wife, daughter, and granddaughter had assumed they had more time with the man they adored and had come to lean on so heavily.

Just as I knew he would, Bryan reassured me that I was more than able to give Kyra the support she needed and that he was there if we needed him. I held the phone as he encouraged me, so that I might encourage her, and we ended our conversation with Bryan telling me how much he loved me. Although I didn't say the words, what I felt for him went without saying. Right there on the phone, he began to pray, and while I closed my eyes and listened, my heart swelled. Even after he said amen and told me that he loved me, I embraced his words and allowed them to soothe my being. There was a saying that a family that prays together stays together. We weren't a family yet, but it was my heart's desire that we stay together. I picked up my briefcase and purse and walked out of my office. I had already explained the situation to Kandi, so I passed her desk and nodded that I was on my way. When I got to the elevator, I met Wanda. She seemed pretty pleased with herself. Obviously, she was thinking our ordeal from earlier was what had me so visibly upset. I didn't have the energy or the desire to tell her that she was giving herself too much credit. She had indeed started a battle, but I would be winning the war. The fat lady had not sung. In fact, she hadn't even entered the building yet.

Chapter 10

When I arrived at Kyra's office, the young lady at the reception desk hardly looked up at me. She was too busy playing solitaire and blowing bubbles with what looked like grape bubble gum. It must have been ghetto receptionist week or something, because this was the second incident today. Here she was, looking home girl fabulous, sitting smack-dab in the middle of the reception area, in an office of higher education to boot, looking a mess.

"Hello. I need to see Professor Simmons." I stretched my head over the desk a little since she was acting as if she hadn't heard the door open and me clear my throat.

She sucked her teeth and threw her bright burgundy braids over her shoulder. "She's in there." She pointed her neon nail in the direction of Kyra's office.

I was about to say something else and remembered the reason why I was here in the first place. I didn't have time to school this chick or hip her in ten minutes or less on how to work in a professional environment.

The door was open a crack, and I took a deep breath before I entered, preparing myself for whatever state I might find Kyra in. Knowing her, she would probably be throwing herself into finishing up something. A stressful situation had a way of converting pain into nervous energy, so there was no telling what she could be doing. I pushed the door open and walked in, expecting her to be sitting behind her desk. Instead, she was sitting in one of the chairs across from her desk, and there was a man occupying the chair next to her. I looked on as he held her hand and caressed her back. Neither of them had heard me come in. I cleared my throat.

He was the first to stand. I did my usual quick inspection. He was in his fifties; had salt-and-pepper wavy hair, a dimpled chin, deep, piercing brown eyes, and a broad nose; was about six feet one; weighed around 180 pounds. He wore a crisp white French cuff shirt with black cuff links, black slacks, and black, square-toed Italian leather shoes. Very distinguished, well put together, and judging from the gold band on his ring finger, very married.

"Hello," he said and held out his hand toward me. "You must be Patrice Henderson. I offered to take Kyra home, but she mentioned that you were on your way. I've heard a lot about you, Gwen, and some of Kyra's other close friends."

I looked him up and down. "Oh really? And tell me. How do you know Kyra?" I didn't mean to be quizzing this man when I should have been consoling my friend, but here he was, telling me how much he knew about us, and we didn't know a darn thing about him. At least when I left today, I would know who he was and would figure out if he was the mystery man that Kyra was sneaking around with. If that was the case, we were going to be having a long talk as soon as the grief subsided, because unless he just liked wearing a gold band on his ring finger, there was a Mrs. Whomever somewhere. I noticed out of the corner of my eye that Kyra had stood up and was moving toward the other side of her desk.

"Oh, please forgive me. I'm Dr. Anthony Warrington, but please just call me Tony. I'm Kyra's new boss. When she called me to tell me about her grandfather, I rushed right over to see if there was anything I could do."

I watched closely as he shifted a little. He appeared to be a little nervous that I was questioning him. Kyra must not have told him that her circle of friends had her back and were honorary members of the inquiring minds club.

"Well, it's very nice meeting you. And thank you so much for taking care of Kyra until I got here," I said. I turned to Kyra. "Sweetie, do you have everything together?"

"Yes, just about," Kyra whispered. She looked up from what she was doing, and I noticed how red and swollen her eyes were. "I haven't had a chance to download my lesson plans for my classes, and I have several meetings scheduled. I guess I need to tell them that I won't be able to attend." She had her BlackBerry in one hand and was frantically flipping through the pages of her organizer with the other.

"Don't worry about any of that," Dr. Warrington said and walked around the desk and stood beside her. Again, he wrapped his arms around her and pulled her close to him. "If you don't mind me going through your computer, I will download everything for your graduate assistant and look over your meeting schedule. If there is something that I can attend in your stead, I will. If not, then I will let them know that you have a family emergency." He kissed her forehead, and I watched as his lips lingered there affectionately. "Don't worry about anything, Kyra. I just want you to go home and get a little rest before you travel to Mississippi."

Kyra acted as if I wasn't there. A definite indication that this guy had her sprung. "Thank you so much, Tony. I'll check the flights when I get home and let you know what time I can get a flight out."

I had been quiet too long. "You don't need to worry about that. I will get us a flight." I looked directly at her boss to make sure he didn't miss the *us,* since he probably preferred just her. "I don't know if Gwen should be traveling, but there is no way that I'm letting you go down to Mississippi alone."

"I don't want you to interrupt your schedule. You were just promoted," said Kyra. "I'm sure they need you there." Tears began to fill her eyes.

"I've already cleared all that," I replied. "So, finish getting your stuff together. We'll pick some things up from your house and go home. Thanks again, Dr. Warrington. I appreciate what you've done." That was my way of dismissing him.

"Oh, okay. Well, Kyra, you have my numbers. Please call me after you've rested a little," said Dr. Warrington. "I'll be there for the funeral, but if you need me before that, just say the word."

What? I thought. Did he just say that he was flying to Mississippi? If my memory served me correctly, she had mentioned having a new boss just a few short months ago. How could they have gotten to know each other that well in such a short period of time? A floral arrangement, a monetary contribution to whatever cause the family had earmarked, those were the expected expressions of condolence. But, this man had arrived on the scene before any of us, had held her hand, rubbed her back, and kissed her forehead, and was getting ready to board a plane to be there just for her.

"Patrice, please take care of her," he said.

I nodded and watched him exit the office. The minute

the door closed behind him, I turned and watched Kyra
collapse hopelessly in her chair and sob uncontrollably.
A heavy cloud of pain settled in the office, and I swallowed hard to keep from crying along with her. As if in
slow motion, I walked around the desk and leaned down
and held her in my arms and just let her cry. More than
anything else, she needed to shed the tears and not hold
anything back. This was her time, time for her to deal
with the loss of her poppa, and even though this Tony
person was someone of importance to her, he didn't
need to see Kyra lose it, didn't need to see her out of
control. He seemed to be a nice guy, if you looked
beyond the gold band that announced to onlookers like
me that he was married to someone. He might not have
known that I had figured out his agenda. I knew he
wanted Kyra to find comfort in his arms so she would
be beholden to him. Kyra didn't need to be in his debt;
she had us, and what she needed in this space of time
was to let go, with no one counting the cost. I wouldn't
rush her solace. I'd wait as long as she needed me to and
allow her this time.

It must have been too early in the morning for most
travelers, because we were able to breeze through the
electronic ticket counter and each airport checkpoint
without delay. Wouldn't you know it, though? I was all
about business, trying to handle things for Kyra and to
keep Gwen from moving around too much, and along
came a mack.

"Hello. Haven't I seen you someplace before?" The
security guard, who should have been checking lug-
gage and ensuring the safety of those in and outside of
the airport, had stopped performing his assigned duties
and had picked me up on his mack radar. Aside from

his occupation, I would have possibly considered him my type, long ago. He was a tall chocolate wonder with handsome features and a nice body.

"I don't think so, unless it was at church." I looked at him directly and dared him to use another pickup line.

"Maybe so," he replied and walked around to the other side.

"What?" Gwen came closer to me and spoke in a whisper. "Once upon a time, you would have gotten his number just because."

"That's true. I mean, he was an attractive guy, but I have Bryan. I may not know what I want, but I do know who I want." It felt good saying what I just did.

"I'm so proud of you," Gwen said and picked up her purse from the other side of the scanner. Her tote bag was placed on the push cart, and she waited for either Kyra or me to steer it.

We didn't think that Kyra had taken in any of what had just happened. She was standing there, but it seemed that her mind was a thousand miles away. Then she spoke. "I've always admired that you've called your own shots, regardless of what everyone else thought. I know that for you lots of times it was fun and games, but if any woman made an honest assessment, she'd say you were bold enough to do what so many of us only dream of doing." She grabbed the handle of the cart and fell in step behind Gwen and me.

"Thanks, I think," I said. She was right. I had called my own shots. Hindsight was twenty-twenty, though. There were a few things that I would do differently. Sometimes the lifestyle you lived came back to haunt you. Jason had made me see that.

Scott had told us to request wheelchair assistance for Gwen. We didn't exactly follow his orders after Gwen put the fear of God in us for even bringing it up once we got to the airport. Scott really didn't want her to travel to Mississippi, especially under such stressful circumstances, but Gwen had explained that it would be worse if he didn't let her go. She would only worry about Kyra, and that wouldn't be good for her or the baby. Reluctantly, Scott had finally given in, but not before advising me to keep a close eye on Gwen. Tucked away in my tote bag were detailed orders from Scott and the numbers of two of his friends who practiced obstetrics in Jackson, along with the number of another obstetrician in the next county, should I have trouble reaching the first two. I understood completely and appreciated the extremes he'd gone to.

We were seated on US Airways flight 4399 and had only one stop, in Atlanta, Georgia, before arriving at our destination. Kyra frowned the minute we got settled.

"What's wrong?" Gwen asked as she turned to her, with a look of concern.

"I should have gotten a seat someplace else. I don't want to make you two uncomfortable," Kyra replied. She touched Gwen's shoulder. "You don't need to be crowded. I usually travel alone and sit in one of the aisle seats."

I listened as Gwen assured her that she was fine. "Kyra, it's cool. And I'm fine. We are fine." She rubbed her stomach. "You are just sensitive because of the stress. Trice is okay, and we don't want you to think about anything right now."

I chimed in. "That's right, girly girl. The flight is not that long, so why don't you get the sleep you didn't get last night? You really should have taken one of the pills Scott gave you to help you rest."

"No, I'm okay. I just need to get to Mississippi," said Kyra. She attempted a weak smile and listened as we were instructed to get ready for takeoff.

I knew that getting to Jackson as quickly as possible was the number one priority for Kyra. With each call she had received from her mom, it seemed that Kyra's grandmother had fallen apart more. Kyra was the glue that seemingly held the family together, and her grandmother had refused to do a thing until she arrived.

Gwen had slept downstairs, and Kyra and I had shared my bed upstairs. While Gina had been willing to give up her bed, Kyra hadn't really wanted to sleep alone. We talked until she finally fell asleep, and even then she tossed and turned. I didn't want to say so, but when the alarm went off, I felt as restless as I knew she was. While it had only been less than twenty-four hours since she'd received the call about Poppa, she had told Gwen and me while we waited to leave Richmond that every hour she had to wait seemed like it was shackled to a pit of pain that her grandfather would never be able to soothe.

I remembered how back in the day, every time something happened and whenever Kyra was going through something, the first thing she did was call her Poppa. I vividly remembered the time when she was head over heels over this bright-skinned guy named Keith Emerson. He was a cutie, and the one thing that bugged us all was that he knew it and reminded her of it every time they hung out with us. He had a reputation for liking and leaving, and we kept urging Kyra to open her eyes and see him for the dog he was. She wouldn't hear of it and insisted that we didn't want her to be happy and have an opportunity to have someone like Keith like her. So, we stood by silently and watched him lead her on and pretend to be as into her as she was into him. That is, until he embarrassed her in the cafeteria, in front of his fraternity brothers, by saying that he was just trying to get into the drawers and could never be into no fat girl. Andre and Marcus were prepared to kick his butt, but Kyra begged them to let it go. Instead, she called her poppa and told him all about it. The minute she hung up the phone, we were there to reinforce what he had said, that "everything would be all right." That night we picked up pints of Ben & Jerry's in five different flavors and a bag of Chips Ahoys. We went back to our room and listened as she vented and cried until the heartache didn't ache as much.

Shock ran through our dormitory quickly when the word hit that Keith had been kicked out of school for having drugs in his room. No one had ever known him to be a drug user or seller, but that hadn't stopped the cops from confiscating all his belongings and hauling him away in the back of the police cruiser. We all stood on the sidewalk, wondering what was going on. As he passed by us, he looked at Kyra with a sorrowful look on his face, and she gave him a cold stare and assumed a stance that said she welcomed the revenge.

Gwen didn't say a thing, but I knew that traveling through Atlanta brought back memories. I was bothered for that simple reason, but the stop in Atlanta was the shortest route and we needed to get Kyra to Mississippi. Gwen hadn't traveled to or through Atlanta's airport since Tiffany's death. Her sister had died from complications of the AIDS virus, and because of this, Atlanta would always remind Gwen of losing Tiffany. We had prayed hard and begged God to grant us more time, but it was not to be. I remembered the rainy day we left Atlanta to carry Tiffany's remains back home for burial. Grief had consumed all that we were and had threatened to take what sanity my best friend had left. I held her all the way back to Virginia as we traveled the distance back to bury the third musketeer.

When we rushed through Atlanta's airport, I watched

Gwen withdraw and go through the motions, with not much to say, because her surroundings obviously hit an emotional nerve. Maybe this was a little too much for Gwen to endure. The sting of death was still too fresh. I watched Kyra withdraw for a different and yet similar reason. Atlanta marked the reality that she was halfway to her destination. It was almost time for her to deal with the reason we had made the trip. On both counts, I felt like I was seesawing between my friends and feeling them, because that was what close friends did. I had just enough time to call Bryan before our flight was ready to leave Atlanta.

His cell phone rang only once before he picked up. "Hey, Patrice. Where are you guys?"

"In Atlanta, but we are getting ready to take off." I looked over and noticed both Gwen and Kyra on their phones as well. Gwen was obviously talking to Scott, and Kyra had actually stood up and walked a distance away from us. The person on the other end of her call was, in all likelihood, Tony. I had slipped into the bathroom while Gwen showered last night and had told her all about the office scene. The description she'd given me matched Mr. Married Man to a tee. Yet both of us knew that now was not the time to question Kyra.

"Well, you call me the minute you get to Jackson," said Bryan. "And, Trice, I know you are there for Kyra, but when you return, we need to revisit our future. I can't do it like this anymore." There it was. The unstated had just been stated. I thought his silence regarding our issue was his way of giving me time, but obviously time was ticking away.

"Okay." I didn't want to just say nothing. I had played that card, and the game had ended before I'd even known what the stakes were.

"Well, don't forget to call." He had switched gears

just that quickly and now was sounding all busy. Being a businessperson myself, who often got so focused on her work that nothing else could penetrate her concentration, I understood his need to return to his task, but at the same selfish time, I wanted his undivided attention.

"Don't forget to go to Gina's band concert tonight," I said. I had never missed any of her events, and I needed him to stand in for me.

"You know I wouldn't forget Gina, and I will drop her off at Kennedy's house. In fact, I just texted her a few minutes ago and asked if she and Kennedy wanted to go to dinner with me." I could hear voices in the background.

"And did she respond?" I was holding him up because I needed to hear him tell me he loved me. It would have been easy for me to say it first, but I was still hung up somewhere between crazy and sane.

"Of course. Your child would never turn down T.G.I. Friday's. Look, Trice, I hate to rush off the phone, but they are waiting for me in the conference room. Call me when you get to Jackson." He disconnected the phone and didn't tell me he loved me. I couldn't really understand why I needed to hear him say it. I guess I just did.

Before we knew it, we were looming over Jackson, Mississippi, and being told to prepare for landing. I had been a lot of places, but I had never been to Jackson before. I just wished it wasn't under these circumstances.

"Kyra, did you tell your mom to meet us at the airport, or should we get a car?" I asked as I pushed Gwen along in the wheelchair. She had finally given up on being dead set against this measure. I didn't know what Scott had said to her in Atlanta, but when I brought it up, she only nodded. To make light of the situation, I joked with her about getting one that was powered. That way I wouldn't have to use my energy to push her. She let me know quickly, she was only doing it so her husband wouldn't have a fit and so I wouldn't have to report back that his orders had not been followed to the letter.

"Yes. I called her early this morning, when Scott got there to pick us up," said Kyra. She cleared her throat. "She should be here already. I'm sure she will need to add us to the mix for sanity's sake. Mema has been driving her completely crazy and Mom, needing to transfer the negative energy, will be driving us crazy."

Transfer negative energy, I thought. When did she start talking about energy being negative or positive? I looked at Gwen, who returned the same confused look to me.

"Your family can't be that bad," I said. I continued to the baggage claim, with Kyra on my heels. I was actually talking over my shoulder. There was no way that they could be as dysfunctional as the Henderson clan in the backwoods of Virginia. The first time we met Kyra's mother was at our graduation ceremony. We had all been excited to share the culmination of our four-year achievement with our loved ones. Everyone except me. I had invited my family only because it was the right thing to do. I had hardly pulled off my graduation regalia before I was packing them back up in the van Uncle Sonny had rented and directing them to the interstate due north. That was after my mom had reminded me that they had come all that way to see me just walk across the stage and that money didn't grow on trees. I got the hint and offered her money to fill the gas tank up and to cover the bridge toll. She gladly accepted it and didn't even bother to look back.

While I was dealing with them, Kyra's mother had packed her bag, called a cab, and caught a flight, needing to return to her affairs in Jackson. Kyra had never talked about why her mother didn't visit more often and hadn't really opened up with any details about her family life.

This impromptu visit would be like a curtain being raised to reveal a side of Kyra that we didn't know. Since Hurricane Katrina, her grandparents had been among those that had become displaced and had lost everything. Luckily, they had been transported to an area that had not been so severely affected, but it took a while before they could get a message to Kyra's mother and inform her of their whereabouts. Like many who had lost everything in New Orleans, they hadn't wanted to leave until they had seen the disaster for themselves. They needed to view the remnants of what had been, so they could force themselves to move on. From what Kyra had said, they were still waiting for the day when they could return to the place where they had put down roots and rebuild.

Up until Katrina, New Orleans had been the place they called home and to hear Kyra talk, there was no place like it for them. They had never visited her, or her mother for that matter. They'd always been too busy with the family business. Funny, she had never told us what that business was. Whenever we asked, she would just say that it was a long story. Long or short, we had never heard it. If nothing else, maybe talking to somebody attending the funeral or at least reading the obituary would shed some light on what they did. We could always corner that one person at the repast who had had too much to drink. That distant cousin or a friend from around the corner, someone would definitely be in their sauce and ready to spill their guts. After all, they had lived in the city that never sleeps, and since it didn't sleep, I'm sure it had many, many stories to tell. Hopefully, a few of them would be about Benjamin and

Katherine "Kat" Laurent, affectionately called Poppa and Mema by Kyra. Either way, I was curious to meet the extended family, since everything about them and Poppa and Mema had been kept sealed and away from us, behind Kyra's private wall.

"You'll see." That was all Kyra said before calling her mother on the cell to find out where she was. Once she had located her, she maneuvered in that direction, and we followed her. We were in unfamiliar territory, and for right now, we would let Kyra guide us.

From a distance, we saw Kyra's mother walking toward us. She had her head wrapped up in a brightly colored scarf, and even from the distance, I could see the heavy make-up she always wore. The make-up was what I remembered. What I didn't remember was the head wrap. I immediately wondered why it had to be that bright and colorful. Maybe it was a Jackson, Mississippi, by way of New Orleans thing. Had Gwen been standing up and had she caught a glimpse of Kyra's mother, she would probably be wondering the same thing I was. But, since she was sitting down, I had to wonder for both of us.

Kyra's mother began waving her arm wildly over her head. Kyra put her head down a second and lifted it back up and took in the sight of her mother still waving frantically. "I'm glad I accepted the pills that Scott offered, even though I didn't think I'd need them at the time. Staying here to help bury my poppa is going to be the hardest thing I've ever had to do. Being around my mother and Mema is going to elevate my blood pressure and will be very taxing to say the least." She stopped speaking in midstream, and we stopped along with her. Without looking at us, she continued. "Gwen, Patrice, promise me you two will still be my friends when we return here in a few days to go back home?"

"Girl, stop tripping. We are friends for life. There is nothing that could happen that would cause us to want to end our friendship with you," Gwen said.

As Gwen spoke, I wondered why Kyra would say something so drastic. I was not the one totally consumed with grief; my thought pattern was pretty clear. If she was talking about being friends at the conclusion of our stay, I needed to know what could possibly happen that would cause us to abandon her once we were back at the airport and on our way back home. Gwen must have sensed that I was mulling over Kyra's request. Because I had not said a word of reassurance, she pinched my hand.

"Ouch," I yelled.

"What's wrong?" said Kyra. She hadn't seen Gwen pinch me.

"Oh, nothing," I said nonchalantly. "Kyra, we are here with you because we love you. Whatever goes down, we will handle it as friends. Like always." I had cosigned for Gwen, and I hoped she had us prayed up for the unexpected. Not that I hadn't prayed for us on my own. But you can never be covered too much, and somewhere in the pit of my being, way past my love and concern for Kyra, beyond Bryan's need to know what our future held, there was a feeling that we were walking straight into a world we were not prepared for.

Chapter 11

"Sweet spirits, there is my girl!" Eva Simmons wrapped her arms around Kyra and kissed both her cheeks twice.

"Hey, Mom. I'm glad to see you, but not under the circumstances," said Kyra. She pulled away from her mother's grip and looked at her.

I was still fixating on the bright scarf. She also had on large hoop earrings and a ton of bracelets, up both arms. She reminded me of the fortune-tellers they had on hand to read your palm at fairs.

"Mom, you remember Gwen and Patrice," said Kyra. She moved away as her mother exchanged hugs with us.

"I know you talk about them all the time," said Eva as she returned her attention to Kyra. "What are we going to do without Poppa?" She started crying. Kyra comforted her mother and let her know that she was there to handle everything and do exactly what her poppa would have wanted her to do. Instantly, they assumed the family roles they had played, and Eva Simmons clung to Kyra and cried softly on her shoulder.

Looking on, we could see that Kyra was the rock, the

anchor, and the one that had inherited the strength to carry the family through this storm.

Gwen and I climbed into the backseat of Eva Simmons's Honda Accord, and we all headed out of the airport parking lot. I was still so fixated on the bright head wrap she wore. I couldn't take my eyes off it until Gwen pinched me and disciplined me with a stare. How could I help it? There were more colors on the wrap than there were on a color wheel, if that was possible. Eva's clothes were in disarray, and she just seemed to have pulled herself together barely in order to pick us up. At least that was what I hoped. I didn't want to believe that this was her everyday attire and that the bags under her eyes were a constant. I hoped this was just evidence of the emotional upset of losing her father.

Kyra was driving. "Gwen, do you need to stop to get something to eat? I'm sure Mema has something stirred up for us, but if you need something to tide you over before we get there, there are several places along the way." She glanced at Gwen in the rearview mirror.

"Actually, I'm fine. A little tired," said Gwen. She yawned and rubbed her eyes under her sunglasses.

I reached for her hand and squeezed it. "I'll help Kyra with whatever she needs. After you get something to eat, you need to rest a while."

"Please don't tell Scott how worn-out I am. He will be on the next plane to pick me up and carry me back to Richmond," said Gwen. She tried to sound light-hearted, but I could tell she wanted to reassure Scott that she was okay and yet she realized that maybe she should have listened to him. I could tell she was a little concerned and hadn't expected the trip to take such a toll on her.

"I won't. Just promise you will tell us exactly how you feel. No covering anything up and thinking you are Wonder Woman," I said.

"Promise," Gwen whispered. She leaned her head against the seat of the car and closed her eyes. "I'm going to rest my eyes for a second or two."

"I'm not pregnant, but I'm a little tired myself," I said and closed my eyes.

"Mom, tell me. How is Mema holding up?" Kyra asked.

"As well as can be expected, I guess. She is going on and on about wanting to bury Poppa in New Orleans, even though the burial site for the spirit callers is no longer there. She's worried that the spirits won't be able to find him here in Jackson and that he will not be able to make his final transition and return to stand guard."

I had reclined my head against the seat, taking Gwen's lead and hoping to take a quick nap before getting to the house. That is, until I tuned in to the conversation in the front seat. My eyes popped open, and I raised my head up so quickly, I felt like I had given myself whiplash.

"Mom, we will talk about it later," Kyra mumbled. Again, she glanced in the rearview mirror, and instead of the closed eyes she had probably expected, she found both Gwen and me looking right back at her.

"If we don't talk about it now, you can forget talking about it when we get home," Eva remarked. "Mema will be hanging around every corner, lurking in the shadows, and trust me, she is in rare form. She has already consulted all their workers, and some of them will be arriving as early as tonight. A few will stay with other callers that relocated here from back home, some at my house, and since Mema wants to be close to Poppa, we will be staying at the funeral home."

"What? The funeral home?" I gasped. I sat up and leaned my head across the front seat in one fluid movement. Somebody needed to tell me something. No wonder Kyra had been so concerned about how we were going to react. Spirit callers, standing guard, staying in a funeral home . . . she was getting ready to be left in Jackson. If something didn't make sense real soon, I was taking my butt and Gwen's right back to the airport, and we would be boarding the next plane heading to Richmond. *Wait a minute*, I thought. This was my friend, and she needed me. That was all that mattered. I told myself that as I sat back in my seat and waited for Kyra to fill in a couple of details.

"Poppa's brother owns the funeral home," Eva informed us. "His house is actually connected to it, and that is where Mema wants to stay. Not actually in the funeral home. She believes that Poppa will rest better if we are close by."

Again, friendship was a special thing. If it weren't for that, the comment Eva had just made would have been all I needed for a quick round-trip.

Kyra spoke up. "It's not exactly like that, Trice. Mom, we won't be staying at Uncle Bart's. My friends will be more comfortable at your house, so I will be staying there with them."

"Mema won't hear of it," cried Eva. "The energy will not be the same if you aren't in the house with us. Your power is needed." Eva continued talking, throwing her hands all around her head in wild circles.

Gwen cleared her throat. "Kyra, sweetie. If you need to stay with your family, Trice and I can get a hotel nearby. That's not a problem at all. We didn't come to disrupt anything or to alter plans."

"I'll work it all out. I'll talk to Mema and tell her how everything is going to go," Kyra promised. She attempted a weak smile.

Sleep would come later. I was too busy keeping a close eye on the bone-throwing voodoo sisters in the front. Neither Gwen nor I closed our eyes for the remainder of the trip to Kyra's mother's house. It was even difficult to take in the sights after what I had heard. All the red stoplights gave me a chance to observe the people that walked up and down the sidewalks. They appeared to be mere images: nothing about them stood out or made an imprint on my mind. All the streets and buildings looked alike, and all the businesses seemed to repeat every other block. My mind was consumed in a haze of confusion, and I couldn't shake it off. Obviously, Kyra's poppa and mema dealt with some dark stuff. That much was clear. My faith was strong enough to deal with whatever came my way, and although it was definitely something to digest, none of it mattered or made me view my friend any differently.

When in doubt, you do what you know. So, I prayed like Job and quoted scripture like Paul all the way to the house. It might have been under my breath and inaudible to other ears, but I was giving it all I had and then some. I even texted the first lady of our church and asked her to pray for our strength in the Lord. Of course, I didn't tell her about this latest occurrence; it wasn't my business to tell. She knew about the sudden death of Kyra's grandfather and that we would be joining Kyra on her trip home. Kyra had become close to the pastor's wife, who was also a tenured professor in the English Department at Virginia Commonwealth University. They were more than just lunch buddies; they leaned on each other heavily, knowing that politics existed in every realm and that there was always a need for someone to watch your back. They worshipped together when the chaos of the week had ended and their obligation to educate bright young minds had for another five days been fulfilled.

Now that we were in no rush to get to Kyra's mom's, we pulled in front of the house much too quickly. Kyra and her mother got out the minute the car was shifted into park and the engine was turned off. They paused in their tracks, waiting for us to get out.

"Come on, guys. This is my mom's house," Kyra mumbled. She looked at us, and her eyes were telling us that she was sorry. Sorry to bring us into her world. A world that had come to make sense to her, but that on-lookers standing on the outside would never understand.

"We're coming," said Gwen. Just as quickly, she turned slightly in the seat and mumbled to me under her breath. "Come on. Let's go in. We'll find some way to stay someplace other than a funeral home."

"I know that's right. I get the creeps just going inside one," I whispered. She was on the money with that. There was no way I was going to stay in a house that was connected to a funeral home and help keep watch over an old man who wasn't going anywhere without the assistance of about six escorts.

Eva held the gate open and waited for us to walk through it. Like the four steps that led up to the side-walk, it had seen better days. It was held in place only by a connector at the bottom, which was covered par-tially by tall grass and weeds. It didn't appear that Eva spent a lot of time maintaining things on the outside. What little grass she had in the front yard was in need of mowing, and the bushes and hedges could have used trimming. I wasn't a garden-care kind of woman, but I wouldn't necessarily let the grass, hedges, and bushes take over my yard. I would head to Home Depot and arm myself with enough tools to fight back. Further in-spection revealed that the porch needed some of the wood replaced. Several rails and some edging had rotted. I could barely tell what color the house had been, but it looked to be some shade of green. Looking across the street and at the two houses next door, I noticed that Eva's house didn't fit in at all. Every other residence was well maintained, the lawn mowed, hedges trimmed, and each of them had a warm, inviting aura.

"Come in here, sweet darling girl, and give you Mema a big ole hug." A plump lady with salt-and-pepper, wavy hair pulled back in a bun swung the door open. She was the color of warm honey, the same complexion as Eva and Kyra. I tried to recall if Kyra had said that Mema was eighty-five or eighty-seven, but the lady that stood in the doorway, with a jean jumper on and a green and white apron wrapped around her waist, didn't look a day over fifty. If it weren't for the gray strands mixed in with her black hair, she could have passed for forty, even with the added weight.

"Oh, Mema. It's so good to see you," said Kyra. The minute Kyra wrapped her arms around her grandmother, silent tears eased from both their eyes. Eva looked on and wrapped her arms around herself and rocked. They held each other for a while and Mema spoke into Kyra's hair, but what she said was obviously meant for Kyra only, because while we saw her lips moving, as close as we were standing, we didn't hear a word.

Kyra pulled away, and her grandmother resisted a second before letting her go. "Mema, these are my best friends, Gwen and Patrice." She moved from in front of her grandmother and allowed her to walk toward us.

"Oh, two beautiful ones. Come and let Mema embrace you."

Gwen moved freely and I followed suit. Mema smelled really good, like some type of natural oil and some other fragrance that I had never smelled before. It created a strange yet welcoming scent, and I closed my eyes and hugged her back.

"You are tense. You need to relax," Mema informed me. "I know you came for a funeral, and we will bury my Benjamin, but staying here with Mema will be good for what ails you."

I looked at Mema and then at Kyra and Gwen. I didn't want to offend, so when I looked at Mema's smiling face again, I smiled back and nodded my head. "I don't know what to say."

"I know you don't, beautiful one. You never do," replied Mema. She chuckled softly and took my hand and squeezed it.

"So true," Gwen quipped, and she laughed along with Mema.

"Come on in, guys. Let's go and relax for a while," said Kyra as she walked behind her grandmother.

Eva had ducked in while Mema was exchanging greetings with us. The inside of the house didn't match the outside. Everything in the house was tidy and organized. The furniture was outdated, but it was well kept and showed that the occupants cared about its longevity and its appearance. The floors shined, and the smell of clean quickly entered my nostrils. I positioned myself beside Gwen on the love seat that faced the sofa, which Kyra had fallen onto.

"I'll go get you something to drink. You all should be thirsty. I just made some freshly squeezed lemonade," said Mema, and she disappeared down the hall.

Kyra looked at us, noticing that while she was reclining against the sofa, it took us a few minutes to do the same. "I know I have a lot of explaining to do. But all of it is difficult to discuss with anyone. I just didn't want to defend or protect what it is they do and how they have lived all their lives." She looked down at the floor.

"You should have known that we are better friends than that, Kyra," Gwen scolded. "We may have had questions, but with us, you wouldn't have had to defend them or protect them from judgment. Who are we to judge?" Gwen rubbed her stomach and frowned.

"What's wrong?" I asked. I leaned over and placed my hand on top of hers. "Are you in pain?"

"No, actually, the baby is just moving around," Gwen explained. She started giggling.

Kyra had jumped over to where we were, sat on the arm of a chair, and placed her hand near ours. We must have made a sight, because Eva came in with a tray of sandwiches and started laughing. "When Kyra told me that you three were as close as they come and did so much together, I thought the girl was exaggerating. But look at you three. You'd think you were all carrying the child."

Kyra and I answered at the same time. "We are." We laughed and just held each other. I could feel Kyra's embrace and could only smile. She needed us, and we knew that it was important that we get her through this trauma and, more than that, that we didn't judge. If I had learned anything else personally, I had learned not to judge. My faith was strong, and nothing or no one could sway me into believing anything other than my Messiah lives; Jesus is the way, the truth, and the light; and all the other things that I had learned throughout the years. But in all that, I knew God didn't want me to judge. Maybe in addition to being here for the funeral, this was a mission trip for us, and maybe Mema needed us.

Mema smiled at us. "This, too, is a scene. My darling girl and her two friends, who are now my girls, too. You girls will be friends long after Mema goes to join Benjamin, and when I go, Benjamin will come get me, and we both will watch over you, this baby, and the babies that will be born from you two." She pointed to Kyra and me.

I couldn't speak for Kyra, and I didn't want to

disappoint Mema, but my childbirth ship had sailed.
I had taken an alternative route, and it had worked
out well for me. Mema seemed to be a sweet lady,
and I could see her in Kyra. That made her special.

"Eat up, girls," Mema urged. "We have much work
to do and lots of plans to make, Kyra. Others will come
soon, and the ceremonies will begin before we know it.
I know your friends think this strange and a bit crazy,
but, beautiful babies, this is our way. I know you don't
believe, and I know you are spiritual. I sense that
strongly, but our ways are not really that different. But
Mema is different. I don't try to convert, and you don't
judge my ways. I'll keep everyone from you, and we will
all be all right in the end. Benjamin is glad to have you
beautiful babies here, and he say you are good people for
his grandbaby. You love her and would never do her
harm. For that, we love you. He is already enjoying your
company." She looked over her shoulder and smiled.

All righty then. She was stepping up the crazy talk
and speaking to Benjamin, who was supposed to be
getting ready for his final showing at Uncle Bart's
place. I smiled at Mema as Kyra and Eva looked at us
to see what expression we had on our faces.

Once Mema left the room, talking to Benjamin we
presumed, Kyra spoke. "See, she goes off like that sometimes. She sees him, and to her, he is here."

"I hate to ask you this, and if you don't want to
answer, I will understand," I said. "Do you see him?"

Kyra looked around and put her hand on her left
shoulder. "I don't see him, but I do sense his presence.
Can I just leave it at that?"

"Sure," Gwen answered and reached for a sandwich
from the tray, which sat in the center of the coffee table.
She lifted the bread from the top of the sandwich to see
what she was about to bite into. Pleased with what she

saw, she took a large bite and started smiling. "This chicken salad is so good."

"Mema can throw down, guys. Wait till you taste some real food. This is nothing," said Kyra. "You will leave here well fed and will carry a few pounds back to Scott. Look at me." She pulled at the fat around her stomach area.

I mellowed out a little and reached for a sandwich myself. Once I took a bite, I had to agree it was very good. It had a hint of something, and at this point, I didn't feel like trying to figure out what seasoning it was. I was hungry and it was good. That was all that mattered. To safeguard things, I held the sandwich up in the air and said a quick grace over it. When I opened my eyes, Kyra and Gwen were looking at me. "Amen," I murmured. I really meant no harm. Kyra knew I liked to have fun, often at their expense and sometimes at my own.

Chapter 12

"Room service? Yes, could you send up a couple of grilled chicken salads? Both with ranch dressing. And two bottles of water. And could I get a couple of lemon slices? Oh, and tell me, what do you have for dessert this evening?" I listened as the lady listed the array of desserts they had. "How about two slices of cheesecake with strawberry topping? No, that will be all. Thanks." I hung up the phone and leaned my back against the fluffy pillow.

Gwen came out of the bathroom in her night attire, complete with ankle socks and a wrap scarf. I could see her navel peeping through the cotton fabric of her nightgown. "I feel like a new woman. The shower was great. And the fact that I didn't have to wait made it that much better," she said as she flopped down on the double bed next to the one I was lying across. My head dangled over the side as I lay on my stomach, with both legs crossed up in the air. I was flipping through my Black-Berry, checking e-mails, messages, and reminders.

"I can't wait to hit the shower myself. When I was trying to take a shower at Eva's house, the water was cold, and someone was knocking on the door, saying they needed to get in real bad." We had spent the first night at Eva's house with only Mema, Eva, and Kyra. It had been very relaxing, actually. We'd looked on as they went through family photos and gathered the information for the obituary. Mema had continued to talk to her Benjamin, and we just watched to see what direction she looked in, indicating to us that in her mind's eye, he was standing right there.

Before the sun had even risen the next morning, the doorbell had gone off, and loud thunderous voices had filled the house. There'd been crying, yelling, and then laughter. I had looked over and noticed that Gwen had slept through it all. That was a relief. I knew she needed her rest, and I didn't want anything to cause her to stress. Shortly after that, yet another group had come in, and there'd been the same loud voices, tears, and then laughter. This time Gwen had responded by placing a pillow over her head. The rest of the day had been a true experience. Around every corner props were being set up and meditation was taking place. The kitchen had been converted, and Mema and Eva had entered a zone that was off-limits to us. We went out with Kyra for a couple of hours and had dinner at Red Lobster. For that short time, she'd laughed and joked and listened to us keep her company. We'd talked about everything we could think of and even called Andre and Tori and put them on speakerphone. The icing on the cake had been Andre Jr. telling us he "lobbed" us. That was priceless. Just as the conversation was ending, Andre asked to speak to Kyra. She held the phone and listened, with a hint of a smile on her face. No doubt he was assuring her that everything would be okay. Marcus had already called earlier that morning from Italy. He had just arrived there for a location shoot for one of his artists and had called Gwen the minute

Mama Bea had told him about Kyra's grandfather. While he understood Gwen's reason for coming, he'd been as upset as Scott that she hadn't stayed back.

We returned to more madness, and it was Kyra who decided that it was too much for Gwen. It was a sad revelation, because truly Kyra didn't want us to leave her, but she understood and knew her place and knew that we didn't need to be a part of it. She pulled Mema to the side and explained. For a few minutes, she came out of the zone and walked into the room where we were. "My beautiful girls, I'm sorry this is too much for you. As I said, it is our way, but I don't want Gwen to be sick. So, you go with Kyra, and she will take you to a nearby place to stay. We need to make sure Benjamin has a place to rest. I want him to go back home, but they tell me there is no home for him in New Orleans. So, I must find another place where he will be able to be found when the time come." What had started off making sense to us, ended up being a conversation she was having with herself.

Kyra realized it and kissed her grandmother's cheek and hugged her tightly. "It will be okay, Mema. Poppa knows all." She was about to say something else but stopped short.

We packed up the few things we had brought, and Kyra took us to the Hyatt not far from her mom's house. After she got us settled and we fought over her paying, she kissed us and told us she had to go finish some things with Uncle Bart and handle a couple of other family matters. I felt bad, because we were supposed to be there for her. But I knew she was concerned about Gwen, and because of that, she wanted me to stay and watch over her. I watched Kyra retreat and looked out the window as she walked toward her mom's Honda. She wiped at her eyes and got in the car. I was torn between both friends. I knew Kyra needed someone, and yet Gwen needed me as well.

So here we were. "I ordered a couple of salads. I didn't think you wanted anything really heavy," I said.

"You were right. I just want a little something, and then I'm going to attempt to get a good night's sleep." She lay down on the bed and placed one pillow under her legs and the other one under her head. Her phone went off, and she started talking to Scott. Suddenly, I was not in the room. I understood perfectly.

I took this time to call my sweetie. "Hey, you. What are you doing?"

"I just walked into your house. I needed to get a folder from your office. I left it there before you went to Jackson. I brought in the mail, too."

"Thanks. I talked with Gina earlier, and she was telling me that she was going to Midnight Madness at the church tonight."

"That's right. She mentioned that to me when she called the office earlier. She has been calling me every few hours. If I didn't know better, I'd think she was checking up on me for you."

"I didn't ask her to. She adores you and sees you as a father, even though we haven't come to that point yet."

"Regardless of what happens, I'll always be there for her," he said.

I didn't like how that sounded. I was miles away, and he was talking like we might not work. Where had that come from? I wanted to say something, but my stupid ego got in the way. My ego was telling me that if he was talking about a worst-case scenario, then who was I to think about the best-case scenario? So, I let it go. "We are all settled in the hotel."

"Good." I listened closely for disappointment over

my lack of response to what he had said; however, I didn't pick up on any. "Is Gwen okay?"

"Yes, she is resting. We are actually waiting for room service to bring us some dinner. After that we will watch a little television and crash early. I'm sure Kyra will be picking us up early tomorrow."

"You mentioned that there will be a ceremony before the funeral."

"Yes. On Sunday there will be a ceremony conducted by someone who is like their big gun. Then the funeral is Monday morning at ten. Then he will be taken to Biloxi and laid to rest there. It seems there is a special cemetery there for the callers."

"You are beginning to sound like an authority on how they handle their dead." Bryan started laughing.

"Not that I want to. Bryan, do you miss me?" It was out before I knew it. I wasn't even sure where it had come from, it had just come. A part of me was tired of holding on to my independence; I needed to be a part of someone emotionally, someone other than my child and my friends.

"Yes, Trice. I miss you a lot. I would think that you wouldn't need to ask me that. It sort of goes without saying."

"I guess I just needed to hear you say it." I didn't know where to go with the conversation next. So, I began to talk about other things. Gwen had answered the door for room service and had placed our food on the nearby table. I continued to talk nervously to Bryan about everything and nothing.

"Trice, why do you do this?" Bryan asked, annoyed.

"Do what?" I was getting irritated. I sort of knew what he was talking about, but I didn't want to say it. I preferred to play like I didn't know. I stood up and walked to the table and sat across from Gwen.

She put dressing on her salad and glanced at me with a questioning look. She could tell that somehow I had backed myself up in a corner and Bryan wasn't going to let me get out of it easily.

"You express some emotion, and when you realize it, you retract quickly, like it never happened. One minute you act like you want to walk down the aisle with me and allow me to take your hand and be your husband, and the next, you act like you just want to be my friend. I can't say 'my sexual partner' since we don't do that anymore."

"Whose fault is that?" It was out before I knew it. I looked at Gwen, hoping she would say something to get me off the phone.

"It's no one's fault. It's just the way it should be. Wasn't that a decision that we made together? Or was that something you just agreed with? Maybe deep down you didn't understand or feel the same way I did about it."

"I'm not that naïve. I know what we agreed to, and I'm also intelligent enough to know why we made the decision we did. Look, I'm going to eat, and I'll talk with you later." Before I could change my mind, I hung up. A conversation that should have brought me comfort had made me feel worse. He was right. I was scared of saying certain things and scared to express certain emotions. I just didn't know why it was that way with Bryan. I trusted him totally, and still, I couldn't completely let myself go emotionally with him.

"What happened?" Gwen held her fork in midair and waited for me to reply.

"Don't want to talk about it. How is the food?" I ripped the dressing pouch open and poured the dressing over my salad. With pent-up frustration, I grabbed the knife and fork and cut my salad.

"Well, if you want to know what I think . . ." Gwen

stopped talking and allowed me the opportunity to agree. Because I knew her well, I knew that she wouldn't stop until I allowed her to share her ten cents.

"What do you think, Gwen?" I pushed my food away for a minute. My appetite had left me when I'd hung up from Bryan. If only he knew that I was here in Jackson, missing him terribly and on the verge of saying "ask me again." A scene from *Diary of a Mad Black Woman* flashed across my mind and lingered for a minute.

"I think that Bryan is getting tired of your yo-yo emotions. I know that you've loved him for a while, and yet you waited years just to tell the man. You act as if marrying him is like attaching yourself by chain to a ball and jumping in the river." She smiled. "Marriage is not that bad. In fact, I like being married, not because I finally gave in, but because I love Scott. At the end of the day, loving him and trusting him with that love should be enough." Gwen reached across the small table and rubbed my arm.

"I know, Gwen. He should know I love him. And Bryan knows my hang-ups, and I have to believe that he understands. I was like this when he fell in love with me." I pulled the salad back in front of me and started to eat.

"Maybe he thought you would change. You got to stop assuming that he is okay with your decisions and your tactics. Stop for a minute and switch places. Would you be okay if he was all over the place with his emotions when it came to you? I'll answer that for you. No, you wouldn't be. You are a direct person, and you don't like anyone not being direct and on point with you. I'm with Bryan. In addition to being here for Kyra and keeping a close eye on me, per your commitment to Scott, you should take the remaining days you have here to think about your future with Bryan."

"If he loves me, he will accept me just the way I am.

I can't let Bryan call all the shots and change me. I know my worth, and I recognize who I am. Why should I change or adjust for a man?"

"It's not called changing or adjusting. It's called compromising. A relationship is give-and-take. Please don't get mad at me or take this the wrong way, but with Bryan from day one, you have taken more than you have given." She took the last forkful of salad and placed it in her mouth. With her mouth full, she spoke again. "Now, I'm going to take my cheesecake and curl up in the bed and eat it before you take a big bite out of my behind."

"Whatever." I couldn't believe what she had said to me. How could she call me out like that? After I went through the typical black woman's degrees of anger, I thought about what Gwen had said.

Her words rang in my ears while I undressed and did my daily inspection in the mirror. They got louder when I stepped in the shower and allowed the hot water to flow over my body and wash away my doubts and a few of my fears. If they whirled around and went out with the lather and suds of my scented body wash, I would be rid of some of what I felt. I toweled myself dry and moistened my body with my usual staples, baby oil with vitamin E and aloe, followed by my scented bath and body lotion. The smell of blackberry and vanilla blended in the air and wafted out of the bathroom the minute I opened the door.

All the lights had been turned off, and the only light in the room came from the television. I walked over to Gwen and noticed that she was already asleep. Lying on her side, with her hand on her stomach, she looked so peaceful. Quiet really looked good on her. I removed the portable CD player and the earphones she had placed on her stomach. It had become their ritual to play something soothing for the baby every night. I placed the earphones on my ears and listened to "I'm Gonna Be Ready" by Yolanda Adams.

I sat on the side of the bed and started the track again and really listened. The words soothed my soul and spoke volumes to the pain that I realized I had created within myself. Gwen was right, Bryan was right, and as I listened to Yolanda sing, I realized Gina was right. I needed to trust my heart. My heart was singing along with the lyrics. It didn't know all the words, didn't exactly hit the up tempo or the down tunes, but it echoed one part in perfect harmony. *I'm going to be ready*. I hit repeat and stretched out on the bed and cried, a release that loosened every emotional knot throughout my being. I didn't have to worry about anyone seeing me cry or exposing this very vulnerable side to anyone. I could be me, just Patrice. The pain lifted, and somewhere in the lyrics I let go of the fear, discarded the control, and just as I closed my eyes and allowed sleep to come, Bryan came to meet me in my dream world. Tonight, I would rehearse giving him my heart. Just as I reached for him and allowed him to carry me away, I cried one last tear, because I was finally ready, and it felt so good.

I was sitting in the backseat, and Gwen was riding shotgun. We were on our way to order flowers. Kyra had let us sleep in, and our day with her hadn't begun until 12:00 p.m. I had ordered a full breakfast for Gwen, and I had eaten just a cinnamon raisin bagel with cream cheese and orange juice. Gwen had fussed that she wasn't that hungry, but by the time I got out of the shower, her plate was so empty, no one would have been able to tell what she had eaten. There wasn't a crumb of anything on it.

"Kyra, how did you rest?" Gwen asked.

"Not so bad. I didn't get to bed until two, but I bounced right back up at six. Tony woke me up." She stumbled over the last part. I didn't think she meant to tell us that part.

"Oh, did he?" I replied instead of Gwen. "We were wondering how he knew so much about us and we knew so little about him."

"That's because I talk about you guys all the time," Kyra informed us. "And I just never got around to telling you all about him. He's a nice guy." She smiled, and I noticed it immediately.

"How well do you know him?" I asked. I might have been prying, and Bryan had warned me against it, but she seemed to be willing to talk some. I didn't want to lose out on the opportunity. Gwen sat there silently, and since she didn't open her mouth to interrupt, I knew she wanted me to continue.

"Well, he took the position in January, but I met him when I was away for the fellowship," said Kyra. "He was at Rutgers University prior to coming to Richmond. So, it's been a while." She cut it off too quickly. I had to dig deeper.

"That's the when, but I was asking how well you know him," I said.

"We get along pretty well," Kyra replied. "He's a fair person and great to work for. There are many things I admired about his management style, and he's open to fresh ideas, of which I have plenty. You guys know me." She laughed lightly.

We joined in. "He sounds nice, and I could tell that he is fond of you by the way he carried on in the office before we left town," I said. "Almost like, I don't know, a better than good friend."

"Girl, I'm an English professor, and you are talking like that?" yelled Kyra.

"Get beyond the grammar, Professor Simmons. And

talk to us," I said. I stopped, sensing that Gwen wanted to say something.

"Kyra, we don't have secrets. So, I'm going to come out with it. I saw you with him outside Hunan a few days before your grandfather died." She paused. "I saw him kiss you. When Trice described him, I figured it was the same guy."

"What's going on between you two?" I added.

"We've been involved since last year," Kyra informed us. "I'm the reason he accepted the position at VCU. And since you already know I'm not into casual relationships . . . I'm in love with him, and he loves me very much."

I needed to approach the rest with caution. "That's great. We are happy for you. Girl, you could have shared that pertinent information. You know how nosy Gwen is?"

"Me?" Gwen snapped her head around. "All by myself, huh?"

"I know that Trice is just as nosy as you are," said Kyra. She pulled in front of the florist and put the car in park and turned the engine off. But she didn't get out, so we stayed put and waited.

"He's married," Kyra said softly.

Gwen spoke first. "Really? Is he separated?"

"No. His wife is still in New York. He is planning to tell her about us."

It sounded like the same story too many women had shared. I just couldn't believe that as intelligent as Kyra was, she had fallen for it. I wanted to shake her, and I knew that Gwen did, too.

"So, in the meantime, you are what? His mistress?" I asked. That might have been harsh, but she needed to feel the sting so that she would wake up quick.

"That's ugly, Trice," Kyra snapped. She jumped out of the car.

I thought to myself, *Here we go*. She had to know how we would respond, which was probably why she'd kept it to herself for over a year.

"Wait, Kyra," Gwen called as she got out of the car. "We don't want to upset you. Just be careful and think about what you are doing."

"I *have* thought about it, Gwen," said Kyra. "I love him, and he is going to tell his wife he wants a divorce. Then he will be free to marry me."

I wanted to ask more questions, but I didn't want to push it. "Okay, well, you know we love you. We can't support you fully, because it's wrong, but we are here."

"I understand," said Kyra. We followed her into the flower shop and waited for a friend of her mother's who would be handling the arrangements.

We helped Kyra order all the floral arrangements for the family, coordinating everything with the color of the casket and the head "spirit calling" outfit her poppa would wear. I knew that wasn't the formal name for it, but it was a lot easier to say than the long term Kyra had used.

No expense was spared, and Kyra went deep in her pocket to add to the money her mema had. From the details she gave us after we left the florist, it was clear her poppa had a generous policy and enough money to take care of Mema. She added that the family business had made a lot of money, and he and Mema were good at what they did and had a lot of clients. It seemed that their business worked like Amway: for every caller that they trained and set up in business, they received a cut of the profits. It was clear that they had a number of people in the tiers under them. We never asked Kyra for an exact count, because, honestly, I didn't want to think of that many lost souls.

The funeral chores for the day ended. "I'm tired,

Kyra," Gwen moaned as she rubbed her feet while we sat in the chairs in the back of the viewing room. I had gotten a look at Poppa, and he was a strikingly handsome old man. His calling gear consisted of what looked like a robe, and he had a scarf on his head that was shaped like a crown. Several gold chains hung around his neck, and one had the symbol of a snake. His arms were crossed upward across his chest. Several colorful markings were on his face. It seemed like a whole lot of extra stuff to me but was routine for them. It seemed that Uncle Bart did a good job. I didn't have to worry about quizzing some family member to find out what the family business was. I knew. Poppa had been the leader of a spiritual group that believed in spirits, transactions, and karma, and that was the nice stuff.

"Okay. Let me tell Mom to tell Mema we are leaving, and I'll take you guys back to the hotel," said Kyra.

"Do you think they can do without you for tonight, since so many people are here now?" I asked. I had heard that it was an all-night event.

"I'll find out," Kyra replied. She walked away.

I moved to sit closer to Gwen. "I know what you are up to," she said. "You want to talk about Tony."

"Actually, I do. But not tonight. I just think she needs a break."

I smiled as Kyra walked toward us. She had been crying off and on for the past two hours. Sitting in a viewing room was extremely hard on any loved one. Death was something that you just couldn't get used to.

"Let's get out of here," Kyra said.

"We are right behind you," I assured her. And we were.

Chapter 13

I was dressed and waiting for Gwen to use the bathroom for the third time. My outfit was simple: a pale green Donna Karan suit and Vera Wang slings to match. I was pulling the loose strands of my hair up again and twisting it into the updo that one of Kyra's cousins had done for me the night before.

Someone knocked on the door, and I said, "I don't know who that could be. No one knows we are here but Kyra." She had left the car with us to get back to the house since she would be riding in the limousine, so I figured it couldn't hurt to check. Maybe it was housekeeping.

I swung the door open, and there stood Bryan and Scott, all smiles. I was getting ready to scream, but Bryan covered my mouth.

"Shhh. Just because you know, Scott would still like to surprise Gwen," Bryan whispered. They walked in behind me, and all I could do was smile.

Gwen was looking down at her skirt. "This thing is too tight, Trice. I feel like a whale. Everything I put on is too tight." She was on the verge of tears.

"You look good to me," Scott said as he walked up behind her.

"Oh my God," Gwen gasped. She threw her hands around Scott's neck and started crying. Scott began to kiss her tears away and tell her how much he missed and loved her.

I turned to Bryan, and he was looking at me. He was getting ready to say something, but I touched his lips with my finger. "No, I need to say something. Bryan, I missed you, and I love you so much. I'm so glad you are here, and you are the best part of me. Sweetheart, you mean the world to me."

I was on a roll, but before I could finish, Bryan touched my lips and spoke. "I missed you and, Patrice, I love you to life."

That was all he got out before I pulled him down until my lips could meet his. I kissed him and wasn't concerned about it stirring something within me or him. I just needed to feel him, if only for a minute.

The funeral was long, and we sat with the family at the request of Mema, not far behind where Kyra sat. There beside her on the bench was Tony, holding her and allowing her to cry on his shoulder. The ring was gone, and despite being sad, Kyra was comforted in a way that neither Gwen nor I could comfort her. Obviously, she needed the touch of a man, and that man just happened to be this untouchable, already married man.

Everything else passed like a blur. Scott held on to Gwen, Bryan was a constant at my side, and Tony didn't let Kyra out of his sight. That is, until we were ready to leave and Mema called us, the three girls, into her bedroom.

"I needed to talk to my girls before you go back to your city." She sat on the bed and patted it, urging the three of us to sit with her. "I have much to say, and you all need to listen close. There is wisdom in this old lady's mouth and much love in my heart. What I share don't just come from what I read, but it come from what I feel right here." She touched her chest. "First, you, Kyra, because you are my darling girl. This man you bring here is not your own. No one need to tell me. I feel it. You lean on him because you think no one else care for you. No one else can because you think you are unattractive. If the weight bother you so, lose some of it. But don't lose you being a true woman. It's all you have. If he love you, he will get it right and come back when he is free to love you. For now, you drink this three times a day and watch some of the weight come off." Kyra looked too shocked to say a word. If she knew her grandmother dealt openly with issues like that, she should have seen the whole thing coming.

"On to you, pregnant one," said Mema. "You going to have a beautiful baby, just like you and the sweet man you married. Don't worry so much. She will come some early because she eager to see the world, but her eyes will be opened 'cause she don't want to miss a thing. When illness come, don't get scared but remember Mema words. Nothing bad will come to you. This is not the spirit talking, but only what my heart feels." She rubbed Gwen's back and smiled.

Mema turned to me. "You are full of wonder, and no one ever have to tell you that you got it, as they say, going on." She threw back her head and laughed loudly as she looked at me. "But there comes a time when you have to give up all of that and just be the you, you are afraid to see. You think it make you vulnerable and easy to hurt, but it only make you smart enough to see that it's time to let someone in. This one you have, you can trust him with your heart. He love you and the child you have taken as your own. Don't be afraid to be happy, and don't be afraid to love."

The entire plane ride back, I leaned against Bryan's shoulder as he slept and thought about Mema's words. What she'd said was right. She had not merely told me my fortune. She'd been like a mother who had been watching everything and waiting for the right time to say something to gently nudge the young one in the right direction. I'd been a little concerned at first, not knowing if Mema had talked to her spirits and found out about us, or if Kyra had shared information about us. That is, until Kyra told me that many of the details about our lives, Mema had gotten from her. I just wasn't sure if Kyra had said that because she didn't want us to judge or to run scared. I would just go with it.

There was so much I needed to say to Bryan, and although I had cracked the door, it was time for me to walk all the way through it and trust that I would not have to retreat and hide my feelings for fear of losing my way or being led in the wrong direction.

I walked leisurely through my bedroom, barefoot, allowing my feet to sink into the ivory-colored plush carpet. Strolling around my brightly lit room, I felt totally free and uninhibited in my birthday suit. No one to catch a glimpse of my nakedness but me, and since I was okay with the body I was in, I didn't mind looking at myself. That is, with the exception of the gray intruder. It was long gone and totally removed, thanks to a pair of tweezers. Now, if there was any truth to the belief that two hairs would grow in the place of one, I'd be in serious trouble.

I wasn't ready to go for a total wax job, but if I had to, then I'd just let it be.

Our flight touched down after 10:00 p.m., and we were all exhausted from the constant affairs that had claimed Kyra's attention. We had tried to be of assistance as much as possible and when Gwen was feeling up to it. For the most part, Kyra hadn't been without our company, even though we'd camped out at the Hyatt after the first night. I'd been willing to stay anywhere but Bart's Funeral Home. For the life of me, I couldn't understand why he hadn't named his funeral home Laurent's Funeral Home. What had possessed him to go with his first name was a mystery. It sounded like a quick place to get a funeral service, but Bart's was anything but a quick funeral spot. Mema had mentioned that everyone that came through had a reservation. There were no drop-ins, no one asking for a family member to be picked up. Bart knew the exact date and time that each of his clients would be coming in. Being in Jackson to help put Poppa Laurent to rest, or to rest until it was time for him to return and stand guard, had indeed been an experience. I just didn't know what kind of experience it had been.

I sat at my vanity and dabbed at a zit that sat on the end of my nose. It had to be the rich food I had been eating. Everything from red beans and rice, gumbo, and spicy fried chicken to curried goat. The goat I hadn't been crazy about; I'd only tried it because Mema had stood there and put a forkful into my mouth. I'd wanted to spit it out, but she kept telling me how good it was and how she'd cooked it especially for us. My mind fast-forwarded to last night. Neither of us had known what to say when Kyra gave us a big hug, touched our cheeks with hers, and said good night right before walking arm and arm with Tony. She knew how

we felt and knew we had planned to have her stay
with one of us or to drop her off at her house. Without
saying a word, she had decided to go home, with Tony
as her escort. Now that we knew his wife was still in
New York, we figured that he would probably be an
overnight guest. If what her grandmother had revealed
didn't cause her to ponder how she was living, then the
chances of her listening to me and Gwen were slim.

I went into the office late. I needed more rest and
wanted to laze around the house, maybe hang out with
Gina at the mall, catch a movie, or just walk through
the park, but I also needed to get to the office. At the
end of next week, I would be taking off again to take
Gina to UVA. She had been at Kennedy's when I got in,
and our conversation had been short since she was already in bed. The conversations we'd had while I was
in Jackson had been filled with her concern for her
auntie Kyra, but between her worries and consoling
comments, I could tell that she was having some anxiety. She just wasn't her bubbly self.

"Good morning, honey," I said. I had to call and hear
Bryan's voice before my afternoon began.

"Good afternoon," he snickered. "You are about
eleven minutes late for it to be morning. Did you get
enough sleep?"

"No. But I'll be okay. As soon as this day is over, I'm
crashing. I just hope Gina will be down for takeout and
maybe a couple of reruns of something really fun." I
walked into the elevator, closed my eyes tight, and
leaned my head against the cool interior. I needed
something carefree and fun.

"You didn't say anything about me joining you guys.
Or is this a mother-daughter evening?" I could hear
him flipping through some papers.

"You have a standing invitation, always." I smiled.

The elevator stopped and opened on my floor. The America Investments seal was in plain sight on the wall behind the reception center. My stomach flipped, and I knew it would be just a matter of minutes before my afternoon took a nosedive and the sight of Wanda reminded me of what had happened before I left.

"We need to talk about making the standing invitation permanent." He must have stopped flipping through the papers, because the phone line was filled with silence.

The night he'd arrived in Jackson, we'd taken a long walk and talked for hours. I'd talked and he'd listened. Everything I'd said had sounded rehearsed as I'd blurted out what I had been repeating mentally. Despite all that I'd shared, when it came down to it, I still couldn't say that I was ready. I'd felt it, I'd known it was there, and still it wouldn't come. I could hear myself saying everything but "Bryan, I'm ready to be your wife." Hadn't I settled that matter?

"Yes, sweetheart, we do need to talk about that." That was all I could say.

"Good. I'll see you at the house then. And, Trice, I love you, and don't let anything stress you today."

By the time I clicked my BlackBerry off, I was in my office and standing behind my desk. *First things first.* I needed to take care of Wanda. I had talked with Chris and John while I was gone and had told them everything that had happened. They'd supported me by reporting the incident to our HR office and writing her up. When I was away, I couldn't think of anything else but getting back here to write her butt up, and now I teetered between documenting the occurrence or verbally reprimanding Wanda. I needed to think about it for a moment.

I sat down and began going through my mail. I was separating it into three piles, things to respond to, things that could wait, and junk mail. Halfway through the mountain of mail, I came upon a padded mailer envelope addressed to me. It smelled of cheap perfume. I reached in the drawer for my silver monogrammed letter opener and slid it down the envelope until I could remove the contents. It was a DVD. I didn't remember ordering anything or a client telling me they would route a report or some other documentation via DVD. I turned around in my chair, slid the DVD into my reader, and waited for the screen to tell me I could open it. Once it did, I sat back and sipped my coffee, curious to see what it was so I could move on with my afternoon. I watched two women on a sofa, getting busy. As I leaned forward, I immediately noticed that the woman looked an awful lot like me, even from the side, although the camera didn't get close. What was obvious was that the room they were in was my office. The sofa was positioned right under the print Chanel had made for me. In shock, I immediately zeroed in the sofa across the room and the print. I jumped up and walked over to the sofa and really looked at it. They had been in my office and on my sofa. It took only a minute to realize that someone was trying to make it look like I had defiled my office and had slept not with a man but with a woman. It took only another moment to figure out Wanda was behind this. I just couldn't figure out as quickly how she had gotten in my office and who my twin was. I had never seen the woman that my twin was with. Alarm caused me to sit down and view the DVD again. This time I tried to look at the woman more closely. Her hair, her complexion, her build resembled mine. If I didn't know it wasn't me, I'd think it was. I know exactly how R. Kelly felt.

I took a deep breath. I needed to think. I was almost sure that Bryan would receive a copy of the DVD, and

I hoped that Wanda would stop there. But I couldn't be sure. A knock on the door interrupted my analysis.

As soon as I said "Come in," Chris came zooming into my office. He was holding an envelope similar to the one I had opened. I now knew that at least two envelopes had been delivered and if Chris received it, then I believed that Bryan getting one was a definite.

"I would ask you how Kyra is and would welcome you back, but I can tell by the look on your face and the opened envelope, which looks identical to the one I have here in my hand, that you know why I'm here," he said. He fell into the chair across from my desk. "Who would send something like this?" he quizzed, with a concerned look on his face.

"Aren't you going to ask me if it's me?" I leaned forward and looked at him, not wanting him to miss my honesty.

"That goes without saying. But the person you are with is a woman, and I didn't suspect that you were bisexual or a lesbian. Not that your preference is any of my business. But Bryan is in your life, so I just assumed."

"I'm not bisexual or a lesbian. I don't know the other woman, and the woman who looks like me is not me." I leaned back and realized how hard this was going to be to explain, and this was Chris.

"Well, there is some woman going around looking exactly like you. Patrice, she could pass for your twin."

"But I'm telling you that it is not me. Someone went to great lengths to set me up, and I have a strong suspicion that Wanda is involved."

"If you are telling me that this isn't you, and based on the conversation we had while you were in Jackson, Wanda is the only person that hates you enough to do this, we've just got to figure out how."

"So, are you saying that you believe me?" I was looking at him, hoping he did believe me.

"I have no reason not to. I'm not just your boss. We have been friends a long time. But, if it is Wanda, then I am probably not the only person that she sent copies to. I suspect John will be here in a minute, and, of course, Sarah from HR, and you need to prepare what you will say to Bryan."

"Lord Jesus," I said and looked up.

"Yep, He would be the one to call on."

Just as Chris got that out, my phone rang. It was human resources. I looked at Chris. *Here we go.* "Good morning. Patrice Henderson," I said into the receiver.

"Good morning, Patrice. This is Sarah. I have John here in my office, and there is an important matter I need to discuss with you. Could you come down right away?"

"Of course." I tried to keep my voice from trembling. What the heck was going on?

The next moment Chris's cell phone went off. He looked at it and spoke. *Here we go again*, I thought. He listened and then returned his phone to his jacket breast pocket. "We might as well go down together."

"I understand what you are saying, but while you know it's not you and we as a team support you, this puts the company in a very negative light should this get out," said Sarah as she held the DVD up. "Whoever is behind this is targeting you for removal. What reason, other than humiliation, would they have for circulating this DVD?"

"I agree, Sarah," said Abbie, who was the firm's public relations director. "That would pretty much be why I received a copy."

"All this talk, but I need to know what we need to do and what strategy we should take," John said.

The minute we had arrived in the office, Chris had come to my defense, saying he would put his job on the line that it wasn't me. Not because it didn't look like me, but because I'd said it wasn't, and in his book that was enough.

John had taken a similar stand, but he'd also said he had to protect the firm. And he'd asked me to understand that whatever position he took, it would be in support of America. He hoped that it would include my best interests, but if it didn't, he asked that I not take it personally.

"From a public relations standpoint, we send out a statement that we are in receipt of this DVD, that we are examining its credibility, and that we realize that it displays a very negative image of a high-level administrator and a clear disrespect for the workplace," said Abbie. "This could cause a problem for subordinates and our clients as well."

"I'm sorry, Patrice, but I agree with Abbie," Sarah replied. "It would help if you go ahead and admit that it was you and it happened. Apologize and the worst-case scenario is that you will be given a period of leave without pay and a letter in your permanent file. Maybe we'll even throw in a couple of psychological-therapy sessions for good measure. This way John can accept all measures, and you can retain your current position."

"I would be admitting that I'm gay," I said. "What about Wanda? What does she lose, or what statement does she need to make?" I jumped up and put my hand on my hip, not a gesture I made often, but I was getting a major attitude.

"We don't know that she did it," said Sarah. "And right now we can't prove it. There is no recording equipment in any of the administrative offices, only in the hallway, as a security measure. So, someone put it there, but it would take a great deal of investigation to figure out the how and why. The recording only tells us when."

"Yeah, it shows the night before I left town for my friend's grandfather's funeral," I said. "But I left before the time indicated."

"Well, of course, we can have our security team do a complete investigation of all the details. We can even pull the security tape from the camera outside your office, but that would be time consuming," said Abbie. "For right now, the alternative I mentioned is the only one I would suggest." Abbie looked at me apologetically and then looked at Chris and John.

My cell phone went off, and when I took it from my pocket and looked at the caller ID, I saw it was Bryan. Here I was, trying to defend myself to my coworkers, and I still needed to explain everything to Bryan.

"It seems there isn't anything I can say or do," I said. "I'm pleading with you guys to do the investigation and not make this public yet. This puts in question my sexuality. I'm going to call my legal counsel right now. So, Abbie, you may want to hold off on the press release."

John spoke up. "I wish we could do that, but, Patrice, I just can't. If I wait, it will back the company up against the wall, and we will have to deal with the backlash from that. Go on home, and we will handle the rest. For right now, the press release will only include our office here and the European firm. Hopefully, that is as far as it gets. I'm not asking for a statement today, but by tomorrow morning I need to have something on my desk."

"Well, if you send it out, then my counsel will have to react to your reaction, and we'll go from there," I said. I was certain that Felicia, Vince's girlfriend, would represent me and would consult whomever she had to in order to defend me. The main thing was, this tape did not need to be released and the press release didn't need to go out.

Chris said, "John, I don't agree with how we are handling this. I'm going to fight for Patrice, but I understand your point. I'm going to ask that we hold the statement until you give Patrice a chance to consult her counsel and we consult ours to see how both parties can work together. We owe Patrice that much at least."

John looked at Abbie and Sarah.

Abbie was the first to speak. "It's your call, but a couple of hours shouldn't hurt us one way or the other."

Sarah was closest to her computer when it alerted her she had an incoming message. She banged her hand on the desk. "Too late. Whoever the person is, they just put the video on YouTube."

"Patrice, I'm calling security to go get your things from the office and to escort you to your car," said Chris. "As soon as you get home, consult your attorney. I'm calling in some high-profile tech people to investigate, and I'll have Fred, the head of our security team, to get our stuff together. It's not an issue of it being you. It is now an issue that through exposing you, they are putting a negative light on America. John, call the lawyers. You need to take this personally now."

Chapter 14

I had talked to Felicia and explained everything. Of course, she'd assured me that she would handle everything. She'd also told me not to talk to anyone except my close circle of friends, not to answer the phone, and to stay in for a little bit.

Before I could call Bryan, he let himself in with the key. Gina was shopping on the western shore with a couple of her friends. "What is this?" he asked as he threw the DVD on the table in front of me.

The look on his face actually scared me. I had never seen him like this before. "Bryan, it isn't me."

"Girl, do you think I'm crazy? I've been dating you for years. I think I'd know you when I saw you."

I tried to remain calm. "It was made to look like me. But I'm telling you this isn't me." I picked the DVD up and threw it across the room. "Wanda is behind this."

"You can't tell me that she would go to this extreme to get back at you for raising your voice at her. Woman, you sound foolish." He stomped around the room like a wild animal that had been caged or was circling before going in for the kill.

"I called Felicia, and she is already working on this.

The security team at work is checking the security tapes. There is a security camera outside my office that isn't visible. They are hoping the person shows up better there to prove that it isn't me." I had more to say, but he cut me off.

"Is that why you have been going back and forth with me? Because you are gay or bisexual? I just can't believe you've made a fool of me. Here I am, waiting for you to be ready to be my wife, and you have no intention of being with me, because you would rather be with a woman. What? All the time or just some of the time?"

That was it. He had gone too far, and none of what he'd said was true, and he didn't seem to care that it was hurting my feelings. Surely, he saw the tears in my eyes, saw my body language, and knew I was on the verge of passing out. "Get out."

"What did you say?" He rushed toward me and stood in front of me.

It was my turn to raise my voice. "If you aren't going to listen to me and if you don't believe me, then I need you to get out right now."

"That's not a problem." Bryan stormed out the door and slammed it shut behind him.

I fell to the floor and lost all control. I didn't know how long I had been there or what had transpired while I was curled up on the floor, suffering anguish and pain without measure. Kyra was on the floor, pulling me into her arms. I didn't know if I'd passed out, because everything was a cloud around me, and I couldn't really see through my eyes. When Kyra pulled me to my feet, she placed my weak and weary body on the sofa, beside Gwen, who held me in her arms and just rocked me.

It seemed that Chris had called Kyra and told her everything. After Kyra made me some hot tea and gave me something for the migraine, she and Gwen just prayed and held me. Not once did they ask if it was me; not once did they question me. They just allowed me to go through it, and they went through it with me. Why couldn't Bryan have understood, like my friends, that I was not gay and I wouldn't do anything like that. Had that been my preference, I would have told him. I would never have welcomed someone into my life if I wasn't sure I wanted them there and certainly if I was involved with someone else. More than that, God would not be pleased. That was enough for me.

"He didn't believe me," I finally said as I stared across the room, looking at several dots and colors. My vision was completely off.

"Bryan?" Gwen asked.

"He was here, and he called me names and said I'd used him and that he didn't believe I could do something like this. He was just so loud, and he was so angry." I started crying again. Kyra rubbed my back. "I finally told him to leave, and he slammed the door so hard, it broke the crystal vase that Tiffany gave me." I cried even harder. I loved the vase because Tiffany had given it to me, and it was one of the things I held dear. It reminded me of her and our sisterhood/friendship.

"Oh baby. It's okay," whispered Gwen, and she began to rock me again. "I'm going to talk to Bryan."

"Don't," I answered. "If he would think that I would do something like this, then the trust he has been speaking of doesn't exist for him either."

"Oh my God, my feet are sore," I moaned. I sat on the end of Gina's twin bed and pulled my shoe off and rubbed the ball of my right foot.

Gina sat beside me and leaned her head against my shoulder. "Mom, I'm aching in places I didn't even know I could ache. With all the money you are paying, you'd think they'd make sure the elevator was working instead of having us move my things up three flights."

"It didn't help that you brought your entire bedroom from home. I don't know where Courtney is going to put her things." I looked around. The entire room was filled, with not a spot left to add another thing.

"It's just because nothing is organized. Once I put my stuff up, she'll have some space. Maybe not equal space, but she'll have enough." Gina laughed. "Why do you think I arranged to move in a day earlier than I was supposed to?"

"You are too wrong." I started laughing. I hadn't really laughed in a week. Not since someone had decided to exploit me on a DVD and not since Bryan had walked out. The investigation was still going on, and they were putting all the pieces together. So far, they didn't have concrete evidence that the lady wasn't me. Nor did they know who had done it and put it out there for the world to see. I would have to go work for the European firm because my credibility Stateside was ruined. My cell phone had rung so much, I finally had to get my number changed. My home phone as well. Everyone wanted to tell me how disappointed they were and how ashamed of myself I should be. And I didn't want to hear it.

"Hey," Marcus called as he knocked on the door. "Gina, did you forget me?" He was pushing a handcart that was loaded all the way to the top. "You two are up here jawing, and I'm downstairs slaving." Marcus had come home the minute Gwen told him what had happened and that I needed him. He and Mama Bea weren't going back to California until it was straightened out. He had already hired his own personal investigating team and had told me not to worry. While he drove up with me to get Gina settled, Mama Bea was moving in to take care of Gwen. The whole ordeal I was going through had caused her even more problems in her pregnancy. As soon as Gina was settled, I was going to camp out in Charlottesville for a few days, in part to handle financial matters, but mostly because it was our plan. Bryan's and mine. The hotel was already reserved, so I was going to stay there as planned. God knows, I needed the time away.

It was good that I didn't know who had done this. I had never thought about doing another living soul damage, but I would have to pray hard to keep my hands to myself. But as Tiffany used to say, "I trust God."

"Oh, sweetie," I said to Marcus. I slipped my foot back in my shoe and walked over to the door and held it open while he maneuvered the cart.

"You girls are going to have to pay me big time, leaving me downstairs to haul this stuff up alone." Marcus put the black compact refrigerator in the corner and placed the black microwave on top of it. "I don't know where you want any of this. I'll sit a while, and you think about it."

Just then the door opened again, and a chocolate brown young lady stuck her head in the door and looked around curiously. "Oh, hello," she said. A pearly white set of straight teeth peeked out from behind her high-gloss lips. She had probably worn braces for a number of years, and the end result of being able to smile and show all thirty-two was well worth it. Her shiny black hair hung down her back, and a wide red headband sat atop her head. It was definitely all hers. I could spot a weave, good or bad, from a mile away. It had to do mostly with having long hair myself and constantly defending the fact that what I swung was God's gift and was not courtesy of someone who was dead and left behind a little something for those less fortunate to work with.

"Hey, girl," Gina called. She put down the lamp she was holding and walked to the door after slipping her feet back in her Old Navy flip-flops. "I was going to call you last night to let you know I was coming up a day early, but I got caught up packing and saying my goodbyes." I watched to see if Gina's eyes were blinking, a sign that she wasn't telling the whole story.

"I was going to do the same thing," said Courtney. She moved inside the door, pulling a large bright green carryall behind her. She wore a jean skirt with black crop leggings under it, a fitted white T-shirt, and red patent-leather slides. Bright red beads were wrapped around her neck, and a wide red bracelet was on her arm. "My mom and her friend are downstairs loading up a cart. Is this your mother?"

I stood up. "Yes, I am." I reached my hand out toward her. "Patrice Henderson. It's so nice to meet you, Courtney."

"Please call me Coco. That's my nickname." She shook my hand and turned to Marcus. "Are you Ms. Henderson's boyfriend?" Most young people were of few words, but this young lady was quite the opposite. She was inquisitive, and I already liked that about her. If you wanted to know something, I always thought you should ask. I never bought the theory that children should be seen and not heard. I was all about respecting elders, but I also believed that if you were being respectful and waiting for the proper time and acting in the proper manner, you should ask rather than be ignorant of some facts. But, then again, that was just my belief, and I had been outspoken from the time I could jump rope and play hopscotch.

"No. I'm Gina's godfather. It's very nice meeting you, Coco," said Marcus as he stood up.

The door opened again, and a lady, obviously Coco's mom, came in, complaining about the elevator being out of order. "This is a mess. All those steps and humidity outside didn't do a thing for my hair." She rubbed her fingers through her shoulder-length tresses. Like mother, like daughter. She had a nice hairdo, and her hair was her very own.

"It is a pity," I said and stood up again. "You'd think they would have made sure everything was in working order, since parents and the kids they are paying a pretty penny to educate will be in and out of here all weekend." I already had an attitude. Having someone to complain with me was right up my alley. Marcus had already told me a couple of times that it wasn't that serious. That might have been so in his case, but as for me, the extra pounds I had put on were telling on me big time. My usual well-maintained physique had suffered since my trip to Jackson, and I would have to work overtime pretty soon to get it back in shape.

"Hello. I'm Coco's mom, Stephanie. You must be Gina." She walked toward Gina, who extended her hand and smiled politely. I never had to tell her when to turn on the charm; she always knew exactly how to deal with people and when to add the extras.

"Ms. Andrews, it's such a pleasure to meet you," Gina replied. "This is my mother, Patrice Henderson, and my godfather, Marcus McGuire." I listened as she put us on display for her roommate's family.

"Of McGuire Productions?" asked Stephanie. "I've seen you on television. You look better in person than you do on television." She was a very pretty lady. She had the same complexion as her daughter, and her appearance was so youthful. I immediately wondered how old she was. I could usually tell, but she was one that obviously took excellent care of herself.

Marcus flashed his million-dollar smile and put on a little extra charm. He extended his hand to her. "It's a pleasure meeting someone that knows of me."

Stephanie was so caught up looking at Marcus that the gentleman with her coughed several times to get her attention. "Oh, this is my good friend Joe."

"Hello," I said. I was about ready to bust out laughing. Even as she introduced her friend, it was clear everyone else had faded into the background, because she was still looking at Marcus in all his handsomeness.

We all exchanged pleasantries and talked about a little of this, that, and the other thing while Marcus helped Joe bring up Coco's things. Like most men, they instantly hit it off, and talked about sports, Richmond happenings, and fishing. I didn't even know Marcus liked to fish.

We all worked side by side fixing up the room and getting everything organized. Coco had brought as much stuff as Gina, and Stephanie and I had to convince them that if they planned on walking around in the room and doing something other than sleeping, both of them would have to send some things back home. Reluctantly and with long faces, they began to pack some items that they thought they could live without, at least until they could make their first trip back home and sneak them back in some oversized tote bag.

I watched in amazement as the two new college students merged their lives together. Gone were the two young ladies who had depended on their mothers to help make decisions and keep life on track for them while ensuring that they had an abundance of everything. They planned their schedules; organized private times when they would need to study; made out a grocery list of must-have staples, like chips, dip, cookies, soda, and water; and alternated parent pickup weekends. Neither wanted both parents coming up when they could easily ride together. That is, until they brought their cars back to Charlottesville with them. I didn't know if Coco was always this independent, but my child needed to be reminded when to change her linens and to do simple chores around the house. And organizing? She was organized only because I was organized. I had to admit I was relieved. She had worried that she wouldn't get along with her new roommate, but now that the room was all set up, they were laughing, joking, and giggling about stuff they didn't really want us to hear.

Too soon, what we had anticipated happened: they were throwing us out. "Uncle Marcus, I know you want to get back home to everyone."

"Actually, I do," said Marcus. "Patrice, are you ready for me to drop you off at the hotel?"

"Yes, that will be fine. I will order in and relax," I said. "Everything I need is within walking distance, so I'm going to go back in time and pretend I'm a college student and just explore places on foot and see Gina and Coco when they will let me."

"Well, you need to get away," Marcus replied. "Hopefully, by the time you come back, some of the madness will be behind you. I will be back up to get you on Friday. Wasn't that the day you planned to return?" Marcus stood next to me.

"Yep, that's it," I said. It was the time that Bryan and I had planned to return to Richmond.

Coco followed Gina's lead. "Yeah, Mom. You and Joe need to get back on the road. I'm okay and I have everything I need. The grocery is within walking distance, so we are cool there. If I need anything, I'm sure

Ms. Henderson would be willing to take me to get it before she leaves."

"Oh, okay, sweetheart," said Stephanie. She leaned around Coco and spoke to me. "If you'd be kind enough to help her out tomorrow, should she need it, I'd appreciate it. Joe has surgery on his knee tomorrow." She turned to him and held his hand. "He really should be at home, resting, but he would not let his Coco come up without his assistance."

"I'll take care of Coco until I leave. There is so much going on in my life right now, I need to breathe," I said. I felt on the verge of telling this woman, whom I had just met, everything. All about my anxiety about getting married, the three-carat ring that I had almost had, about hanging out with the voodoo posse, about one emotional, pregnant best friend and one who was seeing a married man, and about someone posing as me on YouTube and making love to another woman. But I knew better than to air my dirty laundry. Shucks, even if my laundry was halfway clean, I'd still keep it tucked away. It wasn't nobody's business, anyway. "You go on. I have a feeling our girls will be just fine without us. If Coco is anything like Gina, she's been screaming independence for a while now."

"You know Coco already," Stephanie replied. She nodded in agreement. "Well, it has been nice hanging out with you today."

We said good-bye, and Gina hugged us. Coco walked her mother and Joe to the car. As I got in the truck with Marcus, I watched across the parking lot as Coco embraced her mom. Stephanie had started to cry, and Joe held both of them tightly. That would be the scene for Gina and me in a few days, when I decided to come down off this mountain. For right now, though, it felt good being someplace other than home. I wasn't sure what was going to happen with my job or my love life. Even though Bryan hadn't called me, he had reached out to Gina, who had cut him off because, quite frankly, he had cut me off. She had told him exactly what she felt about him accusing me and how hurt she was. Everyone else in my posse had made personal calls and visits and had told him pretty much the same thing. Kim had even come to the house and told me she'd gone by his office and told him off.

As soon I got up to the room, I decided a good nap was exactly what I needed before venturing out to find a place for dinner. I wasn't sure what I wanted to eat, and I decided to flip through the pages of the tourist magazine when I got up.

I hadn't thought I needed transportation, but on the first day of my adventure, I knew I needed some wheels. And I was determined to drive up to Skyline Drive. I left the room early and caught a cab to the nearest Enterprise and rented a midsize car. I didn't need the extra luxury. I just wanted to get from point A to point B.

"Gina, I will pick you and Coco up in a few minutes," I said through my Bluetooth.

"What do you mean, pick us up?" Gina asked.

"I went ahead and rented a car. I figured it would be easier. And besides, since I need to get rid of some stress, I thought I'd be a real tourist." Gina didn't respond right away. She knew I was completely stressed out, and she knew that the worst of it wasn't the DVD, but the fact that Bryan had turned his back on me. "I'm not going to crowd. I made you that promise."

"That was before . . ." Gina didn't finish what she was saying. "If you want it to be the two of us, Coco will understand."

"No, she is more than welcome. Just be ready and we will hang out a bit and then you two can be back in time for whatever you need to do. Deal?"

"Deal."

At the request of Gina and Coco, I swung by the mall and a nearby shopping center to assure them that their occasional shopping escapades could be satisfied between the two places. Then I took them out for brunch and transported them to the grocery store. By the time we pulled into the parking lot of the dormitory, they were asking me to come in with them. But I didn't want to crowd them.

"Nope. I have plans," I insisted. I attempted to smile.

"What plans, Mom?" Gina started giggling.

"Don't worry, chick. See you two later," I said. I didn't have any plans, and I didn't want to tell Gina that my head was busting.

Thank God for the wonderful world of automation. By the time I got back to the hotel room, I was able to log on to the UVA Web system and take care of Gina's bill. I grimaced slightly as I typed in the figures for her first semester bill. As I looked at the screen to make sure everything was correct, I thought about how much love I had for her. There wasn't another person on earth for whom I would be willing to add that many zeros behind the first few figures. Due to Gina's decent GPA, she was able to get a couple of scholarships to offset her tuition, but I knew after that amount was deducted, I would be flying solo for the rest of it.

Since I was in the financial zone, I decided to check my bank account online. I knew there was plenty of money left over in the account even after the transaction I had just made. Prior to my leaving town, I had transferred enough to cover Gina's tuition from my savings account and had cashed in a couple of CDs I had taken out for that exact purpose. Most of my bills were auto-matically deducted from my checking, but because elec-tronic systems were prone to err, and not necessarily in favor of the customers, this time of month, when my car insurance and mortgage payments came out, I double-checked everything to make sure my account was in order. I was humming a Kirk Franklin tune, sipping from a can of ginger ale, and munching from a bag of party mix, with my feet propped up on the ottoman, while I waited for the Bank of America screen to come up.

Had it not been for the rock—no, check that—the boulder along my career path by the name of Wanda, I would be here with Bryan, relaxing a few days before going back to work. With my mind still wandering over my work scenario, I saw my checking balance before me. I blinked a couple of times and mentally recapped how much I had transferred. I clicked a couple of times and saw that the amount of Gina's tuition was being held and still half of that amount was available.

"This must be a mistake," I said out loud. I immedi-ately clicked again for a detailed report of my deposits and noticed that I had four deposits yesterday. I clicked the line for more details and noticed that Gwen and Scott, Kyra, Marcus, and Andre had made deposits to my account. This had to have been spearheaded by Gwen or Kyra. They were the only ones who had my account number. Not that I didn't trust the men in my life, but they had never had a reason to have my ac-count number.

I called Gwen. "What's up, buttercup?" I logged off the computer and flipped through the pages of the *USA Today*.

"Hey, you! Are you okay?" asked Gwen.

"I'm good. Just relaxing as best I can."

"Well, that is just what we all ordered. I miss you much." I could tell she was smiling.

"Miss you, too. But tell me. When did you have time to share my account number with half of Richmond and have people put money in it, like I'm a charity case?"

"We know you aren't a charity case. We are just taking care of our own. Gina is our child, too. So, it was only fair to pay half of her tuition. Scott and I were going to foot the whole thing, but everyone was here for dinner last night, and when I told them what we were doing, they wanted to split it four ways. Andre called about that time, and Marcus told him, and of course you know that boy can't stand to be outdone."

"I appreciate it. But none of you had to do that. I had saved for Gina's tuition."

"It's done now. You will have your turn," Gwen said.

"That's true. So tell me. What did Mama Bea cook up last night?" I listened as she shared the menu with me, and it made my mouth water. I knew if I'd been there, I would have been right at the table with them, pigging out on her good cooking. After getting an update on how she was, I ended the call. She did share that there was still a Tony in Kyra's life. I wondered, *When will things get better?*

I walked around the downtown area and peeped through the storefront windows at different establishments. It was a very pretty historical area, and just looking around made me feel relaxed and at peace. I'd taken great care in dressing before I'd come out. I wasn't expecting to see anybody, but I'd felt so low in my spirit, I'd wanted to do something to cheer myself up, and I'd thought maybe, just maybe, it would pull me up out of the pit. I wore a beautiful print scarf around my hair. A loose-fitting sundress with a matching print adorned my body. It was one of the outfits I had purchased for Jamaica, and it would have been just right in that atmosphere. Today I was bringing Jamaica to Charlottesville.

I thought of everything but home. Home meant decisions and uncertainties. I didn't feel like pondering either of them. Felicia had given me an update. It seemed that the security camera outside my office suite had revealed some information, and she was on her way to meet with the attorney for America. I didn't allow myself to get excited or to feel relieved. I wouldn't do that until the whole ordeal was over.

Here I was, hanging out at the mall again. I had only one more day, and since I had driven up to Skyline Drive yesterday, taken in the beautiful sights, and snapped a bunch of photos, I needed something different to do today. Being up in the mountains and looking out on all of God's creation had made all my problems seem small, especially when I realized that who I served was so big that my issues could be swallowed up.

I decided to get a bathing suit and hit the pool for an hour. I held up a one-piece in a jade-green color. It wasn't really revealing, but it would expose a little back. I just thought it was cute and simple. I wasn't entering a bathing-suit contest; I was just going to take a swim. I put it back and picked up a few more, turning them around and standing before the nearby mirror, with each of them up to me. Then I held up a gold two-piece halter suit. The top had a plunging neckline, and it tied at the neck and mid back. I actually liked it a lot, because the bottom of the halter top would hang loosely over the bikini bottom. I said to myself, "I like this a lot. Not too revealing, but very sexy. I'll take it." Okay, I had been by myself too long. I had just had a conversation with myself.

By the time I left the mall, I had exactly what I needed for an afternoon at the pool. I was looking forward to a relaxing afternoon poolside. I was even thinking of just getting in the lazy river section and floating along. Swimming would require a little more effort than I was up to putting in.

The chlorine wasn't good for my hair, and when I went in to shower, I knew I needed to wash it out immediately. I decided to do something I rarely did and let my hair air-dry. I'd blow it straight later and tame the frizz with a flat iron. But for now I just wanted to relax and curl up with a book. I carefully picked out a cute baby blue lounger with splits up both sides. I was dressing to impress no one but myself.

My phone rang, and I watched as Bryan's number flashed across the screen. I didn't know whether I should answer it or not. Scott had told me that they had played pool together a few days ago, and now that his anger had died down, Bryan realized how wrong he'd been in his accusations. If I'd had to rely on Bryan to help me through the recent mess, I would have been lost. Thinking about that, I hit the button to silence the call and turned the light out. I didn't want the television or any other sounds to keep me company. For my last night in this haven, I wanted it to be quiet.

Chapter 15

My time in the Charlottesville hotel near Gina was much too short. The room was beautiful, and the view from my window was picturesque. Usually, I would have missed the conveniences of home, but had Marcus not called to inform me that he was on his way, I would have easily extended my stay another day.

Just as Marcus and I had anticipated, tears flowed when Gina and I said good-bye. Coco stood beside my child and rubbed her back as she tried to control the tears, which came more rapidly than her tissue could wipe. My heart felt like it was breaking in a thousand tiny pieces as I helplessly watched her weeping, knowing that it was a daughter having to say good-bye to a mother who had always been there to nurture and care for her. Although our parting was only temporary, I cried tears of my own.

Silence kept Marcus company on the way back to Richmond. All I could do was look out the passenger window and catch a glimpse of whatever we passed. I wondered if I needed to commit any of it to memory. I mentally told myself no. There were shopping malls, shopping centers, and convenience stores popping up all over the place; by the time I remembered a few landmarks, they would more than likely change. As if my empty nest needed a little more gloom surrounding it, the sky became dark and a light rain began to fall.

It seemed that morning came before my head hit the pillow and I had a chance to even close my eyes. Last night I'd waited for bedtime noises to come from Gina's room. The mumbles from her after-midnight phone conversations, the noise of her channel surfing, doors closing, and her going up and down the stairs: I missed it all. Then there'd been the occasional outburst of laughter, which had always caused me to yell for her to keep it down. The response had always been the same. "Sorry, Mom. I'll keep it down." But none of that had kept me company last night. For the first time in a long time, I was alone. Gina had never slept over at anyone's house unless I was out of town. Instead, she would invite her friends to come over to our house, as if she didn't want to take a chance of leaving her house and not being able to return. Certainly, she'd known that her stay with me was permanent. The legal powers that be in Virginia had said so, and we had sealed it all with a bond so strong, it was hard to tell that we weren't blood.

I stood inside my walk-in closet and searched for something to wear. Nothing jumped out at me. Usually, I had some idea what I wanted to wear, whether I felt like a power suit with slacks or I wanted to expose a little leg. I had been told by many that my legs were one of my best assets. I had to agree. They were well toned and curvy, no thanks to a regular workout. Exercise was not a part of my daily, biweekly, or weekly schedule. In fact, I couldn't remember the last time I had worked out. Right now, though, I needed to pick out something to wear. I'd think about working out much, much later. At this moment, I had a meeting with Felicia and America's lawyer.

My phone rang. I looked at the caller ID before answering. It was Abbie. I counted to five and tried to determine if I wanted to answer it. My conscience made me give in. "Good morning."

"Hello, Patrice. This is Abbie." She paused.

I couldn't figure out why she'd bothered to tell me who she was. She should have known that I recognized her voice. "Yes, Abbie. What can I do for you?"

She fumbled over her words. "Oh, hmmm. Chris mentioned that you took Gina up to school. How did everything go?"

This lady was talking like we were friends. The only thing we had ever been was two professionals that worked for the same company. On top of that, wasn't she the one that wanted me to tell all of Richmond, and anyone in any other city that knew about America, that I was gay and was so hard up for some gay sex that I'd made love to a woman in my office? Talk about crazy. "Things went well. And your reason for calling me is?" Okay, I knew that was mean, but what the heck did she expect? Me to invite her over for tea and cookies? I took a seat on the stool in my walk-in closet.

"Well, I wanted to let you know that your friend's security team discovered something."

Why did she stop there? "Okay, what did they discover? I haven't talked to Marcus today."

"They did some alteration of the tape, and they know it wasn't you. It seems your twin was turned at a close angle at one point, and they were able to see her left breast. When you shared with human resources details regarding birthmarks and any other special markings, you said you had recently gotten a tattoo of two connected hearts on your left breast. Ms. Twin didn't have the tattoo." She slowed down. "The only thing that is left to figure out is who she is, who the other person is, and who was in on this with them."

"I can answer one out of the three. Wanda." I didn't have to second-guess myself again. The same tattoo that the girls had thought was crazy had ended up saving my integrity, and hopefully, when all was said and done, my credibility would be restored.

"Well, I just wanted to share that information," Abbie added. "Patrice, I really am sorry about all of this."

I put my head down, knowing the information she'd shared was great news, but the damage in part was done. And right now, all the other pieces of the puzzle had to be put together. "So am I." I clicked the end button of the cordless phone and just looked at it.

I had decided on the ivory pantsuit with a simple black camisole and black leather slings. The weather would be changing soon, and on top of that, Labor Day would be upon me, and my window of opportunity to wear this new suit would be gone until next year. I didn't believe in wearing cream or white after Labor Day. Call it old-fashioned, but no amount of television fashion advice would persuade me to do otherwise.

My phone beeped, letting me know I had a text. It was probably Gina; she was the only person that texted me. I read it once and then twice. *Let me say I'm sorry. At least give me that.*

What did he want from me? Yes, I still loved him. I'd loved him the entire time he'd stood in my living room and told me that he believed that I was gay. Believed I could betray our relationship. How was I going to erase that?

I glanced at the nearby alarm clock and noticed that

I was actually ahead of schedule. I had two hours before meeting with Felicia. Before I could change my mind, I picked up my BlackBerry and replied to Bryan. *I needed you to understand, and I needed you to believe me. Your sorry is coming a little late.* I hit SEND before I could change my mind. After a few minutes, I felt a little better. At least he knew how I felt. It just shouldn't have been a mystery to him.

An hour and forty-five minutes later, I walked into the Donovan Building. My D & G shades hid my eyes, and while I knew I was inside, I wasn't quite ready to take them off. I was making a fashion statement, and I needed to feel the confident persona I was displaying deep down. My body language was talking loud and demanding its usual attention, but if someone had said boo, I would have tucked my tail between my legs and been out of there with the wind at my back.

"Good morning, Ms. Henderson," said one of Wanda's sidekicks as she gave me a quick once-over.

If she was looking for fear and for someone who was going to recoil from embarrassment, she could look someplace else. I was not the lady, not today and not as good as I looked. I had come into the office today for one reason and one reason only: to meet with John, Chris, and their legal counsel. According to my voice mail, Felicia should already be here.

"Hello," I said coolly and gave her a fake smile. When the elevator door opened, I stepped in and hit the button for my floor. She got on with me. Being the kind person that I was, I looked at her and grinned a wide cheesy grin.

She stared at me on the sly, looking me up and down. She probably thought I wasn't cutting my eye at her or that my sunglasses shielded me from her careful inspection of me. At any rate, I saw her and I didn't care.

She should have just taken out her camera phone if she had one and taken a photo. That way she could catch my image in still life and check me out whenever she needed to see what a real woman looked like. The elevator stopped on almost every floor. Before it got to our floor, it opened, and in walked one of Wanda's other sidekicks, one that worked for an insurance firm in the building. I had seen the three of them hanging out together a time or two. They'd either hang out in our staff lounge, which I only frequented long enough to get a quick snack or heat water for a cup of tea, or at the corner deli. From those sightings, I figured that they were as thick as thieves or at least workplace chums.

Obviously, the entrance of her partner gave the first sidekick the guts she needed to direct a comment my way. She moved a little until she was right beside her friend. "Girl, these lesbos out here these days are something else. Getting their groove on in the workplace." She looked at me with a frown. "It's just a shame."

"Girl, I know that's right," said the second sidekick. "Just because they got a big-time position and think they some hotshot bigwig, they need to know that they ain't so high and mighty that they can't come down off their high horse. Thinking their stuff don't stink, and all the time on the low."

I shook my head. Hopefully, she wasn't charged with the duty of answering the phones for the insurance company. She had just broken the English language up. I didn't say a word out loud, but neither did I look around as if they weren't talking to me. I took my shades off and looked directly at both of them. They needed to know that they had not accomplished their goal of embarrassing me and that I was not going to beat them down right here in the elevator for talking about me to my face. When we got to our floor, I let them walk out first, but before they could slither away to Wanda's office, I offered a little something for them to take with them. "Excuse me, Dot. Your name is Dot, isn't it?"

One of them turned around and looked at me like she was ready to run in the opposite direction. I couldn't believe it after she had just made fun of me in the elevator. "Yes, it is."

"I just wanted to make sure," I said as I looked at the other mouthy ghetto chick. "And I believe you work for Vantage Insurance. I can get your name later." That was enough. I knew they wondered why I had asked, and if it had their underwear in a bunch and had them on edge, I would keep on letting them wonder.

If this was an indication of how the rest of my day was going to go, I needed to take a deep breath and, as my great aunt used to say, "spit in my hand and take a firm grip." It didn't sound too productive, or clean for that matter, but thinking about what she used to say, and knowing that it meant to buckle down and be prepared for the worst, was enough for me to take her words to heart and be prepared for battle.

I didn't walk swiftly down the hall. I thought that might make people stare at me more. It didn't matter, though. All eyes were on me. And the whispering started. I wanted to cry, but that was something I didn't do in public. I had spent my growing-up years crying because I was embarrassed about my clothes or not having lunch to eat while everyone around me ate. Those experiences had made me somewhat callous, but I had learned how to handle a bad situation with my head held high.

Kyra had invited herself, not wanting me to go alone. So had Marcus. But I didn't need a bodyguard, and going alone sent a statement that I really hadn't done anything. I was just ready for it all to be over.

The conference room door was open, and I walked in. Chris rushed over to the door and hugged me. "Hey. I've missed your beautiful face," he said.

"Hi to you." I hugged him back. I spoke to everyone in the room and waited to sit down as Chris pulled a chair out for me, beside Felicia.

On the other side of the table, John, Abbie, Sarah, and Chris were seated. I don't think any of them knew how to react or how to start things off. There was a tension in the room that really couldn't be described. I just wanted to get the meeting over with and be out of here. What happened next as far as my professional career was concerned was a question only the good Lord could answer.

"Patrice, it is good to see you," said John. He attempted a smile. "This has been a terrible ordeal for you and for us as well." He watched me carefully. I didn't say a word. Felicia had already advised me not to talk; she got paid to do that for me.

"Abbie has informed me that she called to let you know that due to the expertise of Mr. McGuire's investigators, it was discovered that the woman on the DVD is not you. Additionally, they just informed us minutes ago that they have the names of the two women that are on the DVD. So, we are hoping that shortly we will know exactly who hired them and what that person hoped to accomplish." He was breathing hard, as if it took all his energy to share that information.

Abbie picked up where he left off. "On behalf of America, we are sorry that you had to go through this. With this all behind us, once we have connected this horrific ordeal to a person, you are free to come back to work."

Chris smiled and nodded his head. "Of course, we understand if you need more time to, well, get yourself together. Take as long as you need."

Felicia leaned over and whispered in my ear, and I nodded.

"That won't be necessary," Felicia said. "My client is resigning effective immediately, and we will be pressing charges against the company. I don't feel that my client was treated justly, and the investigation that was done was actually done by an outside agency, hired by us. When the guilty party or parties are found, we will deal with that part of the equation. For now, we will see you guys in court." She placed her folders in her Coach briefcase, removed her glasses carefully, placed them in her purse, and motioned for me to leave with her.

Chapter 16

"Hey, guys," Kyra called as she waved from a table in the corner. She was smiling from ear to ear. Neither Gwen nor I had seen her since the funeral, as sad as that was. We had been reaching out; she just hadn't been reaching back. The ritual of a three-way call once a week was the one thing that hadn't fallen by the wayside. I personally didn't know how she even made time for that with her busy schedule and her attendance at every conference or convention related to English, higher education, or her sorority. She had to be racking up some serious frequent flyer miles. The wonderful world of academia must have changed drastically. When I compared the time she spent locally with the time that she was away, it didn't exactly add up to the hours a full tenured professor and the head of a department should be contributing. But, hey, who was I? I wasn't approving her timesheets or her travel forms, and I sure enough wasn't signing her paycheck.

"Oh my God, Kyra. You look good," Gwen squealed and threw her hands up in a shocked gesture. She had been in the house too long, watching too many drama shows. Her reaction was just a little too preppy.

I was standing right behind Gwen, and my extra inches gave me the advantage of looking over her shoulder once I stood on tiptoes to see what the heck she saw. Before I could get a good look, Gwen moved swiftly toward Kyra and I got a good look at her. "Look at you. You look fabulous," said Gwen. I didn't bother to sit down first but instead walked around to Kyra's side of the table and gave her a big hug. I guess I needed to check to see if she was just an illusion or if she was the real thing.

She hugged me back tightly and kissed my cheek. "Thanks, diva. I got tired of you two prancing around like top models and me wobbling behind you. That's sort of why I've been ducking you guys. I was determined to look different by the time we got together."

"Well, stand up," Gwen ordered. She held the menu against her chest and checked Kyra out. Kyra wore a black and white wrap dress, and all of her was fitting into the dress. I looked down at her feet and noticed that girlfriend had on the cutest pair of Gucci slings. The heels were slightly wide and had to be at least three inches. She had never liked wearing heels, but when she catwalked around the table, she was handling things and her confident stride let those at nearby tables know she was in control. The shy Kyra was gone, and this girl could have easily been my diva twin.

She turned around a couple of times and took her seat. "Girl, what kind of exercises did you do?" I asked. I didn't know what else to say. I was in complete shock.

"Actually, I did a combination of working out with a trainer friend of Tony's brother who lives here in Richmond, eating healthier food choices, and controlling my portions. I make every attempt to keep a positive state of mind," Kyra replied. She giggled like she knew a secret that we didn't. If she was able to lose what looked like fifty or sixty pounds in a month or so, she definitely had a secret that I could patent and that would allow me to retire to the Caribbean.

"Well, girl, it looks good on you," Gwen declared. She motioned for the server to come and take our drink orders.

"What can I get you, ladies?" An older lady with a terrible hair-color job seemed eager to take our order.

"I'll have water with lemon," I said first, lifting my head up from the menu for only a second.

Kyra spoke up next. "I'll have the same."

"Dag, you'd think the person that summoned the server would be the first to place their order. Jesus Christ," said Gwen. She flipped the page again and ordered. "I'll have water, too, but put my lemon on the side. Also, could I have an order of wings and the Bloomin' Onion? Make sure I get them before my dinner arrives."

We both looked at her and didn't say a word. Just like Kyra had a new look, Gwen had a new attitude. I was just praying that in Gwen's cranky case, it was only temporary. "My, aren't we testy? Tell me, sweetie. How you feeling?"

"Big," Gwen said. She leaned back in the chair. "If I look like this at seven months, what in the heck am I going to look like next month? I feel like I'm carrying a whale."

"That is not nice. Don't call my godchild a whale," I joked. I laughed only because she was laughing.

"I know that's right. You know, the baby can hear everything you say. He or she would probably not think kindly of their mommy calling them an animal," said Kyra. She looked around and then back at her menu.

"I can't believe that you and Scott still don't want to know the sex of the baby." I said. "Forget all that craziness. I don't know why you two are waiting, but I'm going to the next appointment to look for myself. At least one of us needs to know what this baby is. If we don't start calling them a he or she, they are going to have a complex. The very last thing we need is a confused baby."

"My baby is not going to be confused," Gwen insisted. "We just thought it would be fun to wait and find out at delivery. That is the way they did it back in the day. Way before all these modern-day devices."

The server came with the drinks and placed them on the table. "Can I take the rest of your orders?" She smiled, although she looked tired. I didn't know the lady from Adam, but her body language was saying that she needed some rest.

"Let me place my order, but remind me to tell you two something," said Gwen. She lifted her menu off the table and flipped it open. "I'll have the mixed grill. The sirloin medium well and the crab cake. And could I have a sweet potato instead of the au gratin potatoes?" The server had placed the wings and the Bloomin' Onion on the table, along with a warm loaf of bread. "Oh, and can I have mushrooms on my steak? I've been craving them all week."

I placed my order quickly, not wanting to delay the arrival of our food and risk Gwen going in the back to help prepare it. I listened as Kyra ordered the tuna chopped salad with the vinaigrette on the side. She grabbed all our menus and placed them in the center of the table. Then she took a sip of water and folded her arms, seemingly pleased with her selection.

We had already blessed the food, so I took a piece of the Bloomin' Onion and glanced at Gwen, who was humming some tune and acting as if this was her first meal of the day.

"Trice, please tell us what happened yesterday," Kyra said.

"Well, on my way up to the conference room, two of Wanda's friends attempted to embarrass me on my elevator ride up. Calling me a lesbo and pretty much telling all those in the elevator about the DVD. I believe if they'd had a DVD player, they would have shown it on the wall." I placed my elbows on the table for balance. I knew it was not the polite and classy thing to do, but I needed the extra support.

"I told you that I would go with you," Kyra mumbled. "I wish I had now. You didn't deserve that, and they know nothing about what really happened." Kyra had turned red. "You should sue them for slander. No doubt Wanda told them and anyone else she could tell. She needs to be put to sleep."

"I'm not normally violent, but I agree with you one hundred fifty percent," Gwen said, while chewing.

"It was horrible, but I got through it," I moaned. "I guess I had enough practice when I was young. I let that mess roll off, and I kept on moving. Anyway, when I got upstairs, everyone was gathered, and our girl Felicia was right on time, looking classy, intelligent, and cute to boot. It's hard to believe someone so young would be handling law like that child does." She wasn't even thirty and Felicia was already one of Richmond's top ten lawyers. I believed every African American in the area called upon her to represent them. It was no secret that in no time at all, she would be able to start her own firm. And I would be referring anyone that needed a good attorney.

"Can you continue?" Kyra said.

"I'm sorry." I blinked a couple of times. "Anyway, they told me that Marcus's investigators had determined that it wasn't me. It seems the tattoo you two told me I should not have gotten saved me."

"How?" asked Gwen. She stopped eating and raised an eyebrow.

"Well, when they zeroed in on the women on the DVD, they could see my twin's left breast. I had to give a description of any significant marks that I had that stood out. Of course, I told them about my tattoo and belly-button ring."

"You got that stuff because you are still nasty," joked Gwen. She started laughing, and Kyra laughed with her.

"Do you want me to finish, or are you going to talk about how I used to be?" I asked. I tried to keep from laughing with them. They knew me well. There was still a part of me I was keeping under cover until I could let it out with my husband. Just the thought of that made me think about Bryan. I had hoped it would work out, but I guessed it just wasn't going to be. There was one thing, though, I had decided last night, while I had dinner all alone and listened to some oldies and goodies: no one would get as close as Bryan had. Everyone had thought I was crazy to protect my heart the way I had been, and look what had happened. The first strong wind, Bryan was out like the clothing line from the nineties.

"Go ahead. We are listening," said Kyra.

I went on. "Anyway, they know the woman wasn't me. A further investigation by the McGuire Productions people identified the two women that were the stars. They have yet to locate them, but they will, and then hopefully, they will find out who is behind all of this. Although I know it's Wanda."

"What about your job? When are you going back?" Gwen quizzed me. She had finally stopped eating.

"I resigned, and at the advice of Felicia, we are suing

the company and a pending suit will be filed against the person that orchestrated the DVD."

"Oh, snap," said Kyra as she sat up in her chair. "Felicia don't play."

"She is the real deal. There is only one problem now. What am I going to do with the rest of my life?" I asked in a joking manner. But I really needed to know what the next chapter of my life was going to include. I didn't have to worry about doing anything tomorrow, but once the lawsuit was over and things were back to some semblance of normalcy, I would need to put my hands to something. I was too young for retirement.

"I got a feeling it's going to all work out," said Gwen. "You know, He didn't bring you through this storm to leave you out in the rain. He's just making a pitcher of lemonade instead of a glass."

I reached for Gwen's hand and held it, and then I reached my other hand out to Kyra, and she reached back. "You two are my lifeline, and I thank you," I said and fought back tears.

Gwen was not able to fight back, and she started to cry. "Don't be so serious."

"Let me change the subject. How is Gina?" Kyra asked.

"She is doing well," I replied. "Actually, she will be home next weekend. Her roommate's mother is driving up Friday afternoon to pick them up, and I'll carry them back on Sunday. Would you like to ride up with me?"

"We'll see," said Kyra. "I don't have my calendar with me. But I'll check early this week and let you know. I did call her last week, and she gave me an update on the classes she was taking. She managed to get in Professor Smith's creative writing class. I was pretty pleased about that. She is an excellent professor, and being a famous playwright, there is usually a waiting list."

The server came with our food and placed it on the table and was out of our way. Everyone busied themselves with seasoning their entrées and preparing to enjoy what looked so delicious. Even Kyra's salad looked good. I felt a little bad. Maybe I should have ordered a salad instead of the baby back ribs and grilled chicken breast. The minute I took a bite, the guilt was gone.

"Mom called," Gwen said.

"What? What did she want? I know that sounds bad, because a mother shouldn't have to want anything to call. Except my mom, she always needs something," I responded.

"She actually wants to come up a few days after I deliver," Gwen said and frowned. I could tell by the look on her face that this was something she really didn't want to have to deal with.

"What did you tell her?" Kyra asked carefully, sensing what I had sensed.

"I told her that I would talk to Scott about it." She wiped her mouth and put her napkin back in her lap. "That is the way it is supposed to be. But my mother hasn't exactly been a mother to me since Tiffany died. I mean, I've been respectful, but what she is asking me is a bit too much. And Scott agrees. He will have nothing or no one upset me. I can't even imagine the two of us being in the room together. I mean, what kind of conversation would we have? What could she say to me, and what could I say to her?"

Both Kyra and I only hunched our shoulders. From my standpoint, there was nothing to say. Too much water had flowed under that bridge of sorrow. It had kept Gwen in therapy for months and had caused her to question her own existence. What real mother would do that to her child? I loved her mother, had forever, but wrong was wrong and hurt was hurt. The hurt she'd subjected Gwen to was so unnecessary.

"You move the relationship at your pace and on your terms," Kyra instructed.

"I agree," said Gwen. She looked at me. "Speaking of relationships, Trice, Bryan called me this morning. He said he sent you a text, to which you gave a short response, pretty much telling him to leave you alone."

"Sure did," I said. "I don't know what he expected. Look how long he said nothing. Stupid is in the air. No harm, but you just talked about your mother wanting to visit after treating you like a stepchild for years, and he turned his back on me when I needed him."

"But you have to know that he loves you," Gwen replied sympathetically. "What would you have done if the shoes were on your feet?"

"I want to say that I would have listened to him before I passed judgment," I replied. "He walked out. Which I understood initially, thinking he needed some space. But when he cooled off, he could have talked to me."

"Well, he will probably be finding out that the person wasn't you. If he's calling now, then I'm sure he will be calling later. Either way you've got to deal with him," Kyra said matter of factly.

"I don't really have to," I said. "But I won't say that I will never. After Wanda eavesdropped on my conversation, I thought of ways to get back at her. Maybe my plan of getting back at her brought all this on. Maybe it's God's way of letting me know I was reacting out of anger."

"She's a very sick and immature lady, with nothing to do and no one to do it with," Kyra said.

"Trice, I didn't say this before, but maybe all of this has brought you to a crossroads, of walking away from corporate America and venturing in your own direction," said Gwen. "That wouldn't be so bad. And if you and Bryan work things out, there is the partnership." She pushed her food around, already half finished. "I think he was just so hurt, he didn't know how to respond. My heart is saying he needs another chance. Don't get me wrong. I want to beat him down, but the person that is calling my house like a telemarketer loves you."

I cut my eye at her before I replied. I couldn't say "but" so much, because she was right in part. "God, why am I being punished?" I looked up.

"Girl, I don't think God is punishing you," said Kyra.

"Well, I know Bryan is busy opening the firm, per my husband," Gwen added when she saw my frown. "Don't look at me that way. He and Scott are friends. And I already told you he calls daily, sometimes two or three times. Any who, he told me that Ms. Edna accepted his offer to come work for him. So, there is no hot hoochie walking around the office, trying to get his attention. You know the kind." Gwen pushed her large boobs up with her hands. "Preppy breasts and upright, round hips bouncing all around the office. With Ms. Edna, you only have to worry about her fattening him up by bringing him homemade desserts. And that is not a bad thing, since he shares."

"Why would I worry about him being fattened up? It wouldn't be for me," I responded.

Gwen threw her hands up. "I'm just saying." She had leaned all the way back and was rubbing her stomach. She wasn't frowning, so she was probably just feeling very full.

Kyra broke into the conversation. "Tony is moving in with me."

A dead silence fell all around the table. It seemed

that the nearby table had become just as silent, unless it was my imagination. Given what she had just said, it could have been that I felt the entire restaurant went silent to give her a chance to say "psych."

"Did you hear me?" Kyra asked. She looked at Gwen and then at me. "I'm trying to share a happy moment. That's actually why I invited you two out, to share this moment with me, complete with dinner and dessert. I can't believe that you two are just going to sit there and get all quiet on me. After chatting about everything under the sun."

"I don't know what to say," Gwen murmured as she wiped her mouth with the cloth napkin.

"Of course, we are concerned, because you are our girl. But if this guy makes you happy, then that is all we want," I said. I paused and then continued. "Is he divorced yet?" It didn't matter, because we would support her either way. It was just that if she was this into him, I was hoping that there was a real future for them.

Kyra looked disappointed. "Well, he filed. It will take a couple of months for it to be final. They have a lot of assets, and she is contesting the divorce. But as soon as it's final, we will be getting married."

Gwen smiled. "We want you to be happy. Now, if living together is what you want and you've really thought about it, go for it."

"I love him, and I know he loves me," said Kyra. "You two know what it's like to finally meet someone who is not only wonderful but so loving and kind. I mean, you both have that. Why shouldn't I?"

She had a point, but she had forgotten to add that the catches Gwen and I had made didn't each have another fish dangling on the line with it. "We know you want the love of your life to enter stage right and sweep you off your feet," I said. "Just don't compromise." I reached for her right hand, and Gwen reached for her left.

As if summoned, the server came and asked if she could remove everything and get us dessert. Gwen ordered the Cinnamon Apple Oblivion, and I ordered the Chocolate Chocolate Tower, with plans for Kyra to eat at least a little since it was her favorite.

I didn't want to rain on her parade, but I wanted her to be ready for the inevitable. "Did you tell the pastor's wife? What happens if she comes over for a visit and Tony opens the door in a T-shirt or something?"

"I haven't said anything to her. She never comes by without calling first, anyway," said Kyra. "Once Tony is divorced, I'll tell her everything."

"Just be prepared to say something. You never know how it will come out," I advised. I was trying to be a good friend and throw out all the possibilities. Obviously, she hadn't thought of them all. It was upsetting to see someone playing a game that they had no idea how to play. She was trying to handle her underground stuff, and she was barely keeping a cover over it. I had done my share of dirt back in the day, and all of it had been part of my deep, deep underground. Shucks, I could have worked with Harriet.

"I'll deal with that when or if it happens," Kyra replied, still displaying an attitude.

The server brought the dessert. Kyra must have really been pissed, because once I started eating some, she grabbed the spoon the server had placed in front of her and took a spoonful and licked her lips afterward.

There was no more talk of Tony. We changed the topic to something less stressful. While Gwen ate and seemed okay, I didn't want this to upset her. Scott had given her a pass to go out with me for a couple of hours, and I didn't want him to regret it. We listened as she added the afterthought about the baby quilt her mother had made and mailed to her. That was probably to warm Gwen up before she posed the question of coming to stay for a couple of days. Gwen told us how her eyes had got misty when she saw pieces of fabric that had once been clothing items that she and Tiffany had worn. I knew the quilt would be a keepsake, and despite her mother not being able to say much, creating it spoke volumes.

I pulled in my driveway and hit the garage opener. As I closed the garage door, I rubbed my hand across my forehead. It was a little warm, and my throat had been scratchy for a couple of days. I knew I needed to go to the doctor. The headaches weren't completely gone, and I knew I needed to get a checkup, if only for that. But if I was coming down with a cold, I wanted to head it off. There was no time for me to get sick. It wasn't like I needed to be in the office, but I needed to be able to think clearly and contemplate my next move. Gina had been a trooper a few nights ago, listening as I shared everything with her. She, too, was disappointed with Bryan, but she did say before she hung up the phone that she could forgive him and she hoped that I could, too. I usually tried to respond to her, but when she finished that statement, I just couldn't. There was no need to tell her I could when I wasn't sure that I would be able to convince my heart.

I walked through the kitchen and hung my keys on the hook by the door. I felt I should be able to say, "Honey, I'm home." But whom would I be talking to? Maybe I needed a pet. I detested cats, so maybe I would consider a dog. But that would be something I would get attached to, only to have him run away or die.

"Hey, you." Bryan was sitting in the living room in the dark.

I jumped. "What are you doing here, and why are you in the dark? And where is your car?" I asked quickly, still half shocked out of my wits. A black man in the dark was not a good thing, unless you knew he was there.

"I parked down the street. I figured if you saw my car, you wouldn't come in." He didn't move but just sat there, with his head down.

Come in? What was he talking about? Why wouldn't I come in? It was my house. "What do you want, Bryan?" I asked.

"I just want you to know how sorry I am. I never meant to walk out on you, but seeing a person I thought was you being handled by a woman and doing things to another woman was too much for me. I kept thinking that I must not have been man enough to ever please you, unless waiting for me had driven you to that extreme."

This was going to be a long one, so I sat down. Here he was, feeling inadequate or experiencing some kind of male inferior thing. A person's preference had nothing to do with someone being inadequate or unable to meet another's needs. Bryan was an intelligent man, and he should have known better than that. "Bryan, you were man enough to please me. I know it's been a while, but surely you remember that." I watched him. He was still slumped over. This was not the Bryan I knew. "But beyond that, with us, it was not just the physical."

With that, he started smiling. "I shouldn't have walked out. I stood at the door and listened to you cry, and my pride wouldn't let me come back in to hold you. You've gone through hell and back with America, and I stood by and just let it happen. What kind of man who says he loves a woman does that?"

"Bryan, you are tripping me out. All the lines you are using should be coming out of my mouth." I couldn't believe it, but he was actually beating himself up worse than I ever could have. I reached to turn on the light, and I couldn't believe how he looked. His clothes were wrinkled, he needed to shave, and I could see bags under his eyes through his glasses. I dared not get too close, because I figured that as bad as he looked, he might smell. I mean, Gwen had told me he was going through hell, but I hadn't believed it. And here I stood, beaten up on the inside but still looking good on the outside. There was some truth in women handling struggles and issues better than men. That had to be why God allowed us to give birth and them to watch. Only a woman could endure hours of labor, cuss everybody out, kick, scream, and have her booty stretched two ways too big, and then, when it was all over, be ready to do the same thing all over again.

"It's not a line. I feel really bad." Bryan moved toward me.

I stood still and looked at him. My glance must have appeared like a stop sign, because he halted and just stared at me. "I can't do this."

He looked at me as if I had sucked the life out of his body and left him limp. Before I could say another wrong word, he turned and walked out the door. I went to the window and watched him just standing in the driveway. He didn't move; he just looked up in the air as if he were searching for something. After a few minutes, he walked out of the driveway and down the street. I stood there, watching him, until he disappeared out of sight.

I went upstairs, removed my clothes, slipped on one

of his shirts, and curled up in bed. I turned on TV Land, feeling I needed something funny. I watched reruns of *Good Times* and *What's Happening!!* I cried even through the funny parts and held the comforter tight in my hands as I fell asleep wondering if I would ever be able to forgive him.

Chapter 17

There was something to the saying that love hurt. The cold I had dodged came upon me in full force the morning after Bryan walked out. I barely had enough energy to call Kyra. Instead of her, I got Tony.

"Is everything all right? You sound awful," he said.

"Gee, thanks."

"I'm sorry. But you sound like you have come down with something. Listen, Kyra went to DC for her fellowship. Is there anything I can do?"

"No thank you, Tony. I'll be okay. Just tell Kyra I called and I'll talk with her later." I said good-bye, hung up the phone, and rested my head against the pillow.

Tony must have called Kyra, who in turn called Scott. I knew Scott was dealing with some personal stuff, and I truly didn't want to bother him. While he'd been keeping a careful eye on Gwen, one of his friends from the neighborhood had been killed.

Kip, Scott's best friend, had found his cousin Keith in his apartment, with a bullet wound in the back of the head. It had taken all of two hours for everyone in the neighborhood to start talking and pointing fingers. I couldn't believe the fingers were pointing at Gina's ex-boyfriend Q. I knew he was one of the local king-pins and was always in and out of trouble, but murder? From everything I had heard, he was living like a gangster and acting out scenes from the worst drug-trafficking movie. The thought made me shiver and thank God that Gina had gotten out with her life. Scott had shared some of the details with me and Gwen when it happened a few days ago. Apparently, Q had been arguing with Keith, saying he owed him money. He'd even pulled a gun on him a couple of times in front of a few people. When Kip returned to town and was informed about what was going on in the neigh-borhood with his cousin, he'd gone to look for Keith and found him dead.

When Scott told me about it, I'd listened as he described a person with a heart of gold. He said that Keith had been a nice guy who was always friendly and helpful. "The older people in my neighborhood called him the watchman. He would ride his bike, checking on all of them. Even my elderly aunt and uncle loved him. He did repairs for them whenever I couldn't get by there. I mean, he was a straight-up, nice person. Yes, he had a habit. He liked to drink and smoke his drugs. But he worked and kept the peace in the neighborhood as best as he could. He even took Q under his wing, always telling him the right way and trying to get him to stop gaming, even though he was supplying him. He'd tell everybody that Q was just misunderstood, and even when they argued, you would see him days later riding around with Q. He knew better, but for whatever reason, he wanted to see the good. Maybe because he needed to see the good in himself, despite his habit." Gwen had reached for her husband and had held on to him tightly while he grieved the loss of a good friend.

I spent as much time in the bathroom, releasing the contents of my stomach, as I did lying in bed with several blankets over me even though it was sixty degrees outside. By late afternoon I had grown weak. Then the doorbell rang.

"I'm coming." I pulled the thick yellow robe around me tight and pushed my glasses up on my nose. I passed the large oval mirror in the hallway and couldn't stand a second look. The first had let me know I looked a hot mess. The doorbell rang again. I put a little more bass in my voice. "I said I'm coming." My throat was so sore and irritated, raising my voice hurt severely.

I unlocked the door and opened it without looking through the window or peephole. Scott stood there, with his medicine bag. "Dag, you look rough."

"Thank you." I would have ordinarily given him a comeback line. I didn't bother, especially since he was dealing with a lot. "What do you want?"

"I came to check on you. Kyra's orders and Gwen's. She wanted to come, but we both know she doesn't need to catch a cold or the flu. Patrice, you even smell sick."

"How does a sick person smell? Never mind. Don't answer. Give me something and be on your way. I know you have a hospital full of small people to take care of."

"Cranky and grouchy, I can do. I have one like that at home. Come on and lie down on the sofa."

After a few minutes of poking and checking this and that, he stood up straight. "Patrice, you have an upper respiratory infection, a temperature of one hundred and one, and you probably already know you have the flu. A very bad case. You should have started taking something the minute you had the first symptom."

"I was too busy dying of a broken heart," I responded. I threw the back of my hand over my forehead for a dramatic effect. It was a straight-up Scarlett in *Gone with the Wind* effect.

"You know that you and Bryan will work this out. Have you even called him?" He sat on the edge of the sofa, near my feet.

"Saw him last night, and he looks bad," I said shortly. "When he started to come near me, I thought about how he had treated me and I was like, 'Screw you'."

Scott laughed. "I'm sure you'd like to one day soon."

"Whatever. You are just full of humor today. Take that someplace where it is welcomed."

"Trice, you are going to need someone to take care of you. Kyra is out of town, and Gina won't be home until Friday. Gwen can't, so that leaves Bryan."

"Never!" I sat up and screamed. The pain from it hurt so bad, I grabbed both sides of my head.

"See what I mean? What do you want me to do?"

"I'll be okay." I tried to smile.

"I'm calling Gwen. There has to be someone that can come and sit with you today until we figure out something."

I didn't even feel like arguing with him. I closed my eyes to ease the headache, and before I knew it, I had fallen fast asleep.

When I woke up, I was upstairs in my bed, and my television was on the soap channel. Ms. Laurie, one of the church mothers, was sitting next to the bed, in a chair, nodding. Her silver gray hair was curled up tight, and her gold-rimmed glasses were on the tip of her nose. I glanced down and noticed her signature beige nylon stockings were knotted at her calf.

I didn't want to wake her; she looked so peaceful. Without warning, I had a coughing spree and couldn't stop. My eyes began to water.

"Thanks be to God, you are awake," said Ms. Laurie.

"Here, let me get you a sip of water." She peeped at me over the rim of her glasses and put the water glass that was on the nearby nightstand to my lips. "How you feeling, child?"

"I'm a little out of it, and my body still aches." I coughed again. It felt like there were thick pieces of cotton in my throat.

"Scott gave you some cough medicine with codeine and something to settle your stomach. He said it would make you sleepy and light-headed." She reached down and felt my forehead. "He told me to feed you when you woke up and to get you to go right back to sleep. Rest is what you need most of all. That's all we did back in the day. We didn't have all this medicine and such."

"Thank you for coming to take care of me. With Gwen being pregnant and confined to the house and Kyra out of town, I'm lost." I didn't mention Bryan, although Ms. Laurie knew that he was my friend and he was always with me at church functions.

"No need to worry. I brought some clothes, my personal items, and my rollers. I'm going to be here till Gina comes home on Friday. She called this morning, and I had a talk with her. She is worried about you somethin' awful, but I told her not to fret, that I was gonna take real good care of you. Between that medicine Scott has given you and my onion soup with gingerroots, you gonna be up in no time."

I made an ugly face at the mention of onion soup with gingerroot. I had never had it before, and it didn't sound like anything I could get at a five-star restaurant or my two favorite soul-food joints. There was no point saying anything to Ms. Laurie, but she shouldn't have told Gina anything. I always gave older folk a lot of respect, but I hadn't met one that minded their own business. I guess it was too much fun, keeping their noses in other people's business. Every statement that Ms. Laurie made began with "Chile, if I were you" or "You didn't hear it from me." So many times I wanted to say, "But you're not, so keep your know-it-all opinion to yourself" and "I don't want to hear it from you."

Ms. Laurie forced me to eat that dreaded onion soup with the ginger root, and the stuff tasted like onion-covered bark. Just as Scott had said I would, with every dose of medicine and the repeat helpings of soup, I went right back to sleep.

The rest of the week was pretty much the same. At times I faintly heard the phone, and a few times the doorbell, and once Gwen came over with Scott. The medicine made reality and the dream world merge, so Gwen's visit could have been a figment of my imagination. The one person I didn't see was Bryan, and Ms. Laurie had not added his name to the list of callers on the notepad next to the bed. I guess he had taken what I said seriously and had decided to leave me alone. Scott kept saying I needed rest more than anything else. I knew what I needed, but it wasn't rest. It was just that sleeping was the alternative to thinking.

"Hello, sick person." Gina was standing in the doorway.

"Hello to you," I replied. I was sitting up in bed, watching a Tyler Perry DVD. "I'm actually feeling better. So much so, I sent my babysitter home when Scott came to check on me this morning." It was so good to see Gina, I couldn't keep from smiling. That was something I hadn't done in over a week, and it honestly felt good.

"Couldn't stomach Ms. Laurie another day, huh?" She laughed. "She is so sweet, it's almost unreal." Gina came over to the bed and wrapped her arms around me and hugged me tight. "I missed you."

"Don't get too close. I don't want you to get sick." I

hugged her back. A tear tickled my eye, and I rubbed it away quickly. "You look good."

"Thanks, Mom." She held my hand and looked at me. "I wish I could say the same. The first thing we need to do is get you in the shower, and then I'll brush your hair in a ponytail or something. You feel up to that?"

"I think I can manage that with your help." Ms. Laurie had given me sponge baths, not wanting me to stay up long. I was appreciative of any amount of water that hit my body. You could call me a lot of things, but never funky.

She went to the bathroom and started the shower. "Mom, I talked to Bryan, and he wants to come over. I can't imagine why he would want to see you looking ragged." She stopped and covered her mouth before laughing. "Sorry, Mom."

"Oh, don't worry about it. I know I don't exactly have it going on, and God knows, I'm nothing close to a diva right now." I watched Gina go through my dresser drawers and get some things out. "I've never been this sick before." I knew why I was so sick. The physical illness shouldn't have committed me to a weeklong bed rest. No, my heart was sicker than my body.

"He was really worried. When I told him I was coming home a day early, he was relieved. He kept saying he would have come over if he'd thought you wouldn't have thrown him out."

The concern that Bryan had displayed was obviously something between just the two of them. I hadn't talked to Bryan, or had I? Scott must have told him I was sick. "Well, Ms. Laurie did okay, and now I have you."

The hot shower with plenty of bath gel, followed by some body oil and scented lotion, was just what I needed. By the time Gina brushed my hair and pulled it up in a banana clip, what I saw in the mirror wasn't that bad. She relocated me downstairs, saying the change of scenery and the sunlight filtering through the windows would do me good.

After a few days, all my flu symptoms were gone, and I felt a lot stronger. Dr. Elliott confirmed that I was well enough to return to my normal activities, with only a warning to take it slow.

Chapter 18

"This is just what I need," I said. I turned toward the massage table that Gina was lying on and watched as she moved her lips to whatever was coming through the headphones plugged into her iPod. "She can't hear a thing."

Rosa laughed. "You know how this younger generation is. They can't do a thing without listening to some loud bebop music. How is Gwen doing?" Rosa, our usual therapist at Kim's, was massaging all the kinks out of my shoulder muscles.

"She's hanging in there. Tired of being home, but other than that, the doctor says she is progressing along well."

"I know you will be glad when she delivers. Is it a boy or a girl?" Rosa asked.

"We don't know. She and Scott want to wait until the delivery. My plan was to go to the last appointment and see for myself, but I came down with the flu. I'm planning on going to the next appointment to catch him or her on-screen." They might not have wanted to know, but an inquiring mind like mine needed to know. Besides, I was tired of buying green and yellow. I was dying to get something pink or blue, for that matter.

"How is Bryan?" Rosa finished massaging me and covered my back with the sheet. We always passed the time by talking about this or that. But today I just wanted my massage with little conversation. I feared that she would start asking about Bryan. She knew all about our relationship, being Kim's close friend. I hadn't even told Kim what had happened, and I didn't think that Gwen would have shared the information, feeling that it was a little too personal.

"He's okay." I didn't say anything else, wanting to keep it simple. I didn't like sharing information that I didn't know was true; that would be too close to lying. However, what I had shared was the truth. It was just secondhand information.

"That's great. So, when are you two going to jump the broom so you can give Gina a brother or sister?"

Enough. If I didn't say something to circumvent all the questions, I would have to lie. "Gina is too old for a brother or sister. Listen, don't let me forget to get some of the Peach and Apricot Bath Scrub. I am completely out. And I think I'm going to need some exfoliant, too."

"Oh, okay. Let me run and get it." Rosa had already finished Gina's massage, and Gina had been relaxing while Rosa finished mine.

I tapped Gina's arm. She wasn't moving her lips anymore. Whatever she had been listening to had put her to sleep. "Dag, my bad. Was I drooling?" Gina mumbled. She wiped her mouth with the back of her hand. "I wish I could get a massage like that after my chemistry class. That stuff is kicking my butt."

"I'm sure you can handle it. I don't know about a regular massage from Kim's staff, but my credit-card statement is showing somebody's spa that is providing biweekly pedicures and manicure. I even saw a few facials." I wasn't getting on her. I didn't mind her having the extras.

"Sorry, Mom. Coco found this place not far from campus, and we've been going there. It's very nice, and the atmosphere is so nice. Not as nice as Kim's, but it's not bad at all. Coco got her hair done there a couple of times, and I got my braids tightened once. By the way, I'm going to get Kim to take this out tomorrow afternoon."

We continued our conversation in the dressing room while we put our clothes back on. I was so relaxed. "That's fine. I thought you wanted something low maintenance, and the micros are cute. But it is totally up to you."

"You're right. I just wanted to do something different, I guess." She came from behind the curtain, putting her iPod in her bag.

"Talk to Kim before you leave. She may have some ideas. She's been doing your hair for a while, and she is a wiz when it comes to hair. Whatever you decide, I'm sure it will look good. Come on, and let's go get something to eat. We can check on Auntie Gwen before we go home."

We arrived at Gwen's before one o'clock. Kyra dropped by not long after Gina and I arrived. It was so good to sit back, relax, and talk girl talk. Scott had an emergency at the hospital, and we planned to keep Gwen company. She was glowing still. Kim had been over earlier that morning and had fixed her hair. Her stomach was shaped just like a ball, and now she leaned back and wobbled when she walked. Her nose had spread a little, and she kept showing it to us every fifteen minutes.

"Auntie Kyra, Mom tells me that you don't live alone

anymore," Gina said as she ate double chocolate ice cream with Gwen.

I waited, with wide eyes. Gina could be critical, and I knew she was going to quiz Kyra and pass judgment.

"Yes, and I'm enjoying every minute," Kyra responded. "It's taken some getting used to. I mean, sharing my space with him, but it's been okay." She started smiling.

"So, how is the divorce coming?" Gina asked.

"You are so your mother's child," Kyra said. She looked at me and rolled her eyes.

"Don't give me that look. I didn't say a thing. Nor did I tell this young, impressionable child to ask you if you're crazy," I said in my defense.

"I'm not crazy. I'm just in love. The last time I checked, there was no crime in that," Kyra snapped. She sat with one leg under her. She was dressed in a pair of jeans and a snug burgundy turtleneck. True to her word, she had kept the weight off. In fact, she looked smaller than she had when we'd had dinner with her weeks ago. Gina had freaked when Kyra walked through the door, opening her jacket, lifting her sweater up, and pulling at the waist of her jeans. We had watched her careful examination of her aunt Kyra. Nothing sagged and everything was tight. I didn't voice it this time, but I could only assume it had a little more to do with Mema than we'd initially thought.

"Well, as I said before, and it seems it bears repeating, we love you and are concerned about you. Just take it slow and think this thing through," Gwen interjected. She got up to go to the kitchen to get chocolate chip cookies and dill pickles to add to her ice cream.

"I've got this. You two, no, you three, don't need to worry about me," Kyra said. She had a little attitude, but friendship went beyond feelings, so we didn't take it personally. "So, have you talked to Bryan?"

It was my turn to roll my eyes at her. I could have pulled her wavy black hair from her head. "Well . . ."

Before I could think up a story—which was just another word for a *lie,* but since I tried to live right and holy, *story* just sounded a little less sinful—Gina spoke up. "No, they are still not talking. The only person that is talking is me. I'm eighteen and these two people, my mother and sooner or later my father, are miserable apart, but they won't just come to some kind of agreement to talk it through or something."

"I did talk to him," I answered.

"Longer than ten minutes, Mom." Gina sounded annoyed.

Gwen spoke up. "Oh, no, she didn't. She is sick of you two."

Gina realized how it sounded and started laughing. "Seriously, Mom. I know he was wrong, but he loves you. Isn't that what matters?"

"No. It could happen again. And I'm not putting myself out there in the line of emotional fire," I argued.

Gwen added her two cents again. "I can't believe how childish they are acting. Can you believe your mother called me while she was sick and medicated out of her mind, crying and whining about Bryan? Then the man that will be your daddy, child, called me, talking about how much he loves your mom. The bottom line is, you two need to get your act together. My unborn child doesn't need to be born into all this madness. That includes you, too, Kyra. If you are going to marry Tony, then you need to let him know he needs to speed up the divorce and end this living in sin. I'm not judging, but don't get caught up in his mess."

Before Kyra could respond, I beat her to it. "He's

still calling you guys?" I eased to the edge of my seat.
I couldn't believe it. And when the heck had I called
Gwen? I didn't remember calling her, and I definitely
didn't remember talking about Bryan.

"He called me a couple of times while you were sick
to check on you," Kyra said. "Trice, he loves you, and
I know you don't want to lose yourself loving him, especially after what happened, but . . ."

I could only nod my head. Life was changing, and
whether I wanted to change with it or not, it wasn't going
to slow down and grant me more time to contemplate
matters. I had been acting so foolish. I had spent years
loving Bryan, and yet I had sealed off a part of me so
that all of me wasn't on the line. He didn't deserve that.
Then, when I was ready, he believed a lie and turned
his back. I slid to the floor by Gina's knee and started
crying. I cried because I missed Bryan and I didn't want
it to be too late for us. Gina reached down and rubbed
my shoulder.

Gwen put her pickle down and started crying. "Girl,
you know I'm emotional and pregnant."

Kyra spoke up. "Trice, stop crying so Gwen will stop
crying. Sweetie, the only thing you can do now is work
it out, or you walk away."

"I'm sorry y'all. I didn't mean to lose it, but I'm a
wreck," I moaned. "I just spent a week with Ms. Laurie,
talking about the church folk and everybody's business,
eating onion soup with gingerroot, listening to her
snoring, and pretending I didn't see and hear her and
Mr. Ben in the guest room."

"What?" Gwen managed to say.

"You talking about her husband, Deacon Ben, with
the gold teeth in the front and one leg shorter than the
other?" Gina shrieked. She was on the floor, laughing.
"Tell me Deacon Ben ain't still hitting on Ms. Laurie!"

I was laughing, too. Those two elderly people being together like that was something to think about. "As sick as I was and as much medicine as I was on, I was still in shock when I peeked around the corner and saw Mr. Ben standing there, with his long johns around his ankles and one of his hands on Ms. Laurie's exposed breast. It was a scene that I needed to erase."

"Oh my God," Kyra said. She had leaned across the chair and was laughing uncontrollably. "Go 'head, Ms. Laurie, with your bad self."

"Old folk still doing the nasty," said Gina. "Mom, please tell me that I will never have to walk in on you and Bryan thirty years from now and catch you two still getting busy."

"Girl, all of us are going to be doing it until we can't do it. Divas don't age. They get better," I said.

"I'll drink to that," Gwen said and lifted her glass of water.

Kyra and I lifted our glasses along with Gwen. After we drank, we looked at each other and at Gina and started laughing all over again. I didn't think any of us would be able to look at Deacon Ben and Ms. Laurie the same way anymore.

Chapter 19

I had just dropped Gina off at Coco's house so they could journey back to Charlottesville. Stephanie was kind enough to take the girls back for me, not wanting me to overexert myself. Spending time with Stephanie and Coco had been a treat, and I had even gone shopping and to a movie with them. They were really good people, and I thanked God that Gina was rooming with someone so grounded. They shared many of the same interests, and so far they hadn't clashed. Just goes to show that you couldn't judge people. We had assumed that Coco's private school upbringing would make her stuck-up, and she was anything but. The two got along and had become very good friends.

Tomorrow morning I would be meeting with Felicia again. They had discovered that Wanda had been behind everything, and to my surprise, Chris had helped her. It appeared that they were having an affair. And with me out of the way, Wanda had hoped to be promoted to my position. I guess instead of whipping, Chris had gotten whipped. I was beyond hurt and disappointed. Chris and I had been friends, and I had shared things with him, believing that he had my best interests at heart, and I had been wrong.

Before I could change my mind, I headed toward the interstate to avoid traffic. If I used this route, I would easily get to my destination within fifteen minutes, give or take a few. I didn't need to talk myself out of it; I had done that already the three times I'd started in this direction. The telephone wouldn't do; some things really deserved a face-to-face, and this was one of them. I listened to the gospel radio station and sang along to the familiar songs. We just needed to talk things out.

I pulled into the driveway and took a deep breath before getting out of the car. I armed the alarm and walked up the brick driveway. My feet felt like they were anchored in quicksand. I knew it was probably silly to be experiencing severe anxiety over seeing Bryan and wondering how he would respond to me turning the tables and coming in peace, especially after he had done the same thing and it had ended with him walking out again at my request. By the time I was ready to lift my finger and ring the bell, the door opened. He stood in front of me and didn't say anything right away. There wasn't a smile on his face. In fact, I couldn't read beyond his eyes, and I stared hard to recognize something familiar. My heart sank when I didn't see anything. I swallowed and shoved my hands down inside the pockets of my coat. "Hi."

"Hello." He stood in place.

"I came by to see you. Do you have a moment?" He was making this difficult. This couldn't be the same man that had called both my friends and professed his love. Nor could it be the man that had been keeping in touch with Gina and who only yesterday had taken her out to dinner and given her a check for incidentals, telling her that he wanted to make sure she had a little extra. Nor the one that had come to me a couple of weeks ago.

He glanced at his watch. "I'm actually in a hurry. But, you can come in for a few minutes." Bryan moved back and allowed me to enter the house.

I wanted to go back out and check the door to make sure I had the right house number. My eyes went to the carryall that was near the door. "Going someplace?" I turned around and looked at him.

"Yes, in fact I am." He motioned for me to come into the living room.

I didn't bother to remove my coat, remembering that he said he had only a few minutes. "Bryan, I know your time is limited, so I'm going to say what I have to say and let you be on your way. It would be selfish of me to hold you up." I waited for him to interrupt me. "When you came over to talk to me, I was still hurt, and I couldn't open up to listen. Now, I'm asking that we talk about us."

I pushed on. "Bryan, we've been together a while, and what started as a fling ended once I saw that you weren't going anywhere, and despite my just wanting to have a physical relationship, you wanted more. Dag, it took me forever to see past how good we were together physically and realize that we were good that way because something else much deeper was happening between us. Through my need to be my own woman and my fighting the transition of opening up to love, you loved me. You never questioned when I would be free to love you in return. You loved me and my daughter. We became your world, and I appreciate that so much. Then things exploded, and all I could see was you not loving me as much as you always said you would."

"You are right. And I've missed you. If you are willing

to just try to listen and let me tell you how sorry I am, that is all I'm asking. That's all I came to ask that night."

"Bryan, I love you, and I'm ready to talk."

Before I could finish what I was saying, he stood up and walked toward me. Very gently he placed his finger over my lips. "Don't say it unless you really mean it. I'm catching a late flight to California to meet with Marcus and some investors that he has lined up for me. The minute I get back, we will work all this out. We've wasted time, and I'm ready for us again—"

This time I didn't let him finish. "So am I." I wanted to stomp and have a temper tantrum. Here I was, putting everything on the line and telling him that I was ready to talk, and he was telling me to hold it until a later date. Just as I was getting ready to argue the point, I let it go. It didn't have to be my way. That was half my problem, having things on my terms. I needed to flip the script. "Call me when you get to California." I turned to walk out the door. My heart didn't hurt as bad as it had when I'd arrived, but it was far from totally mended. With my back to him and my hand on the doorknob, I said, "I love you, Bryan."

I didn't need him to say it first. I didn't know if it sounded different to him, but it echoed throughout my insides like I was totally hollow. It gave me a warm feeling, and the butterflies I had felt the first night I'd laid eyes on him and periodically throughout our relationship settled in the pit of my being to remind me that what I'd always felt for Bryan was pure, unadulterated love, even when I didn't know how to define it. And even when he allowed his pain to blind him. Our love defined itself.

* * *

The appointment was exciting. I couldn't believe
how alive I felt looking at the baby on the ultrasound.

"Oh my God, Gwen!" I cried. I held Gwen's hand
and watched the baby, our baby, squirm around.

"Gwen tells me that you want to know the sex," said
Dr. Reese as she moved the instrument across Gwen's
large belly. "Usually mothers and fathers want to know
the sex of their unborn child early. But every time I ask
Scott and Gwen, they tell me no. I am about to bust.
I'm ready to tell somebody."

"Well, I want to know," I said. "But only if Gwen
doesn't mind." I looked down at her.

"Trice, I don't mind. This is your baby, too, and if
you want to know, then go ahead. Just promise that you
won't slip up and tell me or Scott."

"I promise." I smiled and kissed her cheek.

"Okay then. Gwen, look away, and I'm going to
show Trice what you guys are having," said Dr. Reese.

My eyes widened as she moved along and suddenly
pointed to the screen and mouthed the word *girl*.

"That is so amazing," I whispered. Something else
kicked in that I hadn't expected. I felt like I had missed
out. I didn't regret adopting Gina, but standing here in
the examination room with Gwen, I wondered what it
would be like to give birth. Today was full of surprise
emotions.

"Okay, girly girl. Let's go on back to your house and
relax. The carryout is on me," I told Gwen.

"Are you happy?" Gwen asked as we drove toward her
house. We had called Olive Garden and ordered takeout.
Gwen was dying for seafood Alfredo and lasagna, so
I got her both. I couldn't imagine mixing the two, but I
was sure she was planning to eat them both together.

"I am now. I should have listened to Bryan and left

my job when he asked me to help him start the firm. I could have avoided all the stuff with Wanda."

"You needed to leave when you felt you should. If you had left then, it would have been for him and not for you."

"They didn't stand behind me, and that pisses me off as well. I really thought I was more valuable to them as a professional than that."

Gwen rubbed her stomach and grimaced.

"You cool?" I asked.

"He's just kicking." She continued to rub and look at me.

"Oh no, you are not tricking me. I'm thinking on my feet. Continue to refer to the baby as you always have, as Baby Buddles. It's a cute little unisex name." I paused, then said, "I went to see Bryan." I didn't have to look at her to tell her mouth was open.

"And?"

"We talked briefly. He was on his way to meet with Marcus and some investors."

"Oh, that's right. That was last night?" Gwen said matter-of-factly. "Bryan had taken a photo of me that I didn't know he was taking, and he shared it with Marcus as soon as he got off the plane. I'm going to kill him."

"So, you didn't tell me that he was meeting with Marcus?" I sounded irritated, when I was the one who had told her not to share anything about him with me.

"It was you who said, 'Don't tell me nothing about Bryan Chambers. He is absent to me.' So, I took your advice. You know I always do. You are the great wise one, so I try to humble myself and keep my opinions to myself and just follow your lead." She was ready to giggle.

"Well, you could have said something. Anyway, we talked a minute. And we both decided that we've wasted time. The one thing that hasn't changed is that we love each other. Now, all this mess has clouded it, but we both know that it is still there. We will talk the minute he gets back in town. He even called me when he landed, and we talked for hours."

"So, you two are on your way back to normal?"

"I guess you can say that. I just won't be holding my breath on any promises for a while. I know what you are always telling me, but this, what just went down, is why I keep my heart to myself. It hurts too bad. I didn't know a broken heart can give you diarrhea."

"Fool. It can't. I should know. My husband is a doctor."

We laughed together, and since life was almost back to normal, it felt so good.

I slept late the next morning after staying up and talking to Bryan half the night. We talked about everything and nothing, like two teenagers. When I woke up three hours after our conversation had ended, the phone was still to my ear. I couldn't help but smile. It had been a while since I had talked to Bryan all night and years since I had done so until I'd fallen asleep. As I put the phone back in the cradle, I could only giggle. I spoke out loud. "I hope I told him I loved him."

I was bored out of my mind. I had cleaned everything in my house twice. The phone rang several times, and I ran into the kitchen from the laundry room. My hands were covered with suds from the washing machine. I didn't bother to look at the caller ID. "Hello."

"Ms. Henderson? This is Coco."

"Oh, hey, sweetheart. How are you? Is everything okay?"

"I hope so. But I am a little worried, and I thought I should call you."

"What is going on?" I sat down and held my chest. Lord, I hoped my baby was okay.

"Gina didn't come in last night, and she wasn't in our eleven o'clock class, either. I'm worried. She has never missed class before, and she has never stayed out all night."

"When was the last time you saw her?" I was trying not to panic. I had talked to Gina after I'd left Gwen's yesterday to tell her what had happened, and everything had sounded fine. My mind went back to the young black girl that had been missing at one of the universities in the South. They had found her weeks later, dead. I didn't want to mentally go there, but Coco was telling me that Gina was missing.

"After we came back from dinner, her old boyfriend was waiting in the lobby for her. I could tell she was nervous about seeing him. She hasn't told me everything about him, but I know enough to know she never wanted to see him again."

"How did he know where Gina was? Had she been keeping in touch with him?"

"No. He said her mother told him where she was for a blunt and forty dollars. She called Gina every now and then. When I asked Gina if you knew that she was keeping in touch with her, she told me you did. Anyway, he was telling her how much he missed her and was glad that she was doing the college thing and all that stuff. She kept asking him why he'd come, and he kept saying, he wanted to see her and talk to her."

"And did he leave?"

"Yes, he did, and Gina went with him."

"Why did she do that? I mean, why would she go with Q when she knows he is bad news? She could be anywhere."

"He promised he would bring her right back. I

begged her not to go, but she told me it would be okay. I waited up all night. I didn't call, because I didn't want to worry you, and if she came in late, then I would have to tell her that I had called you, and that would have caused another problem. So, I went to my eight o'clock class and didn't get out until eleven. When I went to my next class and didn't see Gina, I knew I had to call you."

"I'm glad you did. Listen, I'm on my way up there. I'll decide what to do and who to call. It hasn't been forty-eight hours, and the cops won't see it as a crime yet. And she is eighteen and she knows him. I'm calling Bryan and the rest of my friends. They may have some ideas. Stay put, and call me if she calls you or comes back. Oh, Coco, did you call her cell phone?"

"That's just it. Her cell phone was charging in the room when we went to dinner yesterday evening. She didn't come back up to get it."

"I'll call you."

"Ms. Henderson, I'm sorry," said Coco.

"It's not your fault. It will be okay." I hung up the phone and started crying. I needed to convince myself that things would be okay. Q had taken my baby someplace against her will. My heart was racing, but I knew I had to call somebody.

I speed dialed Bryan, and he answered on the third ring. "Hey. There's a problem." I hadn't bothered to look to see what time it was there. I had just dialed the phone. "Bryan, Coco just called. Q showed up there yesterday afternoon and threatened to tell Coco all about Gina's past. To avoid him telling it, she left with him. She was only supposed to go out for a little while, but she hasn't come back."

"What?" Bryan yelled into the phone. "Did she call her? Did you call her?"

"Her phone was charging, and she didn't go upstairs to get it."

"What's going on?" I could hear Marcus in the background and Bryan telling him what I had just told him.

"Well, I'm going to the airport, and I'll get there as soon as I can," Bryan replied. "Wait, Marcus is going to get a friend's private plane, and we will both be there as soon as we can. You go ahead up to Charlottesville. See if Kyra can go with you. Marcus is calling Vince now. I'll call Scott and get him to call his boys. They know everything that goes on in Richmond, and they know of Q. In fact, they've been watching him off and on for a while, making sure he doesn't come near Gina. I guess he felt that since she was in Charlottesville, he could go up there. But he has messed up now."

"Bryan, hurry please." I broke down and couldn't stop crying.

"Baby, it's going to be okay. Just do what I say, and I'll be with you before you know it."

I wanted to go looking for Q myself, but I didn't know where to start. My first instinct was to go to his mother's house, but I had promised Bryan I would call Kyra and drive to Charlottesville and wait there. I dialed Kyra's cell. "Kyra?"

"Yeah, Trice, it's me."

She sounded like she was crying, but I knew that Bryan hadn't called her. "Are you okay?"

"It's a long story. Tony played foul. His wife came here last night and told me that there was no divorce pending and that they are still together. Every time he goes to work at a new school, he picks someone naïve like me to befriend and have an affair with. It seems there are two Kyra's on the East Coast. On top of that, they both have herpes."

"That is awful. Did you call the doctor and make an appointment?" I was pissed for yet another reason.

"I just came back from the doctor. I looked okay doing the physical exam, but, of course, they had to test me. I went ahead and got a test for everything else, too," said Kyra.

"Well, I hate to share more bad news, but Q went up to UVA and kidnapped Gina."

"What? What do you mean, kidnapped?"

"He threatened to tell Coco all about her if Gina didn't go with him, and to avoid that, she left with him last night and hasn't been back since. Bryan is calling everybody, and he and Marcus are on their way back to Richmond on a private plane."

"Thank God for money. Hey, we shouldn't tell Gwen."

"We aren't. But I need you to ride to Charlottesville with me. Bryan doesn't want me to ride alone. My first instinct is to go to Q's house and see what they know or if they are there."

"He wouldn't be that crazy. Kip and the boys have been watching his trifling behind for a minute. He knows better. You want me to come over there?"

I wanted to ask why no one had told me Q was being watched, but I'd ask later. "I should be there in three minutes."

"Three minutes?"

"Yeah, I've been driving the entire time we've been talking."

"We haven't been on the phone that long."

"Thank God for turbo and no cops stopping me."

By the time we got to Charlottesville, the troops were out. Scott called to let me know that Kip and his other friends had been to Q's house and had found out that he was out on a run.

"Trice, you don't have to worry. Kip is going to find Gina," said Scott.

"How can you be so sure?" He didn't know it for sure, and I didn't appreciate him filling my head with something that might not happen. Too many girls were turning up dead after being abducted.

"Because it's more personal than you know." A very emotional Scott went on to share it all with me. "Kip and his friends have been watching Q. He was the one that shot Kip's cousin a couple of months ago."

"Why wasn't he arrested?"

"He is still a suspect. But his mother covered for him. So, we are left waiting for more evidence to come back. You know, Trice, especially at moments like this, every mother loves their child. She loves Q to a fault. Everything he does, she covers for him. I believe it is not just because she loves him but also because she is scared of him. This isn't the first time that he has killed someone. Last summer he beat up one of the elderly men in the neighborhood and left my old neighbor for dead. But, God didn't let it go down that way. There are so many people upset with Q's mom. They don't understand why she won't release him to a system that is designed to help him. She needs to give him up. And yet she covers for him, and he keeps getting away with all this stuff."

"Scott, I'm so sorry." As upset and scared as I was about Gina, I could feel Scott's pain and Kip's. I couldn't imagine having someone I loved killed and watching the murderer out walking around like nothing had happened. What kind of animal killed a person in cold blood and acted as if that person's life didn't matter? As if that person didn't have a family that loved them? "Why didn't someone just pay Q the money that Keith owed him? I mean, if they heard them fuss over it."

"That's just it, Patrice. He told someone that Keith didn't owe him any money. He just wanted to kill someone." Scott was silent for a minute. "Kip will find Q."

Scott had told me everything, and at that moment, I didn't care if Kip had to beat someone down to get it. He mentioned that Q's run was up to DC, Jersey, and New York, and he would be back and forth for a few days. But they knew he was in DC and would be there till tomorrow morning. In fact, they had one of his boys call and check his exact whereabouts. Because Q didn't have a clue that his boy was playing informant, he told him his location and also mentioned that he had Gina along to help him with a couple of connections. He didn't want to show his face, and using her would shield him from looking like the low-life street vendor he was.

Even though we had just got to Charlottesville, Scott told us to go back to Richmond. Coco was so upset that she asked her mother if she could come to Richmond with us. Given the circumstances and knowing that Coco was worried about Gina, Stephanie asked to speak to me.

"Hi, Stephanie. I'm really sorry about all this," I said into the phone.

"There is nothing to be sorry about. That boy shouldn't have gone up there and taken Gina against her will. Nor should he have threatened her about anything that she had done, right or wrong."

"Well, I'll drop Coco off the minute I get back to town," I said.

"That's fine," replied Stephanie.

Since we at least knew that Gina was okay, I felt a little better. I prayed that Q hadn't forced himself on her or made her do anything crazy. He needed to be thrown in jail. He had gotten away with all that he had done to her before, but it had to come to an end.

When Kyra and I walked into my house, it was after 11:00. I was tired and mentally worn out. "What did Scott say the last time he called?" I asked Kyra.

"That Kip, Vince, and a few of Scott's other friends are already in DC, in the area that Q is in. It's just a matter of time before he comes back. They didn't want to move too soon and have him do something crazy. Oh, and Andre is on a flight, too. I believe he lands in a couple of hours."

"Bryan should be here in an hour. I'm going to shower."

"You go ahead and I'll wait down here."

By the time I got out of the shower, the front door was opening. Bryan walked in, with Marcus and Andre right behind him. While I hugged Bryan and hung on for dear life, Kyra hugged Marcus and Andre.

"Hey, baby girl," Andre said as he picked me up off my feet. "Tell my goddaughter that if she wanted her uncle to come home, she didn't have to do something so drastic."

"Leave it to you to try to add humor," said Marcus. He hugged me and smiled. "You hanging in there?"

"Yeah, I'm okay," I said. "Scott has been keeping us posted. I just hope Gwen doesn't get suspicious. She is a month from her due date, and she has done well. This may push her over."

"Too late for that," Bryan interjected. "Scott called us a few minutes ago and said he was taking her to the hospital. She was having contractions."

"What?" I cried.

"She overheard Scott on the phone with Kip. He said she was running through the house, looking for her phone to call you, when a pain hit."

"Oh my God. Will this nightmare ever be over?" I shrieked.

Marcus looked at Bryan. "What is the plan?"

"Since they have not narrowed in on Q yet, I say we start that way. Kyra and Trice can go to the hospital," Bryan replied.

We paced the halls of the waiting room. Kyra and I were waiting for Scott to come and get us or tell us what was going on. All I knew to do was pray and I did. I prayed so long that my praying became singing and my singing became praying. Just when I couldn't think of anything else, Bryan rang my cell phone.

"Hey, baby. You hanging on?" he asked.

"I'm trying. This is hard, sweetheart. This is so hard. Gina is God knows where, and Gwen is struggling because they say her blood pressure is so high."

"Well, we know what we have to do." He began to pray. "Father, in the name of Jesus, we come, God, just seeking you. We realize that we don't have control of either situation, but we know who does. We give Gina to you, Lord, and pray that we might find her safe. And, Lord, please go to Gwen right now and allow your healing balm to touch her right now. Give us peace through this storm, and we will be so careful to give you the glory and the praise. In Jesus' name, Amen."

I was crying softly. "Amen."

"You go back in there and wait for Scott to call you. Gwen is going to need you and Kyra to make it through this."

"Okay." I was still crying.

"Trice, I love you, and both of them will be just fine. I think you know that, but you can't let doubt or fear tell you otherwise. Scott told me about Kip's cousin, so you know that they are fired up, and Kip knows how important Gina is to Scott. We may not like his method, but I believe whatever the end is, it will be the way it is supposed to be. You've got to trust that and hold on to that."

"I love you." As I said the words, Kyra came to me and tapped me on the shoulder.

"Listen, Mema just called me out of the blue," she said. Her eyes were big.

"And?" I wanted her to spill it.

"She said she was calling to let her beautiful girls know not to worry about Gwen. She and the baby will be fine. She is having some difficulties, but it is only temporary, and then the baby will come out and be healthy and strong. And she told me to tell you that Gina is okay and this boy will bring no harm to her. She will just forever know to choose a different kind of man. There will be bloodshed, but it will not involve anyone close to us."

My eyes were big. "What?" I had become fond of Mema, and at this very moment, I was hoping she was right.

"One more thing. She said to relax. The baby won't be here until forty-seven minutes after the dinner hour."

We waited forever, walking in and out of the labor room, encouraging Gwen and keeping her spirits up. It was difficult because I was thinking of my baby, who was somewhere and was scared and wanting to be back home with me and my friends, who were her family.

Finally, Gwen gave birth to a baby girl, with Kyra and me helping to cheer her on and Scott telling her when to push. I watched as my best friend's baby girl entered the world and let out a yell that pierced everyone's ears. Her eyes were wide open, as if she knew we were all there. Gwen cried when Scott placed the baby on her chest and rubbed her forehead. The complexion of their baby was a perfect blend of those two. Scott was grinning from ear to ear.

Gwen spoke to me. "You knew the baby was a girl?"

"I sure did. And as you requested, I didn't say a word," I whispered. I rubbed at the tears that flowed freely from my eyes. I was crying because I had just witnessed a miracle and because I needed this miracle to reinforce the idea that another could happen any minute now. I needed them to call and say that they had found Gina. "I would ask if you have a name, but knowing you two, the answer is probably no."

"Actually, we have a name. Auntie Trice and Auntie Kyra, meet Zion Michelle Elliott," said Gwen.

"What a special name," I replied.

Kyra spoke up. "Hey, I need to write the time of birth down and the measurements for the baby book. Patrice, give me a pen."

I fished through my purse and handed her one.

"Scott, what was the time?" asked Kyra. She was all ready to write.

Scott looked at the pad by the table. "Zion was born at six forty-seven and she—"

Kyra yelled, "What?"

"Why are you yelling, Kyra? What's wrong?" cried Gwen. She frowned.

I could only look at Kyra. "Nothing. just something a wise old woman told us," I interjected. I would forever wonder.

Kyra and I left the hospital like two worn-out soldiers. Neither of us had been to sleep in twenty-four hours. A nap in a hospital chair didn't count. Kyra drove me home, and we saw that a few cars were in the yard. I hadn't bothered to notice what Marcus was driving, since it was a rental. Maybe they had come back because they couldn't find Gina and Q. I didn't know what to think. If they had found Gina, they would have called me. The sight of the home I shared with Gina made me even more depressed. I struggled up the walkway and slowly opened the door. Kyra stood behind me but didn't say a word, obviously thinking exactly what I was thinking.

The minute I opened the door fully, Gina came charging toward me and didn't stop until she was in my arms. "Mom."

"Oh, Gina sweetie," I yelled. I pushed her back. "Let me look at you. Did he hurt you? Did he try to do anything to you?"

"I'm okay. Other than calling me a stuck up b and some other choice names, he didn't do anything. He wanted me to make some big exchange for him in New York, and we stopped off in DC to make a pickup. But thank God Kip got there before we could leave."

"Well, I'm glad you are okay. Where is Q?" I asked.

Kip spoke up. "He was shot and killed. The pickup he was making went bad. Gina was out in the car when it happened. He won't be spending time with DC's or Virginia's finest. But he definitely won't be hurting anyone else. And Gina will never have to look over her shoulder."

Gina laid her head on my shoulder and cried softly. This was probably going to lead us back to therapy, but the important thing was that she was safe and she was at home. I looked around the room at all the people who loved us, and I declared at that moment that I was blessed. "I love all of you."

With groggy voices and half-shut eyes, they said in unison, "We love you, too."

Marcus stood up. "I'm crashing in the guest room

upstairs. Andre, you sleep in the guest room down here," he ordered.

"Whose Daddy are you? Navigating traffic in somebody else's house," I said. Andre and Marcus never stopped. They were always comical together.

Kip was already on his way out the door.

"How can I thank you?" I asked. I looked up at him and knew I would never be able to.

"You don't. We family," he said. He was gone just like that. From the moment I'd first met him, he'd been such a no-nonsense kind of guy, and always, always dependable and a true friend.

Once we were upstairs and had got Gina to lie down for a while, Bryan and I sat on the end of her bed and just looked at each other.

"Before something else happens," I said, "I want to tell you that I love you. You and Gina mean the world to me, and I can't imagine myself without you in our lives. I've known I've loved you for a while, and yet I didn't want to lose myself or risk loving someone who would leave me or not love me the way I've always thought I needed to be loved. I think it stems from all that I lacked in my youth. But you weren't there, and I can't expect you to see the hurt and the scars that were left behind."

"I know. . . ." This time I touched his lips.

"Let me finish. Now, I'm ready, ready to be loved and ready to love you. If you will have me, Bryan Chambers, I want to be your wife." I felt like I should be on one knee. This wasn't exactly the way I had dreamed of saying all of this. The circumstances weren't perfect. There was no candlelight or violins playing softly in the background. It was just Bryan and me in Gina's bedroom. My hair was a mess and my clothes were wrinkled, but we were together, and I realized that there was no special moment, no ideal second to tell him that I wanted to spend my life loving him.

"Well, Ms. Henderson, if I'm gonna love you, you have to promise me three things. That you'll love me." He moved back a little to look me in the eye. He kissed my forehead. "Today."

"I will."

He kissed my nose. "Tomorrow."

"Yes."

He kissed my lips softly for more than a minute. "And always."

"Always." I returned his kiss and slipped my arms around his neck and held on tight. "I can do always."

Chapter 20

It had been three months since Gina's ordeal and the birth of Zion Michelle. Scott and Gwen had decided to celebrate her birth every month. They were going above and beyond, since they had decided not to have any more kids. Gwen's body had gone through a lot of changes, and neither of them wanted to endure another difficult pregnancy. They declared that one was enough, and I couldn't say I blamed them. I had played nanny for Zion for a week after Scott's mother left, and as sentimental as I got in the hospital, I was so glad that my baby had come not only potty trained but able to tie her Nikes and slip her feet into her Baby Phat boots.

The phone rang. "Hey, what time are you coming over?" Gwen asked quietly.

"Why are you whispering?" I whispered so she could hear how she sounded.

"Zion is asleep, and she was up all night. Kim is coming to do my hair, and after that, I'm hoping that Scott can watch Zion so I can take a nap."

"Girl, she is wearing your butt out."

"Yes, she is. Thank God for all of you. Here I was, thinking I was going to have one of those television experiences where the baby is put down and she stays there until it's time for a bottle or to be changed. Boy, was I wrong. She is such a sweetie. The minute she pouts her bottom lip, you forget all about her being a little noisemaker."

"Well, I will be there as soon as Gina gets here. She has some place she wants to take me."

"Where's Bryan?" Gwen asked.

"He's at the office. I officially start on Monday. He's all excited, and to be honest, I am, too. I've been doing a few things from home, but Monday is the big day."

"Speaking of big days, I know you two are of one accord and all is well in bliss land, but has he put the ring on your finger?"

"No. And I'm not sweating it. He knows how I feel, and I'm not holding anything back. That part alone feels real good. The ring is a symbol, blessed by God. When the time is right, I'm sure he will pop the question again, and this time I'll be ready."

"Well, come over after you and Gina finish. Oh, I almost forgot to tell you that Kip called Scott last night, and he and Kyra went out again."

"What? Who would have thought? Kip is a cutie-pie, and they make an attractive couple." Kyra had gained some of her weight back, and still, she looked real good. The weight loss really had everything to do with Tony and very little to do with her. The concoction that Mema had given her was simply a blend of natural herbs used to keep your system cleansed. Here we'd been thinking it was some voodoo stuff.

"I agree and she is happy. That is what really matters," said Gwen.

"You ain't never lied," I replied. "Look, Gina just walked in. I'll see you as soon as we run whatever mystery errand she has arranged."

"Come on, Mom," Gina called. She came back through the living room, sipping a bottle of grape juice.

We went to get a manicure and chitchatted about the summer class she wanted to take and about this nice guy she had met. I knew if he had gotten Gina's attention after all she had been through, he had to be special. I was concerned that she would turn out like I had emotionally. Fifteen years later, Ben's suicide still affected me, and it had caused me to never want to give anyone my heart or allow them to love me. Now, as I looked back over the past year, I realized that holding my heart so tight had almost cost me the chance to love a man as wonderful as Bryan. I just didn't want the same thing to happen to Gina.

"Where are we going now?" I asked.

"Bryan wants me to pick him up before we go to the mall. You don't mind, do you?" She glanced over at me and then focused her eyes back on the traffic. "I figured I could get double if both of you go shopping with me."

We drove the remaining distance to the office, talking about this and that. All the way Gina reassured me that the therapy had helped but insisted she felt ready to end the sessions. "The residue of what happened will need time. What Q did was awful, and I really thought he was going to hurt me, but then I prayed real hard that if he felt anything for me, he wouldn't take my life. He didn't. So, I figured that somewhere in his twisted mind, he cared for me, at least a little. I feel sorry for his mom."

I thought about what Gina was saying and readily agreed. "I feel sorry for her, too. I'm also proud that you were able to visit her. I know it meant a lot to her."

We waltzed through the doors of the building. I was totally relaxed and ready to shop. I hadn't really done any major shopping in a while, and the promised trip to the outlets was just what I needed.

"Hey, you two," Bryan called. He was in the reception area, making a photocopy.

"Hey, you," I said and kissed his cheek.

"Hey, Daddy person," Gina said in greeting and reached on Ms. Edna's desk and got a piece of candy. "You ready?"

"Just a minute. Come into the conference room," Bryan replied. We walked in step behind him, and Gina hummed and bounced all the way there.

When he opened the door and turned on the light, he moved to the side so we could go in. Gina went in first, and I went in behind her.

"Surprise!" Kyra, Kip, Scott, Gwen, Andre, Tori, and Jordan all yelled. Yes, Jordan. Gina had brought him to the party to formally introduce him to the family, and I couldn't be more pleased.

"Hey, Marcus. Man, you still there?" Andre asked.

"Yes, I am. Surprise, Patrice," yelled Marcus.

"So, you are in on whatever is going on," I said. Suddenly, a lightbulb went off, and I started jumping up and down. "Oh my God. Bryan, it's time. Is it time, sweetheart?" I knew I lost major cool points, but I didn't care.

Andre spoke up. "Girl, calm your butt down, and let the man handle his business."

"Okay, Andre," I mumbled and sat down.

"Somebody tell me that Trice just didn't do what I suggested without asking twenty-one questions," Andre joked. He looked puzzled.

"That is the new and improved Trice," Gwen added while rocking my godchild.

Bryan came around and stood in front of Gina first. "Gina, I can't marry your mother without marrying you, too."

Everybody chuckled.

"So, Gina Henderson, will you be my daughter?" Bryan asked. He opened a blue velvet box, which held a beautiful sapphire and diamond ring. He reached for Gina's right hand, placed the ring on her finger, and kissed her cheek.

Gina started crying and hugged him tightly. "Yes, I will be your daughter."

Bryan turned to me. "Well, Ms. Henderson, it is time." He got on one knee and looked up into my eyes.

I could hardly see him for the tears, and I was trembling terribly.

Bryan continued. "You are my world, and I've loved you even when you weren't sure you loved me. We've been lovers. We are friends. Patrice, you must know that you are my soul mate in every way. You complete me. It is you that I think about when I wake up in the morning and you that I whisper a prayer for as I lie down at night. I pray our union will be pleasing to our Father above, and that you will always trust me to love you, and in turn you will love me tenderly, genuinely, and until the end of my years."

There were tears in his eyes and in everyone's eyes all around me. Gwen kept repeating "Oh God," and Kyra was looking at Kip like he should memorize all that he was taking in.

Bryan removed my ring from the ring box and kissed my finger. "I guess I should ask you before I put it on. I don't want to assume." He winked his eye at me. "Patrice, will you marry me?"

"Yes," I said softly.

The ring was slipped on my finger, and Bryan stood up and pulled me to my feet and kissed me sweetly. I thought I would lose my breath. Every moment from our lives flashed before me, from the first night at the Top of the Tower, to this very moment and all the years, months, days, minutes, and seconds in between. With every beat of my heart, from the very first moment I met Bryan, I had loved him.

"I have one more thing to show you. You all can come," said Bryan.

We walked down the hall from the conference room and toward the wing of my office suite.

There on the door was a gold nameplate. It read PATRICE HENDERSON-CHAMBERS. He was getting ready to open the door to the office, which I knew he must have decorated, since he hadn't wanted me to help him.

"Wait a minute," I said.

"What's wrong?" Bryan asked. He looked as if he was wondering if I had had a change of heart.

"That is not going to be my name," I replied.

Everybody looked at me, puzzled and perplexed. "What are you talking about, Mom?" Gina asked the question for Bryan.

"You need to have one made that reads PATRICE CHAMBERS. I don't need to hold on to what was."

Bryan looked at me, shocked. "Okay. If you are sure. Now, do you want to see your suite?" He held his hand on the doorknob.

"Don't need to," I said. "Like you, our relationship, and all that we will be together, I know it is special. The only thing that matters right here and right now is that I'm gonna love you."

"That sounds like a plan to me," Bryan said. He pulled me into his arms and the hall became empty, the lights went down, and all I saw was the man that had serenaded my heart with a passion that words could never describe.

Yes, I was sure of one thing. I was gonna love him always.